PRAISE FOR BRANDT DODSON AND THE COLTON PARKER, P.I., SERIES

"Brandt Dodson's writing combines two of the best traditions of the private eye novel: a clean, laconic style and plotting based on believable human emotions and reactions."

TERENCE FAHERTY,
Shamus Award winner and the
author of *Kill Me Again*

"Compelling and thought-provoking, *Original Sin* reads like it was plucked from the police files, and Colton Parker is the kind of hardnosed, bloodhound P.I. you'll want to follow from case to case. Brandt Dodson has delivered a strong, intriguing first novel."

MARK MYNHEIR,
former homicide detective and author of
Rolling Thunder and *From the Belly of the Dragon*

"*Original Sin* is a terrific read, packed with characters—both savory and otherwise—you couldn't forget if you tried. I'm looking forward to the next book!"

JOHN LAURENCE ROBINSON,
author of the Joe Box Mysteries:
Sock Monkey Blues and *Until the Last Dog Dies*

"*Original Sin* is the first in a series that promises a bright future. Fans of Robert Parker's 'Spenser' series will feel right at home. Recommended."

ASPIRING RETAIL MAGAZINE

"I love a good mystery, and *Original Sin* by Brandt Dodson has all the elements of a good mystery; a PI the reader can identify with, and a believable cast of characters and a plot that's right out of the daily paper. Highly recommended!"

LINDA HALL,
award-winning author of *Dark Water*

"Brandt Dodson delivers a one-two punch in his second Colton Parker novel, *Seventy Times Seven.* The plot is a rollicking ride through the darker side of modern-day Indianapolis, and Colton Parker stands shoulder-to-shoulder with other notable hard-boiled P.I.s. With equal doses of humanity, tenacity, and a sense of duty to his client and soul that are rare in today's mystery novels, Parker is a rising star destined to shine for a long time to come."

LARRY D. SWEAZY,
Spur award-winning author of *The Promotion*

"This book is a winner for both mystery and inspirational fans."

THEROMANCEREADERSCONNECTION.COM

"Crisp. Wry. Honest. P.I. Colton Parker is as unexpected as a bullet hole in a brand new Brooks Brothers suit. You're gonna like this gumshoe!"

CLINT KELLY,
author of *Scent*

"You can't resist cheering for this guy and hoping that he'll solve both his case and his personal dilemmas. This was a story that I didn't want to put down until I reached the conclusion...Looking forward to the next novel in this series. Keep 'em coming!"

RICK BARRY,
author of *Gunner's Run*

WHITE *Soul*

BRANDT DODSON

HARVEST HOUSE PUBLISHERS
EUGENE, OREGON

Cover by Garborg Design Works, Savage, Minnesota

This is a work of fiction. Names, characters, places, and incidents are products of the author's imagination or are used fictitiously. Any resemblance to actual persons, living or dead, or to events or locales, is entirely coincidental.

WHITE SOUL

Published by Harvest House Publishers
Eugene, Oregon 97402
www.harvesthousepublishers.com

Library of Congress Cataloging-in-Publication Data

Dodson, Brandt, 1958-
White soul / Brandt Dodson.
p. cm.
ISBN-13: 978-0-7369-2141-1 (pbk.)
ISBN-10: 0-7369-2141-9
1.Police—Florida—Miami—Fiction. 2. Undercover operations—Fiction. 3. Gangs—Fiction. I. Title.
PS3604.O33W47 2008
813.' 6—dc22

2007034822

Printed in the United States of America

08 09 10 11 12 13 14 15 16 / LB-NI / 10 9 8 7 6 5 4 3 2 1

To Nick Harrison

Your love of literature, of fiction,
and your willingness to mentor
have meant more than you know.

I am honored to call you friend.

Acknowledgments

To Karla. You are the love of my life.

To Christopher and Meryl. Thanks, guys.

To my parents, Robert and Wanda Dodson. You're the best.

To the many bookstore owners and managers
who've taken me under your wing. Thank you.

To my agent, Chip MacGregor. Thanks for believing.

And

To all of the professionals at Harvest House.
All of you, too numerous to name,
have made this a truly enjoyable journey.

Author's Note

Although it may seem hard to believe now, Cuba was once considered the jewel of Latin America. The nation's economy flourished under the steady flow of tourists drawn to Cuba's excellent beaches, fine hotels, and the many casinos that had been established through President Fulgencio Batista's ties to American organized crime. But while tourists and Batista's government enjoyed all that Cuba had to offer, many of its citizens did not. It was this inequity that gave birth to the great revolution.

On New Year's Day 1959, President Batista and his family fled the country as Fidel Castro came to power promising new reforms and a sharing of the nation's wealth.

But Castro's rise to power did not fulfill the promise of his revolution. Further, it constituted a great concern for the CIA and the Eisenhower administration which eventually led to an ill-planned, ill-executed invasion. The invaders—Cuban ex-patriots—were soundly defeated at the Bay of Pigs. It was this defeat that gave the new Kennedy administration its first public trouncing. As a result, many of these Bay of Pigs veterans became quite bitter toward Castro and their new country, the United States. One such man was Jose Battles.

Unable to return to his homeland, Battles opted to enjoy all that America had to offer, and began his quest by building one of the largest crime syndicates in our country's history. This syndicate became known as The Corporation, and dealt in everything from drugs to murder for hire. Under Battles' leadership, the organization eventually boasted an estimated 9000 members, and spread its misery along the eastern seaboard as far north as New Jersey. It was only through the effort of a great many police officers and other officials—many of them Cuban—that Battles was arrested and later convicted in federal court. But no sooner had the cell door closed, than a new set of problems began to emerge.

Once Battles was imprisoned, the syndicate he created began to fragment. This led to the birth of many smaller, yet growing, criminal enterprises. Each of these fragments carries within it the potential of becoming as powerful as its parent organization and, if reunited into one, many times as influential.

The head of the snake may have been removed, but the serpent grows. And like the serpent in the garden, this one remains just as viable—and just as deadly.

Brandt Dodson
Southern Indiana
October 2007

Author's Note

Although [illegible]

On New Year's Day, 1959, [illegible]

[illegible]

[illegible]

[illegible]

[illegible]

CHAPTER *One*

Michael Santiago was a wiry, nervous-looking man who wore a pencil-thin mustache because he thought it made him look debonair. Like Errol Flynn or Antonio Banderas. But to everyone else in south Miami, Mikey was just another hustler.

In the evening of the last Wednesday in September, Santiago and a man he knew as Ron Acuna were standing beside Santiago's 1970s white panel van, waiting patiently to close a deal. The van was parked in a remote section of the Florida Everglades, where the sun was going down, and the oppressive humidity lingered like the boot of a Nazi thug.

"How much longer, Mikey?" Acuna asked.

Santiago shrugged. "Any minute now."

The two men had arrived early at Santiago's suggestion, to be ahead of any cops who might be brave enough—or foolhardy enough—to stake out the Everglades. It was not the place of mice and men. On the contrary, the Everglades were a place where the environment could pose as big a threat as any heavily-armed drug lord in any of the rougher sections of Miami.

"Let's hope so," Acuna said. "This place gives me the willies."

Santiago grinned. "Much different than your Chicago, no?"

"Yes. But we have our snakes too. And they don't always wait until after the sun goes down."

Santiago grinned again and pulled a yo-yo from his pocket. He began pumping it up and down while keeping an eye on the dusty, narrow road they had taken two hours earlier.

"You set the deal, right?" Acuna said.

"It's all set," Santiago said.

"And you know these guys?"

"I know them well enough."

"Which means you *don't* know them, right?"

"Relax," Santiago said. "You're too nervous."

Acuna began to pace. "Just trying to be cautious, that's all," he said. "I heard how shaky things have been lately."

Shaky indeed. Since the death of Clarissa Horell, a very popular college basketball star and niece of Miami's equally popular mayor, the public's forbearance toward the city's drug trade had crumbled. Outcries for law enforcement to stop the illicit flow of narcotics had been heard loud and clear. The public outrage, coupled with the mayor's personal loss, gave His Honor all the political capital he needed to enlist the help of the Dade County and Broward County sheriff's departments. As a result, it wasn't long before the federal Drug Enforcement Administration also joined in the effort. The consequence of all this interagency cooperation was the arrest of scores of drug dealers, suppliers, and buyers. And the result of these arrests was a heightened sense of paranoia among the city's drug traffickers.

For the next few minutes both men were quiet. Santiago continued to work the yo-yo and Acuna continued to pace. But as the sun began its final descent, Santiago said, "Mr. Estévez wants me to close this deal—tonight. But if these guys don't show in the next ten minutes," he paused to glance at his watch in the waning moments of available light, "we will have to wrap this up." He shook his head as he resumed working the yo-yo. "He will not be happy."

"Mr. Estévez?" Acuna asked.

"Ricardo Estévez," Santiago said. "He owns the stuff."

Acuna furrowed his brow. "It's his?"

"Yes."

Acuna looked at the van, then back to Santiago. "How much stuff we got there?"

"Five kilos." He smiled. "And trust me, every ounce counts."

"He trusts all of this to us?"

"No," Santiago said, "he trusts it to me."

"Of course," Acuna said. "I didn't mean to imply anything. It's just that when you asked if I wanted to come along, I didn't know there would be so much junk. And I sure didn't know that it would be *his* junk."

"Sorry you came?"

Acuna shook his head.

"You can make some money here, my friend."

Acuna smiled nervously. "Can always use that."

Santiago paused from working the yo-yo. "Then relax."

Acuna ceased his pacing and thrust his hands into the pocket of his jeans. He was a tall man, lean and sinewy, with thick black hair and coffee-colored eyes. Besides the jeans, he was wearing a T-shirt, New Balance cross-trainers, and a Chicago Cubs ball cap.

"I can use the money," he repeated. "People don't want to hire an ex-con. I thought maybe if I came down here, I could get past that."

"People are the same everywhere," Santiago said, resuming his working of the yo-yo. "It don't make no difference where you're from. You got to hold your cards close to your vest." He pumped the yo-yo. "Know what I mean? You got to know when to hold 'em, and know when to fold 'em." He grinned. The metaphor was not lost on Acuna.

The two men had met in a card game several weeks earlier. Santiago had tried to hustle Acuna, but the younger Cuban-American had outwitted his much older Mexican-American cardmate. Within hours, the two had downed several plates of nachos as they discovered their common ground.

"You just drive. I will close the deal," Santiago said. The diminutive Mexican ceased his yo-yo playing and paused to look at his friend. "Okay?"

Acuna nodded nervously. "Okay."

"You told me you could drive."

"Yeah."

"You drove on the race circuit."

"Yeah. I was good enough for NASCAR. Just couldn't get the backing, that's all."

Santiago continued to hold the yo-yo; continued to study his friend. "So driving us out of here in a hurry, if it comes to that, won't be a problem. Right?"

"Right."

"Okay, then," the Mexican said, resuming his play. "Just relax."

Acuna sighed and began pacing again as Mikey refocused on the yo-yo. It was less than a minute before Acuna broke the silence again.

"Do you work for Estévez?"

"No. But he trusts me. I know things, so he trusts me." He stopped bouncing the yo-yo. "His trust is a very valuable commodity to have."

"Right. Sure," Acuna said, nodding as he continued to pace with his hands still thrust in the pockets of his jeans.

Santiago watched his friend a bit longer, before resuming action with the yo-yo. It wasn't long before his play was again interrupted, this time by a tan, four-door sedan that came slowly into view, giving rise to a trailing cloud of dust.

"Here they are," Santiago said.

Acuna licked his lips and glanced into the impending darkness beyond.

The car came to a stop several yards behind the van. Four men, all of them in their mid to late twenties, got out of the car. Two emerged from the front seat and two from the back.

Santiago slid the yo-yo in his pocket as he greeted the man who seemed to be in charge. "Manuel, amigo," he said with a broad grin. "I was getting a little worried."

The two men embraced as one of the others kept a wary eye on Acuna. Another man kept his eye on Santiago's van. The fourth was looking back toward the unpaved road from which they had just come.

"We ran into a little trouble finding the place," Manuel said, "but we're here now and we're ready to deal."

Manuel, like the others, was very casually dressed. He wore a white tank top, jeans, and tennis shoes. His build was lean, and when he talked, a solid gold cap could be seen on one of his front teeth. A bandanna was tied around his head.

"You have the cash?" Santiago asked.

Manuel turned to the man who had been watching Acuna, who now turned back to the car, extracting a zippered gym bag from the backseat. He handed it to Manuel who unzipped it and held it toward Santiago.

Santiago looked at the bundled cash and nodded.

"And the stuff?" Manuel said.

The Mexican smiled and tossed the keys to Acuna. "Open it, my man."

Acuna glanced at the men. The eyes of all four were on him now. "Sure, Mikey." Then he said, as an offhanded remark, "This humidity is about to kill me."

Santiago grinned and thumbed toward his friend. "He's from Chicago. He can't take the heat."

Manuel grinned.

Acuna walked toward the van as he removed his hat and ran a hand through his damp hair.

And that's when things began to fall apart.

CHAPTER *Two*

Three Broward County Sheriff's Department squad cars, lights flashing, came barreling down the road Manuel and his men had just taken.

"You set us up," Manuel said to Santiago.

Santiago opened his mouth to deny the allegation, but was cut off by Acuna.

"Get in," he said, shoving the diminutive yo-yo master toward the passenger side of the van. "Get in!"

Acuna jumped into the driver's seat and turned the ignition just as Santiago, bewildered, scrambled into his seat and slammed the door.

Acuna floored the accelerator and the van lurched forward, heading directly for a fourth squad car that had approached from the opposite direction and was now attempting to close off their escape.

Acuna spun the van to the left, taking it over the berm of the road and around the oncoming squad before steering back onto the road.

Santiago was wide-eyed and breathless. He looked into the mirror at his side. A cluster of deputies had already sprung from one of the squad cars and had Manuel and his men on the ground. Santiago groaned.

Acuna glanced in his rearview mirror. He could see two of the squad cars that had approached them from the rear were now in pursuit, maneuvering around the fourth car, which was turning around to join in the chase. He deftly guided the van along the narrow winding road. The sun had finished its descent and the swath of light coming from the vehicle's headlights was barely enough to navigate the terrain.

"Where does this lead?" Acuna asked.

"I don't know," the Mexican said. "I haven't never been here before."

Acuna shot him a glance. "You never...what do you mean you never been? Didn't you tell me you do deals out here all the time?"

"In the Everglades," he said. "Not *these* Everglades."

"Great," Acuna said, braking for the next turn while glancing again in the rearview mirror. The lead squad car was on him.

Coming out of the turn, he gunned the engine again. They lurched forward, dipping sharply over a pothole in the road. Both men bounced up before dropping heavily into their seats again. Santiago reached for his seat belt.

Just as he finished buckling himself in, the squad car bumped the left rear of the van with the right front side of the car. The maneuver was expertly done. It was only Acuna's skill that kept the pair from disaster.

He gunned the engine again, speeding the vehicle along the winding and uneven road. The lead squad car, followed by the two others, was keeping pace. Then, Acuna stamped on the brake pedal, bringing the van to a screeching halt. The lead squad car did likewise. The others didn't react as quickly. The second car rear-ended the lead car, forcing it off the road and into a tree.

Acuna floored the accelerator again. From his mirror he could see the hood of the damaged car was crumpled and steam was rolling from underneath. He could also see the two remaining police cars were gaining on him. The one that had rear-ended the first was after him with a tenacity that made it clear the officer was now seeing this as personal.

"One down," Santiago said. "But two are still coming."

"His airbag exploded but it isn't slowing him down," Acuna said. "If we don't get out of here soon, there'll be more."

He reduced speed, gently pressing the brake in an effort to allow the officers to gain ground. They weren't falling for it. "Fool them once, shame on me. Fool them twice..."

"Keep this thing moving," Santiago said. "We can't lose this stuff."

"How much coke we got back there?" Acuna asked.

Santiago gave him a quizzical stare. "I told you. Five kilos."

Acuna did a quick calculation. "Get in the back. When I say go, open the door and toss a kilo at the windshield behind us."

Santiago stared at him in disbelief. "Are you crazy? Do you have any idea how much that stuff is worth?"

Acuna glanced at his friend. "Would you rather lose one kilo or five?"

Santiago opened his mouth to speak, but paused. He climbed into the back.

"Wait until I say it's okay," Acuna said.

"Do not worry, my friend. I'm in no hurry to throw away thousands of dollars."

Acuna continued to hurtle down the road. The squad car had to get close enough for the powder to make maximum impact. But he also knew the officer wouldn't fall for the sudden braking maneuver again. That meant that Acuna was going to need a break. And he saw it just ahead.

"Get ready," he yelled to the Mexican. "When I say 'now,' open the door and toss the stuff."

Santiago muttered something Acuna couldn't hear, but he knew it was directed at him.

A sharp curve was just ahead. Acuna and the officers would have to slow down to take the bend, and that would provide the best opportunity to halt the pursuing squad car.

He floored the accelerator for all it was worth. The van leaped ahead of the closest car, whose driver couldn't see around it to the danger that lay ahead. The officer gunned his car, closing the distance.

As the curve approached, Acuna let off the accelerator without stepping on the brake. The van slowed, but not suddenly, and with no telltale brake lights. Before the officer knew it, his squad car had closed the distance substantially.

"Now!" Acuna shouted.

The Mexican opened the rear door of the van and tossed out a kilo of pure cocaine.

The bag ruptured on impact, spreading a fine coat of white powder across the officer's field of vision. He cut to the right, more out of uncertainty than out of true blindness, and like the officer before him, ran off the road. The car immediately sank into the marshy soil, unable to continue the pursuit. Santiago cheered.

"Excellent, mí amigo. Excellent."

"Close the door," Acuna yelled. "Close it and get back in your seat."

The Mexican did as he was told. The third and final squad car was closing the gap.

"We won't be alone for long. We've got to get out of here."

The narrow swath of the van's headlights illuminated several yards of straight road.

"Hang on," Acuna said, jamming on the brake.

The last pursuing officer wasn't about to be taken in. He came to an abrupt halt, as did the van.

Acuna threw the transmission into reverse and jammed his foot on the accelerator. The van shot backward and crashed into the squad car. Its air bag deployed in a visible cloud of compressed gas. He continued to press the gas pedal, slowly pushing the stunned officer's car backward, off the road. Shifting into drive, Acuna stomped again on the accelerator. The van lurched ahead, leaving the driver to maneuver himself back onto the road.

Acuna knew this tactic had only gained him a few extra seconds. He needed something more permanent. He continued to speed ahead as he took the next curve. He came out of it and saw a straight patch of ground to the left that was strewn with gravel.

"Is that a parking lot?"

"No. A turnaround," Santiago yelled.

Acuna brought the van to a skidding halt before jamming the transmission into reverse and backing onto the gravel. He killed the headlights.

Within seconds, the pursuing squad car rounded the curve. Its headlights, like Acuna's before, fell on the turnaround as well as the van. Acuna turned on his lights and gunned the engine just as the squad car skidded to a stop.

The van shot out of the gravel. Flooring the accelerator, Acuna forced the squad car off the road and into the same marshy Everglade soil that had ensnared the other one. Seeing the vehicle sink into the soil, Acuna reversed the van, steered it around, and resumed their escape.

"Wow," Santiago said. "That was something."

"We're not out of here yet," Acuna said.

"Amigo, you can drive," Santiago said, clearly impressed.

Acuna glanced at the mirror. There were no other cars.

"Are you okay?" he asked his companion.

Santiago glanced in his mirror. "I am now."

"I mean...with Estévez. Are you going to be okay?"

The Mexican wiped perspiration from his face with the back of his hand. "He is not going to be happy with me."

Acuna steered the van from the dirt trail onto a paved road that was just as rough. But it seemed to lead somewhere promising.

"Manuel thinks I set him up," the Mexican said. "He will complain to Estévez. There will be trouble over this."

Acuna glanced at his friend, while trying to keep the van on the road. "How do you know he didn't set you up?"

The Mexican thought about it. "You could be right."

"Sure," Acuna said. "For that matter, maybe Estevez handed you over."

The Mexican shook his head. "He wouldn't do that. He wouldn't risk the loss of five kilos of junk."

Acuna fought to keep the van on the narrow terrain.

"If I was set up," Mikey said, "it came from Manuel. If I wasn't, I bungled the deal. And Mr. Estevez will not take kindly to that."

"We saved most of the goods," Acuna said. "And we saved ourselves."

Santiago looked at his partner. Shadows of dark and light crossed his face in a steady parade as the van continued to race along the road. "We don't matter, my friends."

"We saved most of the goods," Acuna said. "And we saved ourselves."

Santiago looked at his partner. Shadows of dark and light crossed his face in a steady parade as the van continued to race along the road. "We don't matter, my friend."

CHAPTER *Three*

Coffee wasn't something Ron Ortega drank, it was something he *did.* It wasn't uncommon for the second-generation Cuban-American to spend hours selecting just the right blend of beans before grinding and brewing them with the same loving artistry a Bavarian brewmaster lavished on his mix of hops and mash. Ortega was a purist about his coffee. He avoided any form of added infiltrates, and detested sugar, artificial flavorings, and creamers of any kind. He preferred to savor the undisturbed flavor of the beans as nature had made them. And he expected others to do the same.

In short, good coffee made for a good day. Bad brew, on the other hand, was an enemy to scorn. But as he started his second hour of waiting in the outer office of the Special Agent in Charge, he began to recognize a far greater enemy, one that held sway over the bitter taste of bad coffee.

He was bored. And boredom was the worst thing Ortega could face.

Since he'd started his law-enforcement career, he had relished the heart-pounding excitement of a well-executed raid, as well as the pure terror of disarming a resisting suspect. He had experienced the infusion of adrenalin that comes with being cross-examined in court and tasted the bitterness of an arrest gone sour. But there was nothing that could cloud his day more than the mind-numbing, soul-robbing demon of just sitting around. Boredom trumped even bad coffee. So as he waited in a chair across from the secretary's desk, he began to ask himself the age-old question that every tempted man must face.

Do the right thing? Or do the desired thing?

The right thing would be to wait patiently until the SAC was ready to see him. The desired thing would be to find something to keep himself occupied.

Acquiescing, he opted to do the desired thing. He decided to pour himself a cup of bad coffee.

He rose from his chair and walked to a coffeepot that looked as though it hadn't been cleaned since Paris Hilton was just a hotel in France. He knew he would regret the decision. But the thought of sitting on his hands for another hour or two seemed a fate worse than using those same hands to poison himself with coffee that was sure to take the enamel off his teeth.

He committed his first sin by pouring himself a large Styrofoam cup of the black sludge. Then he committed his second by pouring in a liberal amount of nondairy creamer. He reached for a stir stick and began to mix the deadly swill.

"There's more creamer if you'd like," the secretary said from her desk. "I've found it kills the taste."

Ortega saw her smile. *Actually smile* about the need to kill the taste of her coffee.

He wanted to shake his head, express some form of pity, but was interrupted by the voice of the Special Agent in Charge.

"Agent Ortega?"

Juan Rojas, the SAC, was a bull of a man. Tall and as solid as marble, he had thinning black hair, the dark complexion of a second-generation Colombian-American, and deeply set eyes. He wore a navy blue suit, a white shirt, and a dazzling red tie. His dour expression made clear the man was angry. The tone of his voice and his labored breathing confirmed it.

"Yes, sir," Ortega said, stirring the creamer into the coffee.

"Would you like to get your tail in here?"

Ortega, who would continue to work undercover as Ron Acuna if all went well, followed his new boss into the office. Like the SAC's office back in Chicago, this one was not fancy, but was still several notches above the squad rooms in which the typical brick agent worked. A large wooden desk stood in front of a window, a wall unit that housed a large screen television and several government manuals lined the wall opposite the desk, and a wine-colored leather sofa stood along the wall that was just to Ortega's right. Two matching chairs sat in front of the desk. One of them held a tall, thin man who resembled Billy Bob Thornton. This man, like the SAC, was dressed in a navy blue suit, white shirt, and red tie—the tie not quite as dazzling.

Two other men were standing in front of the desk, one in a business suit, the other in a Broward County sheriff's uniform. No one was smiling. The two men who were standing seemed particularly peeved.

"Agent Ortega, this is Dillon Foster," the SAC said, choosing to remain standing behind his desk as he gestured toward the man in the chair. "He's the United States attorney for the southern district of Florida."

The man nodded curtly.

"And this gentleman," the boss said, gesturing toward the man in the business suit, "is the sheriff of Broward County. The other fellow there is the watch commander. I believe you ran him into a tree last night."

The uniformed officer was staring at Ortega through narrowed eyes.

The United States attorney said, "Agent Ortega, would you mind telling us, before we fire you and press charges, just what it was—exactly—you thought you were doing last night?"

"Well, sir, I—"

"You're lucky none of my men were hurt," the uniform said.

"You sabotaged a bust that would have taken five kilos of coke off the street," the sheriff added.

"Not to mention a two-bit street-hustling dealer," the deputy said, before adding, "you jerk" for good measure.

"Yes, but I can explain," Ortega said.

"Why don't you do that?" the attorney said. "Help me understand how you could completely blow a major law-enforcement push to get drugs off our streets."

"Well, I—"

"We're waiting," the attorney said. "Why—"

"Hold on, Dillon," the SAC said. "If my agent says he—"

"He isn't your agent," the attorney said. "He's *my* agent. He belongs to me. The office of the United States attorney runs this man. I asked for him because his superiors at the academy said he showed an aptitude for undercover work. I asked for him because he's from the Chicago office and isn't known to the locals here. I asked for him because I thought he could handle it."

Ortega noticed that the man's voice was growing louder with every word. A vein began to protrude along one side of his scrawny neck.

"Let him talk," Rojas said. "I want to hear what he's got to say."

Even though the attorney outranked the other men in the room, the SAC was on his home turf. The government prosecutor waved a dismissive hand at the DEA chief.

"Go ahead, agent," Rojas said to Ortega. "But this better be good. Your career is riding on it."

Ortega decided to direct his comments to the SAC. "I've developed a bond with Santiago."

The USA rolled his eyes. The two sheriff's department officers continued to glare.

Ortega continued. "While we were waiting for the buyers to show, Santiago said something that changed the layout for me."

"Changed the layout for—what do you think this is, *The Sopranos*?" the attorney asked.

"Quiet," the SAC said, holding up a hand. "I said let him talk."

Ortega paused to sip some of the creamer-laced tar. His throat immediately began to burn. "I've spent the past several weeks with Santiago. He was the mark you wanted me to work, so I've worked him. But the whole time I've felt like he knew more. Like he had connections that ran a lot deeper than any of us knew."

Foster was about to interrupt again when Rojas held up a hand. Ortega continued.

"Santiago lives on the fringe. He wants to be a player but just doesn't have what it takes. But he does know the streets. And he sees himself as a linchpin in the drug trade here. I've downplayed to him. Let him think I'm leaning on him for advice on how to survive."

"And he's going for it?" the SAC asked.

"Yes, sir, he is. Last night I held off giving the signal until I knew I had mined everything from him I could get. Then, just before I was ready, he said his supplier was Estévez."

"Ricardo Estévez?" the SAC asked.

"Yes, sir." Ortega glanced around the room but continued to meet with angry stares. "It wasn't long after that," he continued, "before the buyer showed. I knew we'd arrest Santiago and take the stuff, which would mean I'd lose the opportunity to work Estévez. So I made the decision to save Santiago and the junk." The stares continued. "I'm sure I can get inside the Estévez organization. So I made the decision to sacrifice the plankton for the whale."

The USA looked at the SAC in utter disbelief before directing his venom toward Ortega. "You decided to sacrifice the plankton for the whale? Who qualified you to make judgments in the field like that? Santiago is more than plankton to us. And how do you know we don't already have someone on the inside?" He rose from his chair and closed the distance on Ortega. "Who said it was okay to let a punk like Santiago walk?" He began jabbing his finger into Ortega's chest. "Just—where—do—you—get—off?" He punctuated each word with a thrust of his finger.

"Easy," the SAC said. "And for the record, Dillon, we don't have anyone on the inside and you know it."

The attorney continued to glare at Ortega for a moment longer before taking his seat. He sighed and crossed his legs, turning his head away from the young agent.

"I know I should have told someone," Ortega said, "but I didn't have time. My judgment was that you can take Santiago off the streets anytime you want. But Estévez is a much bigger fish."

"And just how would you know that?" the sheriff asked. "You're from Chicago. How would you know who we're dealing with here in Miami?"

Ortega set his cup on Rojas's desk. "Because I'm a good agent."

Foster snorted.

"When I came to Miami, the first thing I did was talk to the locals. I wanted to know who the players were."

"We didn't bring you down here, son, to conduct intelligence operations," the SAC said.

The attorney turned his laserlike gaze back to Ortega. "We brought you down here to make busts at street level. To work with our local enforcement agencies in a cooperative sting. Does 'Operation Street Sweep' ring a bell?"

"Yes, sir."

The SAC dropped himself into his chair. "So you think you can infiltrate Estévez's operations?"

"Yes, sir."

Rojas flashed a glance at the federal prosecutor. The other officers were still clearly angry.

"What do you know about him?" he asked.

"I know he is thirty-five years old, just a bit older than me, and he's Cuban. Like me. I know he owns The Oasis. I also know he's ambitious, and ultimately he wants to revive La Corporación."

The SAC sat with his hands folded behind his head. The hint of a smile flavored his otherwise stern expression. "You've done your homework."

Ortega wanted to accept the compliment, but thought better of it, still feeling heat from the others.

"Estévez is a dangerous psychopath, Ortega," the attorney said. "If he even suspects you're working him he'll have you cut into so many pieces we'll be able to bury you in every city in America."

"Undercover work is always dangerous, sir," Ortega said, "regardless of who the subject is."

The SAC turned in his chair. "He's right, Dillon. This could be our chance to infiltrate Estévez and his organization. More important, it'll give us a chance to find out who the guy is working with and the kind of organization he plans on building. This isn't just a chance to pull Estévez down—it's a chance to disrupt the whole system."

The attorney snorted again.

"How will your wife feel about this, son?" the SAC asked, turning to the young agent.

"She wants me to succeed," he said, just a little uncertain. She *did* want him to succeed...but at what cost? Ron Ortega, along with several other junior DEA agents from around the country, had been asked to come to Miami to assist with the high-pressure sting operation. The DEA's plan was to return them to their original assigned office with a nice letter of commendation as soon as the busts were concluded. At most, the work was not to extend beyond eight weeks. But now, with Ortega's new information, he could be in Miami for three months or more if he were successful. What would Libby think of *that?*

The SAC smiled. "I don't think we should pass up this opportunity, Dillon. We've been trying for the past year to get inside this guy's business. Ever since we busted Battles and his son. Now we have the thing dropped in our laps."

"José Battles and his son were organized," the attorney said. "They had a system in place, even if it was a violent one. With them, we knew who we were dealing with. But Estévez is a wild card. We don't have much intel on him other than he is an admirer of the Italian syndicates and their talent for organization." He sighed. "It might be an opportunity at that."

The SAC nodded and turned back to Ortega. "Estévez is unpredictable, son. When Capone ruled Chicago you knew what you got. When Frank Nitti took over, things changed. The same thing is happening to The Corporation. With Battles and his son gone, the tone of the organization is in flux. You'll be walking into a gas refinery with a match in your hand. Are you ready for that?"

Before Ortega could speak, the sheriff stepped up to the SAC's desk. "Now hold on a second. I have three patrol cars damaged, not to mention a large number of man hours tied up in this thing. I'm not going to just sit around here with my—"

"We'll cut you in on the final bust," the SAC said. "Fair enough?"

The sheriff paused, opened his mouth, before pausing again. "It's not for me. I want my officers to have something to show for their effort." He nodded toward the uniformed deputy, who was still glaring at Ortega.

"Not a problem," Rojas said. He turned again to the United States attorney. "Dillon?"

The attorney sighed as he stroked his chin. The others in the room were quiet with their eyes focused on him.

"He's new, Juan."

"Understood."

"He's already dropped the ball."

"We'll keep him on a tight leash."

"I want a seasoned lifeline working with him."

"I got just the man."

The attorney sighed again, before turning toward Ortega. "You mess this one up and I'm going to have your tail."

"If he messes this one up," the SAC said, "Estévez will deliver it to you."

CHAPTER *Four*

Ron Ortega's seedy ground-floor apartment in the Liberty City section of Miami was the perfect fit for his deception as an out-of-work, out-of-town ex-con on the make.

A single bedroom, one bath, and a small kitchenette were augmented by a cramped living room that opened onto a small terrace through a set of sliding glass doors. The furnishings were third-hand and extremely uncomfortable, and the grainy reception on the small black-and-white television came by way of rabbit ears.

As Ortega entered the apartment, he tossed his keys onto the table next to the door and set his government-issued .40-caliber Glock next to the keys. He was pleased he had been able to convince the chair jockeys in the SAC's office there was value in what he wanted to do. But he also understood he was on a very short leash. And that meant he would have two enemies gunning for him—the USA and his crowd on the one hand, and Estévez and his crowd on the other. But undercover work had always been a two-sided proposition, and pleasing both sides would require walking the kind of tightrope even the Flying Wallendas would avoid. Ortega grinned. The setup would provide just the kind of challenge that would solidify his career. With this under his belt, he could move up. Possibly *way* up.

He flopped onto the sofa exhausted. At the end of last night's affair in the Everglades he had been required to explain himself to a cluster of very angry deputies. Finally he'd been allowed to go home, with instructions to report to the SAC at seven the next morning. Now that meeting was over, he was tired. He yawned as he rubbed the fatigue from his eyes.

The conversation, if it could be called that, with the SAC, the United States attorney, and the Broward County Sheriff had drained him. He had known they'd be hot, and he hadn't been sure he could convince them to see things his way. But he had. At least for now. And that got one monkey of his back. The next one would be far more difficult.

He pulled out his cell phone. His wife answered on the third ring.

"It's me," he said. "I—"

"Is the job finished?"

"No, not exactly."

There was a long pause. "What do you mean, 'not exactly'?"

"There've been some developments. I'm going to have to stay a bit longer." He could hear the apologetic tone in his voice.

"How *much* longer?"

"I don't know. Few weeks. Maybe more."

Her silence trumpeted her displeasure.

"You still there?" he asked.

"Yes."

"Then say—"

"Did you volunteer for this extension?"

"—something. Yes. I did."

She sighed. "You *promised.* You said this thing would be over in only eight weeks and you would come home."

"I know, but—"

"In case you've forgotten, I'm going to have a baby in five weeks. *We* are going to have a baby. Doesn't that mean anything?"

The question hurt. "Yes, Libby, of course it does. You and the baby are why I'm doing this. If I can crack this thing it will boost my career in ways we can't imagine. It'll mean a promotion. It might even mean we can get our OP and get back to Oregon." He paused to wait for a response that didn't come. "You want to go back to Portland, don't you? It might mean we can do that."

"Getting your office of preference won't mean a thing if you're dead."

"I'll be all right."

"This thing is dangerous, isn't it? If it wasn't, there wouldn't be so much glory attached to it."

"I'm not doing it for glory."

"Then why?"

"I just told you."

Another pause.

"Can you tell me what it is?" she said.

"No."

There was another, more protracted pause.

"If it's that big, that means there's money involved. Lots of money," she said, reasoning her way through. "And that means a lot of temptation."

"I'm going to be okay."

"There are a lot of ways to not be okay," she said. "You might be fine physically, but what about...what happens when you get around the alcohol? The money?"

He held the phone against his forehead and sighed. Couldn't she trust him *yet?* Prior to meeting Libby, drinking had ruled his life. Finally recognizing that his goal to become a DEA agent would be jeopardized if he couldn't put the genie back in the bottle, he began attending a chemical-dependency retreat sponsored by a church in Portland. It was there that he met Elizabeth. She had been volunteering in the kitchen, cooking and serving meals for the week-long seminar. For him it had been love at first sight. For her it had taken a bit longer.

His drinking had served not only as a barrier to the career he wanted, but it was also an obstacle to a relationship with the woman he desired. Ultimately, it was his growing love for her that generated the strength to overcome his addiction. But then she began to talk religion to him. And that had been the last straw. Wasn't it enough that he could climb out of the bottle for her? Must he also climb into a pew? Wasn't her dependency on God just as much of a crutch as his alcohol?

The relationship ebbed and they didn't see each other for several months after the seminar. But then Ron began to drift. And he began to drift far enough away that he felt compelled to rely on old anchors. It wasn't long before he was into his old habits just as deeply as the old habits were into him.

In quiet desperation he returned to the church that had sponsored the retreat and turned his will and his life over to Christ without prompting from anyone. And then, shortly thereafter, his relationship with Elizabeth—Libby—resumed with a full head of steam.

"If I didn't think I could handle this," he said, "I wouldn't have suggested it."

"You suggested it?"

He couldn't believe he had been so stupid.

"You *suggested* it?" she asked again.

"Libby, I have a chance to infiltrate an organization that's moving hundreds of pounds of cocaine into this country every year, not to mention all the other stuff they're into. I not only have a chance to bring them down, I have an opportunity to damage their delivery systems. If I have that opportunity, shouldn't I take it?"

She began to cry.

"Libby," he said, "I have to do this. I'm a *cop*."

Silence.

"I'll be okay," he said, reassuringly. "God will take care of me."

"He can take care of you, if you let him," she said. "But it won't be easy. You—"

"It's never easy," he said. "But that doesn't mean I can't do it. I haven't had a drink in four years, have I?"

"No. But if you let your guard down for a minute..."

"I don't plan on letting my guard down," he said. "I'm not just a cop, I'm an undercover cop. Being on guard is what it's all about."

CHAPTER *Five*

The meeting had been requested by Ricardo Estévez. Times were difficult and change was in the air. And with change comes challenge. And Estévez had always believed challenges were best met when they were met in unison—even among competitors.

Julio Lopez, David Michael Salter, Ernesto Torres, and Eduardo Garcia arrived at Estévez's oceanside villa at precisely nine a.m.

Lopez and Salter arrived together in Lopez's Mercedes S400 sedan. Lopez was a short thin man with wavy black hair parted in the middle. In his day the women said he looked a little like Desi Arnaz. But time and tension had taken their toll. Any resemblance to Arnaz now was solely in the thick Cuban accent they shared.

Salter, unlike Lopez, had never been an attractive man—a fact of which he was blissfully unaware. He refused to allow his squat, rotund physique to interfere with his pursuit of the ladies, even as he entered his seventh decade. Neither did he allow the inconvenience of marriage to serve as a barrier between his obligations and his desires.

Behind Lopez and Salter, Torres and Garcia rode in Torres's armored SUV.

Ernesto Torres was a tall, thin man with a graying mustache who had long ago forgotten women in his pursuit of wealth. And he had been amply rewarded.

Next to Torres, Eduardo Garcia was peering silently out the window. Like Torres, Garcia's focus was on making a dollar. He was a tall, solidly built man, with a thick mane of gray hair and deeply set brown eyes overshadowed by bushy eyebrows. At eighty, he still had the stature of a much younger man. But the vigor he had once displayed was beginning to elude him.

In both vehicles, the principals rode in the backseat while two bodyguards rode in front. As they arrived at the villa they paused at a set of wrought-iron gates. Lopez's driver pushed the call button and identified himself. A voice told him to proceed to the house, and the gates swung open.

They drove along a gently sloping, palm-lined driveway toward the mansion that came slowly into view. The two-story Mediterranean-style home was no less than ten thousand square feet, with a balcony that rimmed the upper floor. The windows were ample and many, and the recessed entryway was protected by a wrought iron gate that matched the one through which the men had just passed. From their approaching vantage point, Estévez's guests could see behind the house to a rolling yard that sloped gently toward a large veranda that opened to a breathtaking view of the Atlantic.

As the vehicles approached the front a portly, middle-aged man stepped from the doorway. He wore a Hawaiian-style shirt, white Dockers, and topsiders. A visible bulge under his open-tailed shirt revealed a pistol tucked in his waistband. He paused near the vehicles to allow the bodyguards time to open the doors for their employers.

"Good morning," he said, stiffly. "Mr. Estévez has been eagerly awaiting your arrival." After the men had exited, he said, "This way, gentlemen."

The bodyguards had begun to follow their respective charges when the big man stopped. "Alone, please."

The four principals hesitated, before nodding to their employees that everything would be fine. The guards returned to the vehicles without hesitation as the men followed their host's man into the house.

They passed through an ornate entryway and by a grand staircase as they walked along a highly polished wood floor and came to a set of French-style doors opening onto the veranda. Ricardo Estévez was sitting on a chaise lounge, facing the Atlantic.

The escort cleared his throat and Ricardo Estévez turned to face them. Like his servant, Estévez was wearing an open-tailed Hawaiian-style shirt, Dockers, and loafers without socks. An expensive-looking gold watch wrapped around one wrist and a matching gold bracelet around the other. He was smoking a long thin cigar.

"My friends," he said, rising from the chaise, "I am so glad you could make it." His smile was as crystalline as the sea as he extended a hand to each of the men—none of whom returned his smile.

"Jimmy," Estévez said to the big man who had escorted his guests, "get them something to drink."

"What may I bring you, gentlemen?" Jimmy asked.

The men declined any refreshment. Estévez asked for coffee.

After Jimmy left, Estévez motioned for the men to have a seat around a table on the ocean side of the large patio. "It is warm for so early in the morning, but a nice breeze is beginning to come off the water."

The men followed their host to the table, where they all sat under the shade of an umbrella.

"Let me thank you for coming," Estévez said.

"We are not here because we have a choice," Lopez said. "We are trying to keep our necks and not start a war."

"Right," Salter said. "We all have had enough troubles without turning on each other. Don't you agree, Ricardo?"

"Gentlemen," the Cuban said, flashing his glittering smile, "none of us wants a war, least of all me. A war does no one any good. It is something to avoid, and that is the very reason I have asked you here this morning."

Lopez cast a skeptical glance toward the others. "Then why are you hijacking our shipments, knocking out our mules, and—"

Estévez held up a hand. "None of that is coming from me. I have had my own troubles."

"Then who is behind these attacks?" Salter asked accusingly.

"Kingman," Estévez answered without hesitation. "Of this there can be no question."

Salter failed to stifle his laugh. "*Kingman?* Why Kingman?"

"Who among us has the most trouble?" Estevez asked.

"Right now," said Torres, "I'd say it's pretty bad for all four of us."

"And for me," Estévez said. "I lost a sale last night too."

"We have lost more than sales," Garcia said. "We are losing people. They're leaving, getting arrested..."

"We can't even afford to pay the law anymore," Lopez said. "Things are drying up all over town."

Estévez was about to speak when Jimmy arrived with a mug of coffee, which he set on the table. "Will there be anything else, sir?"

Estévez told him no before pausing long enough to taste the beverage.

"The Colombians," he said admiringly. "They still make the best coffee."

Salter spoke. "Can we get back to the business at hand?"

"Thank you, Jimmy," Estévez said, dismissing the servant.

As soon as the big man was gone, Salter continued. "Why Kingman?"

"We have all had trouble. He hasn't."

The four men glanced at each other, perplexed. It was Salter who spoke next.

"And what's your point?"

"Kingman has been to Havana twice in the past month," Estévez said, taking another drink of his coffee.

The four men exchanged glances again. "And how do you know this?" Lopez asked.

Estévez said, "How I know is of no consequence. It is *what* I know that matters. And what I know is that he has traveled to Cuba on two occasions in the past thirty days. And," he said, pausing for more coffee, "there have been other trips prior to that. In each case, he has met with our Colombian friends."

"'Friends'? What are you getting at, Ricardo?" Garcia said.

"The whole world knows that the Cuban government will eventually stabilize. Raul is not capable of assuming leadership."

"Maybe not," Lopez said, "but Raul is Castro's brother, and who in Cuba will challenge him?"

"The people. They've had enough. They are finished with the Castros."

Salter furrowed his brow. "How does Kingman figure into this?"

"During the early part of the nineteen-fifties, before Fidel, the Mafia, along with some of the other families, was looking for ways to use Cuba for laundering profits. They were going to use the hotels, along with the casinos, to make the trail a lot harder to follow. But that was only one benefit. They could also work those businesses and make a nice sum on the side. And," he added, "without U.S. government intervention. But then Castro came on the scene and the opportunity was lost, along with much money." He paused to taste more of the coffee. "This is really excellent, gentlemen. Are you sure I can't get you something?"

The four shook their heads.

Estévez continued. "It is one of the reasons many people believe the Mafia was responsible for the assassination of President Kennedy. It is said the Italians delivered Chicago for him. It was Chicago that put him over the top during the general election. Whether any of that is true or not, cannot be known for sure. Too much time has passed. But later, when the invasion at Bahía de los Cochinos failed, many of the Cuban expatriates blamed Kennedy because of his lack of follow-through with the military. Without that support, the invasion was doomed to fail, and dreams of a restored Cuba were ended. A little over a year later Khrushchev installed missiles in Cuba, which the president had to force out. The missiles were removed, but only after Kennedy promised to never invade the island.

"The insult was too great to bear. My fellow countrymen lost their country and the Italians lost a lot of money." He shrugged. "So Kennedy lost his life. Whether any of this is true or not, as I said, it has been too long ago to say. But what we can say with certainty is that the opportunity will be resurrected. And we can gain a foothold in Cuba by satisfying a nation full of disgruntled people."

"And you think Kingman is doing this?" Lopez asked. "Trying to set up some kind of deal?"

"I do."

Salter shook his head. "I don't get it. How does that tie him into our problems?"

"Think about it," Estévez said. "As I said, all of us have had troubles, except Kingman." He paused to allow the men time to think. "When we add the Cuban connection into the mix, it seems clear. Kingman is trying to condense his power here to make him one of the big players in the new Cuba. He's positioning himself for a run at Havana."

Lopez reclined in his chair. Salter seemed puzzled.

"But he isn't the only one," Garcia said. "The Italians will want a piece too."

"And the Colombians," Torres added. "And the Asians."

Salter shook his head. "I don't get it," he said. "What does he hope to gain? He isn't a young man."

"But Kingman has a son," Lopez said, mostly to himself, as he began to put the pieces together.

"Besides," Estévez added, "Kingman was one of the invaders at the Bay of Pigs. He wants to see Cuba restored and he wants his share of it before he dies."

"So you think our enemy is Kingman?" Garcia asked. "You think he's behind all of this?"

"Yes," Estévez said. "I believe he is behind our hijacked shipments, the warehouse fires, killing our mules...it all fits."

"You think he is behind the crackdown too?" Lopez asked. "I have a hard time believing that."

"You should, because he isn't. That, my friends, is the circle of life. We've been through it before. Something happens, something that makes news—in this case a college coed who takes too much acid—and suddenly the public is up in arms." He smiled and waved a dismissive hand. "It will all pass. It has happened before and it will happen again. Kingman is not behind the arrests of minor dealers and the raids that are choking our supply lines. On the contrary, this is coming from the politicians and the public. It will only last for a while. The public doesn't really want us to stop. They can't afford for us to stop. But let something happen for which they feel responsible, and suddenly they develop a conscience that bursts in outrage and the police go crazy." He shook his head. "No, Kingman is not behind this. This is a temporary cost of doing business. You toss the police a few kilos, a few mules, a club or two, and it all goes away."

"Let us hope so," Garcia said. "It will be hard to fight a war on two fronts."

Estévez smiled. "We don't have to, my friend. Let the police have their show. Meanwhile, we concentrate on Kingman."

He sipped from the cup.

"And now, gentlemen, you *must* try this coffee. Jimmy?"

CHAPTER *Six*

Michael Santiago was exhausted despite having slept later than usual. His reddened eyes tried to focus on the first cigarette of the day as his hands struggled to hold the match steady. Once he'd lit up, he inhaled deeply.

The Mexican ached all the way from his matted hair to the gold-capped tip of his boots. Stress had that effect on him. But he had slept in his own bed and he was still alive, two things that had not been a certainty the prior evening.

Predictably, Estévez had not taken news of the events in the Everglades lightly. He'd exploded over the loss of his kilo of cocaine and began slapping the diminutive Mexican around the room, before putting the barrel of a loaded pistol to the man's ear and threatening to blow his brains all over the bar. But then Santiago claimed someone had set him up—and it was because of Ortega's quick-thinking that four of the five kilos had been saved.

"Hold on," Jimmy said, as Estevez continued to hold the gun against the Mexican's ear. "If you waste him here it'll ruin the bar. Why not do him in the office?" As Estevez wasa about to pull Mikey away from the bar, Jimmy corrected himself. "No, wait. That wouldn't be any good. We'd never get the stains out of the carpet."

For the next few moments, Jimmy continued his banter with Estevez, each time correcting himself, until the drug lord had time to cool down and regain control.

The volatile Cuban relented. "This doesn't mean that we're okay," he had said, taking the gun from Santiago's ear, "but it does mean you have another day to make things right." From the Mexican's standpoint, "another day to make things right" was a reason to live.

Estévez had told Santiago to bring "the man who saved my product" to the club prior to opening. He also gave Santiago an assignment: find a fresh piece of news—gossip even—that could help further his empire and keep him a notch above his competitors. The former task would not be hard. The latter could be a bit more difficult since the recent clampdown had all but stifled activity, along with the willingness of people to talk about it. Being a snitch was difficult at best. But when there was nothing happening to snitch about, the job became downright impossible.

After finishing the cigarette and downing a bottle of Corona, Santiago left his apartment and began heading west for two reasons.

First, Hokey's was a local hangout for anyone who made their living off the streets. Hustlers, dealers, and con men all ate at Hokey's. But there were also games of chance in the backroom of the restaurant—gaming that provided Santiago with an additional layer of income.

Second, he needed to think, and sitting in the apartment staring at lime-green walls and TV game shows wasn't fodder for the kind of thinking necessary. He needed to be out and about—to oil the process. He needed to be where the talk was happening.

Within a few minutes, he had covered six blocks, bouncing his yo-yo as he walked, when the solution to his second task drove past in a Miami Police Department squad car.

Officers Dowd and Hurst were two of Miami's finest. As their patrol car passed Santiago walking in the opposite direction, Hurst, who was driving, turned in his seat to take a second look at the Mexican.

"That Santiago?" he asked.

Dowd turned in his seat. "Yep. I do believe it is."

Hurst flicked on the light bar across the top of their squad car and made a broad U-turn. As he approached Santiago, he screeched the car to a halt, curbside.

Dowd jumped out of the car. "On the wall, Mikey, and spread 'em."

The Mexican calmly tucked the yo-yo in his pocket and turned to put his hands on the exterior of the building. "Come on, Dowd," he said, the cigarette dangling in time with each syllable, "you guys got no reason for pushing me like this. I ain't done nothin'."

Dowd did a pat down, found a .38-caliber handgun in the man's pocket and confiscated it along with the yo-yo. "No reason?"

The Mexican sighed and rolled his eyes.

"Get in the car," Dowd said, shoving the wiry hustler toward the patrol car.

"Why? I ain't done—"

"Shut up and get in the car."

Dowd opened the left rear door, shoved Santiago into the squad, and slid in next to him. He handed the gun to his partner.

As soon as the door was closed, Hurst pulled away from the curb and drove four miles west before turning into an alley that ran between a restaurant and a vacant building. He killed the engine and turned in his seat to face Santiago. Neither officer said a word.

The Mexican looked back and forth between Dowd and Hurst. "What? What do you want?"

"We ain't been paid," Dowd said. "We ain't been paid for two weeks. By anybody."

"No one's paying," Hurst added.

Santiago flashed a nervous smile. "Guys, come on."

"Two-and-a-*half* weeks, Mikey," Hurst said. "And we've been looking the other way on a lot of nasty stuff. And we're doing it for a lot of nasty people."

"A lot of nasty *illegal* stuff," Dowd added.

"Like this piece you been carrying," Hurst said. "You know convicted felons aren't allowed to carry firearms."

"Hey, come on guys, come on. Things have been a little slow. People ain't makin' the jack like they—"

Dowd drove his elbow into the man's side, driving the air out of him in an explosive sigh.

Santiago groaned and clutched his abdomen.

Dowd got out of the car, leaving the rear door open as he leaned against the quarter panel, working the yo-yo until the Mexican could get his wind back.

"Take a deep breath," Hurst said. "Nice and slow."

Santiago coughed, sputtered, and coughed again.

"We ain't got all day, partner," Dowd said, bouncing the yo-yo up and down. "Why don't we teach this little snit a lesson about holdin' out on us? Nothing spreads faster around here than the word of a busted-up Mexican."

Santiago gasped. His color began to return.

"You feeling better, now?" Hurst asked.

Their victim nodded, gasped again, and attempted a weak smile.

"Okay then," Hurst said. "You can deal with me, or you can deal with him. But you have to deal. Understand?"

Santiago clutched his side as he nodded. He was still unable to speak.

"We haven't been paid in two-and-a-half weeks," Hurst repeated. "Now I know business can be slow, especially during times like these, and we don't want to seem greedy. But a deal is a deal. So it doesn't really matter to us if things are slow or not."

"Which they're not," Dowd said, as he continued leaning against the car, playing with the yo-yo. "Stuff is still gettin' moved and nobody is paying their fair share."

"A lot of stuff," Hurst added.

"Okay, okay, I got the message," Santiago said, regaining his strength. "I'll see what I can do."

Hurst shook his head. "Not good enough, Mikey. We're going to have to have more than that."

Dowd quit rolling the yo-yo and turned to look directly at the Mexican through the open door. "What kind of reputation are we going to have with your friends if we let you walk away from this?"

Santiago was being good copped-bad copped. He knew that. But he also knew that both of these dudes were truly bad cops. It wasn't a game for them. Even the good cop was capable of killing him for holding out.

"Hey, look guys," he said, with a nervous laugh, "there's enough for all of us, you know? Like I said, I'll see what I can do."

Hurst glanced at his partner. "What do you want to do?"

"Kill him. How else we going to send a message that we're not to be messed with?"

Santiago tried to read between the lines. Tried to see how far the good badge-bad badge would go.

"Come on guys," he said, his voice starting to break. "We can work somethin' out. Right?"

Hurst said, "I'd like to, Mikey. I really would. But you owe us two-hundred-fifty—each. And we just can't let that slide."

"I say we kill him," Dowd said again, still peering at the Mexican through the open door. "We can't exactly arrest him, so that doesn't leave us a lot of options."

Hurst stroked his chin, appearing thoughtful, reflective. "That's true. And nobody would care. Besides, we'd be doing our jobs."

"Ridding Miami of the filth that preys on decent citizens everyday," said Dowd.

Santiago looked for a break in their countenance: something—anything—that would give him some glimmer of hope.

"Guys, guys, come on. You know I'm good for it."

"How good?" asked Hurst.

"Good. Real good."

"Good like, 'I can get you officers your money by tomorrow afternoon' good?" asked Dowd. His expression was flat.

Santiago looked to Hurst and saw the same lifeless stare.

"Sure. Sure, guys. I can have it to you by tomorrow afternoon."

Hurst smiled and looked at Dowd. "See there, Frank? I knew Mikey would come through."

Dowd pulled the diminutive Mexican from the car and slammed him against the side of a building.

Santiago fell to the ground and Dowd kicked him, forcing the smaller man into a fetal position.

"Two o'clock, Mikey," Hurst said. "Two o'clock tomorrow or I'm going to let my partner, here, finish what he started."

"And pass the word along," Dowd said. "Tell all of your buddies if we don't get our cut, we're going to be awfully upset." He tossed the yo-yo onto the wilted Mexican before slamming the rear door and climbing into the front seat next to his partner. "And that's two-hundred-fifty apiece," he said. "Comprende?"

"Comprende," Santiago said, pleased that he now had the information Estévez required of him.

CHAPTER *Seven*

Santiago called the guy he knew as Ron Acuna from Hokey's and told him to meet him there. Having the second part of what Estévez demanded of him, the hustler now needed to arrange a meeting between his friend and the club owner. The meeting would fulfill the first part of the implied contract that would allow Santiago to continue living.

It was a few minutes after eleven when Ron Ortega slid into the booth, across the table from Santiago.

"What's happened to you?" Ortega asked, noticing the man's bruises.

"I ran into some business," he said, washing down part of an enchilada with the last of his second Corona of the morning.

Ortega studied the Mexican. His movements were slow, deliberate. He was guarded, like a man who is in pain and trying to hide it.

"Estévez?" he asked.

Santiago shook his head. "No. A couple of cops who aren't getting paid."

"Cops?" Ortega asked, causing several heads to turn.

Santiago's grimace caused Ortega to lower his voice as he glanced around the partially filled diner.

"What kind of cops?"

"What kind of cops? What does it matter? Cops is cops. And when they don't get paid, things get worse. And things is as worse now as they've been in a long time."

"This crackdown has got everybody on edge," Ortega said. "But people still have needs and stuff will still need to be moved."

Santiago agreed. "The problem isn't the demand. It's meeting the demand without going to jail."

"Sounds like there are other problems too. These guys work you over?"

The Mexican shrugged as he leaned back in the booth and began toying with the empty beer bottle.

"How much do you owe these guys?"

"Two-fifty. For each of them."

"You got it?"

"Yeah. I've been busy. Just haven't had time to get it to them."

"They come to you or do you have to go to them?"

Santiago frowned. "What do you care? It's none of your business anyway."

Ortega ran a hand through his hair. "No, I guess not. But I can run it to them if you want. I don't have anything else going on."

"You might," said Santiago. "I'm supposed to introduce you to Estévez."

"I thought we were going to make collections today."

Santiago shrugged. "We were, but things have changed. I told Estévez about the problem we ran into last night and—"

"How'd he take it?"

The Mexican rolled his eyes. "If Jimmy hadn't been there then, I don't think I'd be here now."

"Why do you work with this guy? If he's that volatile, why don't—"

"What do I look like to you, a brain surgeon? I got no choice. I live in the barrio. I do what I got to do to survive."

Ortega sighed. "Okay. I didn't mean anything by it."

"You're not doing so well yourself. Right?"

"Right."

"I mean, you're doing what I'm doing 'cause you ain't no brain surgeon either."

"No."

The Mexican relaxed, slouching in the booth. Ortega watched as he continued to toy with the empty bottle.

"You sure you don't want me to run the money to them? I can if you want," Ortega said. "No reason to have these guys boost you again."

The Mexican sighed. "I don't want to see them right now." His hand trembled. "I really don't want to have to see them—ever. You know?"

"Okay. I'll take it to them. Just tell me when and where."

Santiago told Ortega where to meet the officers, but then grew silent. He seemed distant, lost in a remote part of his brain that served as a sanctuary in troubled times.

"Is the food good?" Ortega asked, breaking the silence and forcing his friend back into the moment.

"It's cheap. That makes it good. Listen, I got to introduce you to Estévez. That means he took note of what I told him." He leaned across the table and dropped his voice. "And that's a good thing for both of us. So don't go messing it up."

"I won't."

"The man throws me work and I don't want it to stop."

"Okay," Ortega said, acknowledging his lower rung on the ladder.

There was another long pause, before Santiago said, "I didn't plan on doing this, you know."

"Okay."

"My mother worked hard for her kids."

"I'll bet she did."

He eased back into his side of the booth as he continued to roll the base of the bottle on the table. "But sometimes you can take a wrong turn in life, you know?"

"I know. Trust me, I know."

Santiago nodded. "You been there. You know what it's like to be down and out."

"Yes."

"Sometimes, you just can't get out. Once the life gets a piece of you, you just kind of…fall into it. No way out."

Ortega wanted to tell him there was a way out. That he didn't have to live as he did. But the job required him to be silent—to follow Santiago's lead into a lifestyle the hustler was now regretting. For now, Santiago was the best guide the agent had through the gates of hell.

CHAPTER *Eight*

The Oasis was located on Ocean Drive in the heart of Miami's South Beach. Like the beautiful people who populated the famous strip, the club was a trendsetter, a wonder to behold.

Majestic palms lined the sidewalk in front of the club. An expertly crafted cobblestone walkway led toward the impressive grand entrance. It wasn't hard to imagine how the place would look at night, aglitter with lights, scores of club hoppers waiting to enter.

But it was noon now, and no lines had formed in front. Instead, the beautiful people ambled along Ocean Drive, carrying shopping bags full of baubles from the city's finest retailers. Others zipped by in sporty high-priced cars. At a stoplight right near the club, Ortega saw an attractive blonde, no older than himself, sitting behind the wheel of a Ferrari. He kept his eye on it until the light turned green and the car sped away. He wondered how Libby would like to drive a car like that and shop in the places these women shopped. She deserved it. And he wanted her to have it. To make her proud of what he had accomplished, to—

"Come on, man, you can check her out later," Santiago said, tugging on Ortega's arm.

"I was looking at the car."

Santiago snickered. "Sure."

The Mexican steered his friend toward the club's huge chrome-accented doors. "We don't want to be late."

Ortega was struck by the grandeur of the place. The inside of the club was everything the outside had promised. The floor was divided into two decks separated by a flight of stairs that spiraled upward on each side. A bar ran along the left side of the lower floor, and it appeared to be made of crystal. A large mirror hung on the wall behind it, and a chrome footrail lined the lower portion. To the right, a large bandstand was outfitted with a series of overhead lights that could have graced the stage of any Broadway theater. Straight ahead was a large dance floor and a smattering of tables and booths, staggered at varying heights.

The deck above them seemed to be equally large, and went back deeper than Ortega was able to see from his position.

"Pretty nice, huh?" Santiago said.

"Pretty nice," Ortega replied.

The Mexican gestured for his friend to follow him as they crossed the dance floor toward a narrow hallway on the other side of the room. Before they could clear the distance, a tall man wearing a black T-shirt and jeans appeared from nowhere. He put his hand on the Mexican's chest. A tattoo of two linking hearts was etched on the man's forearm.

"We're closed, sir," the man said.

"We're here to see Mr. Estévez," Santiago said. He began to move past, but the bouncer moved in front of the Mexican again.

"I said we're closed."

Santiago stiffened. "And I said we're going to meet with Mr. Estévez."

Just then, another man, bigger and also much older, stepped from the hallway. He was wearing a Hawaiian-style shirt, white Dockers, and topsiders. Ortega could make out the bulge of a handgun tucked under the man's open-tailed shirt.

"Mikey?" the man said.

"Hey, Jimmy," Santiago said, clasping the bouncer's hand in a finger-clutch handshake. "What's happenin'?" The Mexican glared at the man who had tried to stop him.

"It's okay," the big man said. "I got this one."

The other man nodded, gave Santiago a once-over, then moved toward the bandstand, where he went to work helping the others suspend the new lighting.

The older man shifted his gaze to Ortega, before looking again at Santiago. "You here for your meeting with Mr. Estévez?"

"As a matter of fact," the diminutive Mexican said, "we are." He slapped Ortega on the back. "He asked to meet my friend, Ron."

Jimmy told the men to have a seat and left. Ortega and the Mexican sat in one of the booths near the dance floor.

"Is this great or what?"

"It's great," Ortega said, glancing around the room. "So, tell me. Is Estévez upset with me? After all, I'm the one who told you to toss the junk."

Santiago shrugged. "Like I said, he wasn't happy. But he knows we were trying to save as much of his stuff as we could. I bungled the deal. Not you. So don't be worrying about that. Just let me do the talking."

Ortega agreed, but told Santiago he wanted him to know he would be willing to take his share of the blame.

"Mikey," Estévez said, smiling as he emerged from his office with Jimmy in tow.

Santiago had been in the business long enough to know that life can pivot on the head of a pin. The man who was now smiling warmly had been the same man who'd put a gun in the hustler's ear just a few hours before. He rose from the booth and clasped the club owner's hand before giving him a light embrace.

"Mr. Estévez, this is Ron Acuna. He's the one I told you about."

Estévez extended a hand and Ortega shook it. Over the drug lord's shoulder, Santiago was gesturing for his friend to stand. Ortega stood.

"I wanted to meet you personally," Estévez said. "Mikey told me what you did for me, and that you're a friend of his. And in this place, any friend of Mikey's is a friend of mine."

Ortega smiled. "I was glad I could help."

Estévez gestured for the men to sit. "Is there anything I can get for you?"

"Coffee would be fine," Ortega said.

"Corona would be better," Santiago added.

Estévez muttered something to Jimmy and the man moved away as the club owner slid into the booth next to Santiago, opposite Ortega.

"Mikey tells me you hail from Chicago."

Ortega nodded. "Born and raised. I did some time in Joliet, but when I got out, I couldn't land a job that was worth having. I thought if I got far enough away that might change."

"Has it?" Estévez asked.

"No."

The drug lord smiled. "Did you expect it to?"

Ortega shrugged. "I was hoping."

Estévez threw an arm over the back of the booth. The gesture made Santiago uncomfortable, a fact that didn't go unnoticed by Ortega.

"Mikey is a good man," Estévez said, gently patting him on the back. "He can show you the ropes. He knows his stuff."

"We met during a poker game at Hokey's," Santiago said. "I was trying to hustle him, but he ended up hustling me."

Estévez seemed impressed. "You must be pretty good if you were able to take Mikey."

Ortega shrugged. "I'm okay, I guess. I can't sing or dance, so I play poker and drive fast cars."

Estévez smiled, but it didn't come from his eyes. "Mikey tells me he's very impressed with your skill. Mikey is not often impressed."

"Thank you. And again, I am sorry for the hasty decision last night, but I was trying to save as much of your…product as possible."

"I will admit I was very unhappy about the deal going sour and the loss I incurred. But none of that is your fault. You made a decision under pressure, and your decision saved me a lot of money. I am grateful."

The Mexican was about to speak, when he was interrupted by a tall blonde dressed in a white blouse, an emerald green vest with the logo of the club, and black slacks. The color of her eyes matched the vest and she had the kind of tan George Hamilton has been chasing all his life.

She set an open bottle of Corona in front of the Mexican, a cup of coffee in front of Estévez, and another in front of Ortega. The cups were transparent and bore the same logo as the vest she was wearing. She smiled at Ortega.

"This is Chipper," Estévez said. "She has managed my bar for over two years now. She is the best in the business."

"Is there anything else I can get for you?" she asked.

Ortega politely declined. Santiago had already wrapped his mouth around the bottle and shook his head. Chipper left with the tray in front of her.

"Do you have a family?" Estévez asked Ortega.

"No. I have a mother in Chicago, but we're not close. I see her once in a while."

Estévez shook his head. "That is too bad, my friend. But I understand your situation. I too have a mother and we are not close either. But I do have a beautiful wife and two daughters. They are the light of my life. It is for them that I do what I do." He paused to drink, blowing on his coffee before putting his lips to the cup. "When you have a family, you will understand."

"I'm sure I will," Ortega said. Like his host, he blew on his coffee before tasting. "This is excellent," he said. "Very smooth. Very good."

"It's Colombian," Estévez said. "I was telling some of my friends earlier today how much I prefer their coffee." He nodded toward his guest's cup. "I see you prefer it black."

"Good coffee should be savored as it is, without additives."

Estévez smiled a wide smile. "I agree. It is something I have said for years."

Ortega set the cup down. "Again, Mr. Estévez, I'm sorry for the loss. Please don't blame Mikey. I made the decision."

Santiago shifted uncomfortably.

"Please, do not apologize further. What is done is done. I'm glad you were there. You acted decisively and I am always impressed by decisiveness. Not to mention," he added, "Mikey has vouched for you. That means something to me."

Santiago smiled.

"He has told me about your driving. Have you driven somewhere before?" Estévez said.

Talking with the Cuban drug lord was like talking with Dracula. On the exterior he was a man of accomplishment. His diction was faultless. His demeanor gracious. His appearance impeccable. By all visible measure he was well-bred, urbane. But Ortega's research had revealed more of the man than his appearance showed. On the inside, Ricardo Estévez was a churning den of vipers.

Ortega shrugged. "I drove on the circuit for a while, but could never seem to make it big. I wasn't good enough, I guess."

"The circuit?"

"State fairs, things like that. I wanted to drive in NASCAR but...I could never seem to get the backing. Things were tight and I didn't want to find a nine-to-five because it could disrupt my driving career. So I started doing what I had to do. Burglaries, mostly. Some residential, but some businesses too. I was pretty good at that and got to the point where I could penetrate any alarm system." He shrugged. "But I guess I wasn't good enough. I got busted and ended up doing a stretch at Joliet. I got out and couldn't find work in Chicago, so I came to Miami."

"Why Miami?"

Ortega shrugged. "Why not? I had to go somewhere and it's as far from Chicago as anyplace else."

"And you could not find work in Chicago? It's a much bigger city than Miami," Estévez said.

"I suppose I could flip burgers in Chicago. Maybe drive a truck or go back to doing what sent me up in the first place. But there wasn't much else. It didn't take long for me to learn that if I wanted to be successful, make some real money, I had to leave."

Estévez swirled the coffee in his cup before drinking. "It is hard to get a foothold on the ladder of success, my friend."

"That's why I'm here," Ortega said. "I'm after a foothold."

CHAPTER *Nine*

Ortega left after the meeting with Estévez ended. By all appearances, so had Santiago. But the diminutive Mexican doubled back, returning to The Oasis within a few minutes. He had news for Estévez and that news was the second part of the deal that allowed him to continue living. The first, arranging a meeting between Estévez and Acuna, had gone very well. The Mexican had high hopes that the news he was about to deliver would be equally well received.

"What is it, Mikey?" Estévez asked, returning to the dance floor with Jimmy following close behind.

"I have some news that might interest you," Santiago said. "It certainly interested me."

The club owner put his hands on his hips and sighed. "Let's have it."

"After I left here earlier this morning I ran into two cops. Dowd and Hurst." He paused to see if Estévez had a reaction.

"So? Who are they to me?"

"They're on the payroll," Santiago said. "Your payroll, among others. Except they aren't getting paid. By anybody, including you."

"You know this?"

"They cornered me this morning. Said they are not getting their money. They said they are doing their part by looking the other way, but they aren't going to keep doing it if the spigot doesn't open up."

"Where did you run into these officers?"

He told him.

Estévez turned to Jimmy. "Find out who isn't paying the tab. Bring their names to me."

"Okay," Jimmy said, turning to leave.

"And Jimmy?"

"Yeah?"

"Check out this Acuna too. He said he's done time in Joliet. Check him out."

Jimmy nodded and left.

Estévez then motioned toward the booth in which he and the Mexican had been sitting earlier. As the two men sat, Estevez said, "I'm still not happy about last night's deal, but you have done me a service today. The law is breathing down everyone's neck and it doesn't help our interests if they aren't getting paid."

"I thought this might come at the right time, Mr. Estévez."

"It does, Mikey. And I appreciate it." He handed the snitch a roll of bills.

Santiago feigned lack of interest. "Oh, Mr. Estévez, I can't take that. I owe you for last night."

Estévez shrugged. "Forget about it. What's done is done. Besides, I like your friend."

"He's on the up and up, Mr. Estévez. He could have rolled on us last night, but he didn't."

"Sure, Mikey. But it never hurts to check on things."

"Yeah. That's right. Of course, Mr. Estévez."

"After all," the club owner said with a smile, "if he turns on us I won't be the only one who gets bitten. He'll be biting you too."

"That's right." The Mexican glanced at the cash and licked his lips.

Estévez smiled. "So take the money, Mikey. You earned it. Do something nice for yourself."

"Okay," he said, nervously. "Okay, Mr. Estévez. I can use it. No question about that."

He reached for the roll of money but the Cuban maintained a firm grip on the cash.

"Mikey, I may have some work for you."

"Yes?"

"Yes. Jimmy is going to find out who isn't paying their bills. Then we're going to deal with it."

"Okay. What do you want me to do?"

"I want you to call your friend. He's going to drive Jimmy on his rounds."

Santiago swallowed hard. His hand had a firm grip on one end of the cash while Estévez maintained a firm grip on the other.

"If he doesn't show, we're going to think that maybe he isn't what you say he is."

Santiago laughed nervously. "He's okay, Mr. Estévez. Really."

Estévez maintained his grip on the money.

"He's clean, Mr. Estévez. Really."

Estévez continued to stare, continued to maintain his grip.

"Why would I roll you, Mr. Estévez? You've always been fair with me. I don't have a beef with you."

The businessman maintained his grip a bit longer, then suddenly released it and broke into a dazzling smile. "You're right, Mikey. Thank you. As I said, take the money and do something nice with it."

Santiago smiled nervously and pocketed the bills.

"Jimmy will call you and let you know when to have your friend come around."

"Okay, Mr. Estévez."

"Don't feel bad, Mikey," Estévez said, standing to leave. "If your friend's story checks out, then we have work for him. But if his story doesn't check out, then we have other plans." The Cuban paused to look at Chipper, who was working behind the bar, and then to glance over his shoulder at the men who were suspending the new lighting system. He leaned close enough to the Mexican's face to see the beads of sweat that had formed along his Errol Flynn mustache. "Either way, it is in your best interest to see that he shows."

"He'll be there, Mr. Estévez. I promise. He'll be there."

CHAPTER *Ten*

Ortega opened the refrigerator. Except for the lightbulb, a jar of olives, a case of Sprite, two TV dinners, and a half pound of bologna, it was empty. He reached for a TV dinner but was interrupted by a knock at the door.

Setting the TV dinner onto the counter, he went into the living room and quietly picked up the Glock from the table where he had put it earlier that morning.

"Who is it?"

Someone muttered something, but the voice was too low to be heard. He peered through the peephole and saw a short middle-aged man dressed in a short-sleeved shirt, jeans, and tennis shoes. He was chewing gun and wearing a Miami Dolphins ball cap that revealed thick patches of graying hair. His hands were thrust into the rear pockets of his jeans.

Ortega opened the door as far as the chain would allow. He kept the Glock in his other hand, behind the door and pointed at the man's abdomen.

"Yeah?"

The man pulled a leather credential case from his hip pocket. The credentials identified him as Meryl O'Connor, DEA.

O'Connor was sitting on Ortega's recliner with one leg tossed casually over the arm. He was drinking a can of Sprite he had taken from his host's refrigerator. Ortega was eating a chicken wing from the TV dinner.

"So, Meryl, you're my lifeline?" he asked, biting into the chicken.

"Ain't you the lucky one," the man said in a Boston accent.

"I could use some luck. My big mouth seems to squash what little I have."

O'Connor chuckled. "You got a big break, kid. Take it. They don't come that often. You crack this Estévez thing, and we'll be on our way to shutting down The Corporation for years to come."

Ortega picked a bone from the wing and tossed it into the dinner tray. "There'll always be somebody waiting to take over. I'm just chopping off one of its heads. The snake will live."

"Probably. But that isn't for us to decide. Our job is to meet them head on, ring their bell, and take them off the streets. When the next batch comes into power, we get to do it all over again." He shifted his position on the recliner. "How much do you know about Estévez?"

Ortega shrugged. "Enough. I've talked to a lot of the locals. I know he's an up-and-coming player and his power base is fairly broad. I also know he fronts his operations from a place called The Oasis." He picked up a chicken leg. "I went there today and it's very nice, very upscale." He took a bite.

"That's it?"

"Yeah, pretty much."

O'Connor grinned. It was a grin of superiority. The kind of a grin designed to put the younger agent in his place.

"There was a time," O'Connor said, "when the Cubans ruled the drug trade here. And I don't mean just in Miami. They bought the junk from the Colombians, who were more than happy to let the Cubans bear the costs of delivery and take the hits when a deal went sour. But all that began to change when the Colombians started to rethink things and decided they could control importation of the stuff themselves and do a better job of selling it too."

"You've got to give the cheeky devils credit," Ortega said. "It does make sense for them to take over distribution."

"Right. It truly became a 'cut out the middle man' kind of deal. But as time went by, the Colombians became almost too successful at moving their stuff into this country, and the result was that more and more people began to dip their finger."

"Or their nose, if you want to be accurate."

"Ultimately, an estimated ten percent. Personally, I think the number was higher. Then it wasn't long before crack came along and Reagan launched his war on drugs."

" 'Just say no,' " Ortega said, picking meat off the leg bone.

"That was the public face. The private war was far more effective. Eventually the Colombian government began going after the processing plants themselves. And they were very committed, very successful."

"But not successful enough."

O'Connor nodded. "Right. So the Colombians moved their processing operations to Peru and Bolivia."

"This is a nice lesson, Meryl, but how does this enlighten me?"

O'Connor shook his head. "Your subject is Cuban. He was moving up within The Corporation when José Battles began to fall. After Battles and his son were convicted, The Corporation continued to float along, but only for a while. Without leadership and a cohesive bond, it began to disintegrate into separate but no less dangerous subgroups. The drug trade they controlled began to fall back to the Colombians. And that presented a problem for the Cubans. Most of their enterprises have focused on gambling, allowing the Colombians to keep control of the coke. But with various state governments getting into gambling, the Cubans are seeing their profits erode."

"So they want back into the business that centers on a self-sustaining product."

"Right. Estévez sees himself as the heir apparent to the Battles fortune. If he can reunite the major Cuban players before they completely divide, he may be able to jockey for position and rebuild what is slowly being lost. And make no mistake about it, he has the clout to get it done. He's already extended a hand to the Italians in New York and Chicago, and they're listening."

"So what's stopping him?"

"Henny Kingman."

Ortega bit into the chicken, but paused long enough to see if he could recall the name. He shook his head. "Sorry," he said, "that doesn't ring a bell."

"No reason why it should. He's low-profile compared to Estévez, but tends to do a significant amount of business, particularly along the west side. There's been a sort of unwritten rule that Estévez takes the east side of the city and Kingman the west. There are others, of course, guys like Lopez, Salter, and Torres, but compared to the first two, they're considerably smaller. Their value comes in the fact they control some of the distribution routes that were part of The Corporation's business."

Ortega finished the last of the chicken. "You think there might be a war brewing between Kingman and Estévez?"

"Well, something is brewing, that's for sure. It's in Estévez's best interest to avoid a shooting war, especially over the coke trade. That would surely bring the Colombians into the mix and since he has to get his product from them, there would be a problem. But we also know he will do what he has to do to survive."

"Yeah, I guess," Ortega said, digging into the small pocket of whole-kernel corn. "It seems a lot smarter, though, with all the pressure on them, if they'd set their differences aside and work together."

O'Connor laughed. "How long you been with the Administration?"

"Three years."

O'Connor laughed again, shook his head, and took a long drink of the Sprite. "These guys are big-league. They don't let something like a little bit of pressure from us stop them from doing business. The demand for their stuff isn't going to go away. It's not like they're selling newspapers."

"Then what's the point of all this?" Ortega asked.

"It's politics, pure and simple. Some politician's niece—"

"The *mayor's* niece."

O'Connor acknowledged his error. "The *mayor's* niece, excuse me, OD's on some acid and suddenly we got us an all-out police war. Where were these guys when the last ten people OD'd, huh?"

"Who cares? The fact is, we're in it now, and we've got ourselves an opportunity to do some real damage to Estévez and his group. That's good news even if it saves just one more kid."

"Sure. I agree. But like I said, it's all politics. This thing will blow over and everything will go back as it was. Drugs will get sold, people will use them, and we'll continue to bust them. It's what makes our world go round."

"So we should give up?" Ortega asked, scraping the tray for what was left of the corn.

"Of course not. I'm just saying that your assertion these people can somehow pull together to fight a common enemy—us, in particular—is unrealistic. Money gets in the way, and that's when things start to fall apart. Throw a few bucks at them and their vision suddenly gets all blurry and they start doing things that aren't always in their best interests, which is one of the reasons I'm here."

Ortega consumed the mashed potatoes in two quick bites and rose to toss the empty tray into the trash. "You trying to imply something?" he asked.

"No. I'm stating it outright. You're going headlong into one of the darkest, most violent criminal enterprises to ever do business in Miami. The Corporation was Battles's baby. But since he's left, it has taken on a life of its own. It's become a living thing. A highly *desirable* living thing, even if it is fragmenting."

"I've been with the Administration for three years, now. I've been undercover in this city for several weeks and I'm more than adequately trained," Ortega said, sliding back into his chair at the table.

"Sure. But you're not experienced. I am." O'Connor rose off the recliner and joined Ortega by sitting across the table from his younger counterpart. "You will not only have to avoid the danger of being caught, you'll also have to avoid the danger of being enticed."

Ortega shook his head. "I know all of that."

"No, you don't. You know *about* all of that. For you, it's academic. But it's about to become real. Very real."

"I can handle it."

"I hope so," O'Connor said, "Because it's like that snake you were talking about. If you can't handle it, it will handle you."

CHAPTER *Eleven*

Jimmy Caltabiano, the club's head bouncer, who also doubled as Estévez's chief bodyguard and enforcer, had once been a New York City cop. Until he was discharged for "conduct unbecoming." The charge came when it was discovered he had accepted a thousand-dollar offer to forget what he knew about an armed robbery. An internal-affairs investigation followed closely on the heels of the formal charge, which finally resulted in the disciplinary action that ended his mediocre thirty-year career.

Soon after his discharge from the NYPD, his second marriage ended in divorce and his new battle with the bottle began in earnest. With no skills other than those he possessed with a gun or his fists, he scrounged for menial positions that usually ended as disgracefully as had his primary career, but with much less fanfare. Being fired for drinking on the job carried less prestige than taking a bribe. Not that he was proud of either. But neither was he ashamed. His slide to the bottom had been so gradual that when he finally arrived there, it hadn't come as a surprise. A man is what he is, he reasoned. Why fight fate?

But then he'd met Ricardo Estévez. Here was a man the former New York City cop was supposed to hate. But for Caltabiano, the lines had blurred a long time ago, and he no longer had the stomach for a war that wasn't his to fight. It was much better to take care of one's own immediate needs than to get sucked into fighting the wars the politicians started. After all, anything can be made illegal. All it took was the passage of a law. It happened with prohibition and look how that turned out. A lot of good cops went bad, and a lot of bad cops made money on a law that should never have been passed in the first place. People wanted their booze, just like they want their blow. And as long there's enough desire, any enforcement of well-intentioned legislation will fail.

It had been a hard lesson for the ex-cop to learn, but he had learned it. And if Estévez was willing to pay him for doing a job that helped satisfy the customers' desire, who was he to say no? What was illegal today could become legal tomorrow. All it would take was a legislator's vote—or a judge's decision to strike down a law. And just as it had in the case of prohibition, that vote would ultimately come. To Jimmy Caltabiano, it no longer made sense to be the last man to die in a war that had already been lost.

But Estévez had offered something more—something beyond a paycheck. He offered redemption. And that was something the twice-divorced, disgraced ex-cop desperately needed. He valued the chance to show himself he could do the job; that his work and his life still had worth. And Estévez gave him that chance. And Caltabiano loved the man for it.

"If our people aren't making their payments then we're going to have problems," Estévez said. He was in his office, sitting behind his desk while his enforcer stood before him.

"I can go out tonight and look into it," Jimmy said.

Estévez eased back in his chair with his hands folded casually behind his head. "I want you to do just that, Jimmy. And I want you to take this new guy, Acuna, with you."

"You think that's wise?" Jimmy asked. "With all the stuff that's going on right now, you don't think I should check him out first?"

"All this stuff is the reason for him going out."

"I don't get it."

Estévez smiled. "This stuff has raised everyone's hackles. Everyone's on guard, so it seems stupid for the law to drop a plant on us like this, if that's what he is. On the other hand, if he works with us, we'll get a better sense of it when we see him perform."

"You don't trust Mikey?"

Estévez chuckled. "Mikey's left hand doesn't trust his right. Why should I? Mikey lives on the street. He's a hustler. I don't trust any hustler. But I do listen to him. So if he tells me he got rousted because some cops aren't getting their cut, I'm going to pay attention."

Jimmy shrugged. "Times are tough now. A lot of our guys are just being cautious. Maybe the stuff isn't moving as much as they'd like."

"The demand is still there, Jimmy. People want it. *Need* it. And if we don't meet the need, someone else will." He slipped a cigar into his mouth and accepted a light from the match Jimmy extended. He puffed until the cigar was fully lit before leaning back in his chair and exhaling upward. "This thing we're going through right now is a minor inconvenience. It won't stop us. But it will damage us if we don't keep the right people happy."

"Yes, sir."

"When things get tight our people on the street will react in one of two ways. They will either begin undercutting their protection money, or begin cutting the product to keep their profits up. Either way, we ultimately lose."

Jimmy checked his watch. "You want to go now?"

Estévez shook his head. "Not yet. Let's give Mikey time to get his friend here. We'll let him drive. If he's someone we want, he'll need to see the serious end of business sooner or later."

"And if he's not, then we get rid of him?"

Estévez placed his feet on the desk. "We'll have to, Jimmy. He'll have to go away. And I don't mean back to Chicago."

CHAPTER *Twelve*

Santiago appeared at Ortega's apartment a few hours after O'Connor left. The Mexican's visit was unexpected.

"Mr. Estévez wants you to come by."

"I met him this morning," Ortega said. "What does he want now?"

The Mexican refused to sit. His hands were thrust deep into the pockets of his jeans. "He just wanted me to tell you to come."

"When?"

"Now."

Ortega glanced at the clock. It was nearly seven p.m. "I was just there today."

Santiago nodded. "Yeah, I know. I was there too, remember? But he said he wants to see you again and he told me to bring…*ask* you to come."

Estévez wouldn't have had enough time to investigate Ortega. The request meant the drug lord wanted to see Ortega in action, firsthand.

"You driving?" Ortega asked.

The Mexican shook his head. "You wrecked my van, remember? I took a cab here. You'll have to drive."

The Oasis was open when the two men arrived. They were allowed to move beyond the red velvet ropes, past the throngs of people who had gathered for a chance to party.

Inside the club, the music thumped, the drinks flowed, and the patrons gyrated to the music of a live band.

"Hey, guys," Chipper said, over the din. "It's good to see you back."

"We're looking for Jimmy," Santiago shouted over the revelry. "Is he here?"

The bar manager pointed to an area to the left of the second floor. "He's up there, Mikey. He's dealing with some people."

Santiago turned to Ortega. "Stay here, okay?" he shouted. "I'll go up and get him. I'll be right back."

Ortega waited and watched as the diminutive Mexican weaved his way through clusters of partyers.

"Is this your first time here?" Chipper asked. "I mean, except for this morning?"

"Yeah," he said, over the noise. "My first time."

She nodded, bouncing in time to the music. "Can I get you something?"

"No, thanks. I'm fine," he said, declining with a smile. "As soon as Mikey gets back, we'll probably leave."

She smiled. "Okay. But if you change your mind, ask for Chipper."

Ortega promised he would, and she flashed him a dazzling smile as she went back to the bar.

The dense crowd in the club was mainly young, with all the trappings of the upwardly mobile. At thirty, Ortega fit squarely in the age range of the dancers, and he watched as they partied unaware—or uncaring—that the man whose pockets they lined wouldn't hesitate to kill them if they somehow crossed him.

Ortega shook his head. He was their contemporary, but he had acquired a perspective that went beyond his years. Unlike them, his view of life had been blunted by its realities. His life now was one of responsibilities, and as a husband and soon-to-be father, he would do nothing that would keep him from fulfilling those roles or meeting those responsibilities.

"I found him," Santiago yelled over the noise. The Mexican had returned to the lower level. With him was Estévez's man; the one Ortega had met earlier in the day.

Jimmy—that was the name Estévez had used—had changed clothes since last time. The big man was now wearing a black T-shirt that hung loosely over the top of his dark slacks, and highly polished black loafers. The butt of the handgun was still visible as a bulge under the tail of his shirt.

"This way," he said.

Ortega and Santiago followed the man as he gently but firmly pushed his way through the throng. Once they were across the dance floor, Jimmy turned abruptly to Santiago.

"Not tonight, Mikey," the chief bouncer said. "Not tonight."

Santiago frowned.

"Not tonight, Mikey," Jimmy repeated more firmly.

The Mexican seemed hurt. He glanced at Ortega, then back to the bouncer, before looking down at his feet.

"This way," Jimmy said to Ortega as he steered the undercover agent toward the office.

They stopped at a nondescript door at the end of the hall, a door oddly out of place with the club's extravagant decor.

Jimmy knocked, announced that he had Acuna with him, and entered as soon as a voice inside responded.

The room was large. The white carpeting and blood-red draperies matched the material on two sofas that faced each other across a glass-topped coffee table. A large desk sat at one end of the room. Estévez was sitting on one of the sofas, smoking a thin cigar. There was no smile as he gestured toward the other sofa.

Ortega took a seat across from the man he hoped to put in prison, and crossed his legs. His T-shirt and jeans were clearly out of place with Estévez's sport coat, shirt, and slacks.

"You wanted to see me?" Ortega asked.

Estévez exhaled and nodded. "Yes, I did." He flicked a bit of lint off his slacks. "I have a bit of a problem, which may very well turn into an opportunity for you."

"Oh?"

"The type of business I'm in requires a certain amount of investment."

"Most businesses do."

Estévez paused to inhale on the cigar. Jimmy was standing motionless, just inside the closed office door.

"Yes, but mine has special needs." He threw his head back as he exhaled, but kept his eyes on the agent. "But of course, you already know that."

Ortega felt his palms go moist. "I'm not sure I understand."

"I know why you're here," Estévez said.

Ortega's hands began to perspire. He shifted on the sofa, clasping them around his knee. "I'm trying to get work."

"Absolutely. And I have work for you, if you want it."

Ortega glanced at Jimmy who seemed thoroughly uninterested in the conversation.

"I'll take it," Ortega said.

"Don't you want to know what it is?" Estévez asked.

Ortega shook his head. "It doesn't matter. I need work. I'm tired of TV dinners and an apartment two notches below my cell at Joliet. If you've got work for me to do, I'll do it."

Estévez smiled. "Jimmy, bring the car around. We have some people to visit."

CHAPTER *Thirteen*

Estévez and Ortega met Jimmy in an alley behind the club. Jimmy was standing next to a black Cadillac STS. The engine was running and the right rear door was open.

"You will drive," Estévez said to Ortega as he motioned toward the driver's seat.

"Where're we going?"

Estévez smiled and moved to the right rear of the car, sliding in. Jimmy closed the door and moved to the left side. He climbed into the backseat, directly behind where Ortega would be sitting.

The young undercover agent slid behind the wheel, glancing in the rearview mirror. His eyes locked with Jimmy's.

"Get onto Ocean Drive and turn left," Caltabiano said. "I will tell you where to go from there."

Ortega did as he was told and was soon following Caltabiano's directions to Miami's west side.

After thirty minutes, Jimmy leaned forward and tapped Ortega on the shoulder. "This is it. Stop here," he said.

Ortega pulled the Cadillac curbside and parked.

The apartment building sat less than fifty feet from the road. It was a yellow-brick, two-story structure with individual air-conditioning units embedded in the windows. A small parking area at the rear was partially visible from the street.

"Is this the place, Jimmy?" Estévez asked.

"This is it."

"Okay, I want you to go in and find out why this guy isn't paying out. Take Acuna with you."

"Yes, sir." Caltabiano reached over the front seat and tapped Ortega on the shoulder. "You're coming with me."

Ortega slid out of the car, ahead of the larger, slower man. Glancing about the neighborhood, the agent saw gang symbols painted on some of the other buildings that lined the street as well as the overpass several blocks away.

"And Jimmy," Estévez said, through the open door, "do what you have to do, but know when to stop."

"Yes, sir," he said, closing the rear door.

Caltabiano hooked a finger at Ortega and the two men walked across the thin, patchy yard to the building. Though the sun was down, the night was hot, the air thick enough to be nearly visible.

"This guy is on the second floor," Jimmy said, mopping perspiration from his forehead with a handkerchief. "The apartment is on the right. I want you to knock. Tell him you're the new super and he's got to let you in to install a thermostat for the new air-conditioning system. When he opens the door, you stand aside. Understand?"

The two began to climb the steps to the second floor. By the time they reached the top, Jimmy was sweating profusely and his breathing was heavy.

"Okay," he said, between gulps of air. "Do like I told you."

The television inside the apartment could be heard through the door. From an apartment somewhere above them a man and woman were yelling at each other. Ortega knocked.

"Yeah?" a voice asked.

Jimmy nodded for Ortega to say the line.

"It's the super," he said. "I got to get inside to install a thermostat. You're getting—"

"Later."

Ortega glanced at Jimmy. The Italian was making a wrap-it-up sign with his index finger.

"It's for the new air conditioner," Ortega said. "We're going to install it this week and I need to get this thermostat wired."

The man inside the apartment didn't respond, but the volume of the television came down and Ortega could hear the chain on the door being undone. As the door began to open, Jimmy moved in, shoving Ortega aside as he forced his way through the door, snapping the chain from the door casing and knocking the tenant to the floor. By the time Caltabiano crossed the threshold, he had a .38 snub-nosed revolver in his hand.

"Hi, Mario," Jimmy said. "How've you been doing?"

Ortega moved in and closed the door behind them while keeping an eye on the gun. He was about to speak, about to say something that might cause the big man to put the gun away, when Jimmy tucked the pistol into his waistband without prompting.

"Get on your feet, Mario," Jimmy said.

Mario was tall and thin, with most of his height coming from his legs. His arms were covered with tattoos, and he was wearing a striped T-shirt and jeans. "Hey, Jimmy. What's up, man? Why the visit?"

Jimmy turned to Ortega. "Get him up."

Ortega ran the list of undoables through his mind. He was undercover. He knew he'd witness crimes he must allow to continue in order to build the case he needed to build. But he was not allowed to participate in them, and that included having a ringside seat at a murder. "Jimmy," he said. "Mr.—"

"Get him up. Get him up or I'll kill the little—"

"Okay," Ortega said. "No problem."

He jerked Mario to his feet.

"Take him into the bathroom," Jimmy said.

"Hey, Jimmy," Mario said, with a nervous grin. "What's up, huh? What'd I do?"

Ortega led the man into the bathroom with Jimmy close behind. Once they were in the room, Jimmy plugged the tub and began to fill it with hot water.

"You ain't been paying for protection." Jimmy said, waiting for the tub to fill. "And we got to deal with that."

"Hey, I'm paying. Who told you I wasn't paying?"

Jimmy pulled the gun and struck the dealer on the head hard enough to knock him off his feet.

"Get him up," he said to Ortega.

Ortega kept an eye on the gun. If it looked like Jimmy was going to use it, Ortega would have to take the gun from him and that meant the undercover investigation would be over, as well as any hopes of advancing his career.

"Get up, man," Ortega said, hoisting the bleeding dealer to his feet.

"I ain't been holding out," Mario said, holding a hand to his scalp. "I ain't holding out on nobody."

The burly enforcer struck the man with the open side of his hand.

"You're lying, Mario."

"No, Jimmy. I ain't doin'—"

Jimmy slapped the man again, knocking him to the floor.

"I'm going to teach Mario a few lessons about business," Jimmy said to Ortega, jamming the pistol into his waistband again. "Why don't you get us something to drink?"

Ortega didn't want to leave the room. If things got out of hand, he could be an accessory to murder.

"I can help with this," Ortega said.

"Get us something to drink," Jimmy said, more tersely this time. "I've got to make sure this dude understands we mean what we say." He began rolling up his sleeves. Steam from the filling tub began to condense on the bathroom mirror.

Ortega weighed the situation. If Jimmy lost control of himself, Mario could end up dead. On the other hand, Estévez had explicitly told his enforcer to act within reason. And Jimmy himself had said he wanted to "teach a lesson," a strong indicator that Mario would not be murdered. Lessons, after all, have no value for the dead.

"I'll be right back," Ortega said.

He bolted across the living room to the kitchen and opened the refrigerator. He found a carton of milk and two cans of beer, along with a roll of salami, some spoiled potato salad, and a wilted head of lettuce. He could hear yelling from the bathroom, interspersed with cries of pain. He grabbed a beer and ran back to the bathroom.

When he opened the door, he was immediately engulfed in steam. Jimmy was on his knees, forcing Mario's head into the scalding water until the man seemed to no longer be able to breathe before pulling him out.

"You going to tell me again you don't know about it?" Jimmy said.

Mario sputtered. "I—"

Down he went again, gurgling, sputtering, and screaming under the tub of scalding water.

"Did you get something to drink?" Jimmy asked calmly, looking up at Ortega.

"Found a beer."

"Thanks," he said nonchalantly. "I'll be done here in a minute or two."

He pulled the drug dealer from the water. The man's face was glowing.

"More?" Jimmy asked. "We can do this all day if we have to, Mario. In fact, we can duct-tape you to that chair in there and put the lighter to you if you prefer."

"No, no, I'm okay. Please, Jimmy. I—"

Jimmy shook his head and shoved the little dealer back under the water. This time, he held the man's head long enough that Ortega could no longer hold still.

"Let him up," the agent said.

"What's that?"

"I said, let him up."

Jimmy gave him a stare that was meant to wilt. "You said what?"

Ortega wanted to maintain his cover, but also needed to get the burly enforcer off the dealer before the man drowned.

"Mr. Estévez said to not go too far. Let him up."

Jimmy hesitated, while the man gurgled and screamed beneath the hot water, before relenting by jerking him out of the tub.

"There we go, Mario," Jimmy said. "You can take care of this for us, right?"

The man gasped for breath as he began to cry.

"Right, Mario?" Jimmy asked again, opening the beer.

"Sure, Jimmy," Mario said, through stifled sobs. "I'll see that everybody gets their money."

"Good boy," Jimmy said, handing the beer to his victim. "See to it that it does. And be sure to pass the word along too. Okay? We don't want no more trouble."

Mario nodded, as he started to sip the beer.

Jimmy snapped the dealer's head back by grabbing a handful of hair. "If I have to come back here again on account that you're not paying the cops, I'll set your scalp on fire and use it to burn this place to the ground. Understand?"

Mario broke down. Subdued sobs gave way to wails.

"See?" Jimmy said to Ortega, as he rose to his feet. "All it takes is a little patience and persuasion. They come around eventually."

"Eventually" may be right, Ortega thought. But would it be in time to keep him from going to prison along with his suspects?

CHAPTER *Fourteen*

After returning to the car, Jimmy gave Estévez the story.

"Do you think he'll behave?" Estévez asked. "Or will it be necessary to visit him again?"

Jimmy grinned. "He'll comply."

The drug lord smiled. "One more stop, my friend," he said, to Ortega. "Then we call it a day."

Ortega started the car and followed the directions given him by Jimmy. If there was any concern on the enforcer's part that perhaps Mario *hadn't* been holding out on them, there wasn't any sign of it. But Ortega had his own concerns. Mario had endured torture…and for what? Just to keep silent about not paying the bribes he was supposed to pay? It didn't make sense. Most likely, Mario wasn't holding out, but had confessed to get the burly enforcer off him. And that concerned Ortega. How much more would he have to witness to build a case against these men? How far would you have to go?

The three men drove to a lower-west-side neighborhood similar to the one from which they had just come. The only significant difference was in the color of the despair. This one was predominantly black.

"Pull in here," Estévez said.

Ortega parked the Caddy along the curb by an apartment complex that looked as though it was one step ahead of the wrecking ball.

This building was considerably larger than the other one and considerably more populated. Several groupings of teens had already directed their sullen stares at the Caddy and its occupants. While Jimmy seemed aware it might be best to return later, with more support, Ortega noted that Estévez seemed oblivious to his enforcer's unspoken concern.

"He's in an apartment on the third floor," Estévez said. "His name is Tyrone Banks, but he goes by the name of Hoppity T."

Ortega watched in the rearview mirror as Jimmy surveyed the crowd.

"We might have trouble," the ex-cop said. "There's a lot of them and only two of us."

"Three," Estévez said. "I'm going with you." Without saying another word, the drug lord climbed out of the car and the other two followed. Ortega kept a sideways view on the teens, who were not only eyeing the three of them, but studying the car as well.

The Cuban drug lord lit a thin cigar and shook out the match as he began to evaluate the kids in front of him. Most of them were in their mid-teens. A few appeared to be in their early twenties. One of them, a big kid who stood well over six feet and had a lean, solid build, was standing amid a group of six others. He was wearing a white T-shirt, jeans, and a blue bandanna. He had been dribbling a basketball and talking to the others when Ortega pulled up. Now he had the ball under his left arm as he watched Estévez survey the crowd.

"What's your name?" Estévez asked the kid.

"Gabriel."

Estévez grinned and turned to Ortega and Jimmy. "Gabriel. I like it." He clamped the cigar between his teeth and said, "Come over here, Gabriel. I want to talk with you."

The kid was hesitant, whispering something to the others before resuming his stare at Estévez.

"Come on," Estévez said. "Come on over. I just want to talk."

Gabriel hesitated for a moment longer, but gave in to his curiosity and ambled toward the car, dribbling the basketball in time with every step. He stopped less than five feet from the much smaller, but much more deadly, Estévez.

"See that car?" the Cuban asked.

"Yeah."

"When the three of us come back here, I want that car to look exactly like it does now. There's a thousand in it for you."

The kid frowned. "A thousand? Just for watching your car?"

Estévez grinned.

The kid glanced over his shoulder at the others. Emboldened, he said, "Two thousand."

"Nine hundred."

"Nine hundred? You just said a thousand."

"Ah, but that was before you became greedy. So what do you say?"

"I want a thousand. A thousand or I ain't doing it."

"Eight hundred," Estévez said. "What do you say, Gabriel?"

The kid looked over his shoulder, before turning back to Estévez. "Ain't enough." He bounced the ball.

"Seven hundred, my final offer," Estévez said.

"Ain't enough. I ain't going to do it."

"Jimmy," Estévez said, "show him your piece."

Jimmy raised his shirt tail, revealing the butt of the pistol. Ortega glanced around the yard of the complex. He knew the chances were good that several of the kids were armed too, and with bigger guns.

"See that gun?" Estévez asked.

"I seen a lot of guns. Guns don't scare me. I've been shot before."

"You can be shot again. It would be no problem with me." He removed the cigar from his mouth, blew smoke in Gabriel's face, and said, "But I won't just shoot you. I'll kill you. I'll kill your whole family. And I'll kill them in front of you. And I'll do it slowly and painfully."

Gabriel looked at the car, then at Jimmy, and finally, Ortega. The agent saw something in the kid's eyes change. Something that revealed he knew he was talking with someone who didn't fear him. Someone who was sure enough of himself to drive into this neighborhood and make threats. Someone who had the muscle to back up those threats.

The kid glanced over his shoulder. "Okay," he said. "I'll take the seven hundred."

"Opportunity knocks only once, Gabriel. Now you'll be keeping it safe because I'm a nice guy."

The kid's eyes rolled again from one man to the other. "Okay. I'll watch your car."

Estévez smiled a broad smile. "Thank you, Gabriel. Thank you very much."

He patted the kid on the back and moved across the worn lawn to the building where Hoppity T lived. Ortega followed, noting that Jimmy was close behind and that Gabriel was leaning against the Caddy, giving all three of them daggers.

Ortega followed Jimmy's lead and said nothing. Any sign of disunity between the three of them would most certainly lead to an encounter that none of them wanted.

Once inside, Estévez turned to Ortega. "You can't back down, my friend. You must play the hand you're dealt, and you must play it with determination to win." He said, to Jimmy, "We will visit with Hoppity T. We will see that he understands our concern."

"Yes, sir."

"But that is all that we will do."

"Yes, sir."

Estévez didn't say another word as he moved up the flight of steps to the third floor apartment. The other two followed, and by the time they reached the top Jimmy was near to collapsing.

"I go in first," Estévez said to Ortega. "Then I want you to come in with me. Jimmy, you follow."

The big man nodded, unable to speak.

"Your gun, please," Ortega said.

The enforcer handed him the .38.

Estévez kicked in the door.

Hoppity was sitting on the sofa, cutting a mound of coke with a razor blade. His blank stare contorted into one of fear before he reached for the 9mm pistol next to the coke.

"Don't," Estévez said, coolly. "For I will surely kill you."

Hoppity's hand froze over the gun as he weighed the decision. Slowly, he let his hand drop.

Estévez and Ortega entered the apartment, and Jimmy followed, closing the door behind them.

CHAPTER *Fifteen*

It didn't go well for Hoppity. The beating was vicious, causing Ortega to again struggle with his dual role. Like the choice in the SAC's outer office, he was confronted with both sides of the same bad coin. Do the right thing? Or do the desired thing? Should he be a cop and save one dealer? Or be a cop and save hundreds of kids from the coke these guys brought into the city?

"That's enough, Jimmy," Estévez said, relaxing as the ex-cop struck their victim again.

Jimmy moved off the dealer, breathing heavily, beads of sweat across his brow.

"Now, my friend," Estévez said, to the barely conscious dealer, "you will not hold out on paying for protection any longer. Correct?"

Hoppity T was taped to a straight-backed kitchen chair. His nose was broken, teeth were missing, and both eyes were swollen to the point of closing.

Estévez leaned forward. "Hoppity? I didn't hear an answer."

The man couldn't talk, and Jimmy was about to hit him again.

"Wait," Ortega said. "Give the man a chance."

Estévez held up a hand to halt his enforcer. "I will ask you once more, Hoppity. Will you pay what you owe?"

He was wheezing and unable to speak. The best he could do was to nod his head in acknowledgment.

Estévez leaned forward again. "Tell your partner that if he had been here today, he would have been dealt with in the same manner. Today was his lucky day." He leaned closer and whispered in the man's ear. "Just pay the cops what you owe them. It really is that simple."

He handed the gun back to Jimmy. As the three were about to leave, Hoppity's partner entered. He glanced first at his friend, then at Jimmy, who still had the gun in his hand.

Hoppity's partner immediately slid back into the hallway, ducking behind the door frame. Before Ortega could react, the man's hand curved around the open door. He was holding a nickel-plated .45 and began firing blindly.

Estévez bolted back and dove behind the coffee table. Jimmy ducked behind the wall divider that ran between the kitchen and living room. Ortega dropped to the floor and crawled to the man on the chair as Jimmy returned fire.

Ortega reached the restrained Hoppity and pulled the chair to the floor where it landed with a solid thud. The manner in which gunfire was being exchanged virtually guaranteed neither man would hit their intended target, but stray bullets flying about the room will kill anyone, intended or otherwise.

After getting Hoppity to the floor, Ortega crawled to Estévez laying belly down on the floor behind the overturned table. Loose cocaine was scattered on the worn carpeting.

"Is there another way out of here?" Ortega asked.

Estévez shrugged.

Ortega crawled to the window and peered out. Several trees were standing alongside the building. The three-story drop to the ground could be broken by them.

Ortega was about to tell Estévez to move toward the window when the shooting from the hallway stopped.

"He's reloading," Estévez said.

Jimmy kicked the door closed and stepped to one side, as he also reloaded.

"I've only got five more rounds," Jimmy said.

Ortega looked at the window again. "I've got an idea," he said to Jimmy. "Keep the kid occupied. I'll get us out of the building and as soon as we're out, you follow."

"It's three stories down," Jimmy said. "Are you crazy?"

"It's the only way. There are a couple of trees here. We can climb down them."

Jimmy dropped the last of the cartridges into the gun and flipped the cylinder closed. "Go ahead. I'll cover you and meet you at the car."

Hoppity's partner fired again. His slugs penetrated the door, but landed harmlessly in the wall opposite the apartment's entrance.

"Excuse me," Ortega said to Estévez, as he stood and picked up the coffee table.

He slammed the table into the window several times before the glass gave way. Using his foot, he kicked the remaining shards of window from the frame, clearing the escape route for Estévez and himself.

Before Ortega could speak, Estévez was already through the opening, jumping to the tree that stood nearest the building where he began to scurry to the ground. Hoppity's partner continued to fire rounds through the closed door.

Ortega turned to look at Jimmy, who was standing patiently behind the wall divider. He was not returning fire.

"Get Mr. Estévez to the car," the Italian yelled over the sound of gunfire. "I'll meet you there."

Hoppity continued to lie on the floor, taped to the chair, but out of the path of the stray slugs his partner was firing into the room.

Ortega dropped through the window, sliding down the same tree Estévez had used, feeling every cut and scratch of its branches on his way to the ground.

When he landed, he found the Cuban hiding behind the minimal shrubbery that rimmed the building.

"I don't know if he has any more friends here," Estévez said, "but if we can make it to the car, we can get out of here."

Ortega glanced around the yard. Most of the kids were familiar with the sound of gunfire and knew to take cover. All of them that had been loitering about the yard when Ortega pulled up were now gone. Except for Gabriel.

"Looks like we're in the clear," Ortega said, over the echo of gunfire from the apartment above.

Estévez bolted from the shrubbery and made a dash for the car. Ortega took off behind him.

The two ran for the black Cadillac, splitting apart as they reached the car. Ortega reached the driver's door a split second after Estévez reached the right-rear passenger's door. Ortega unlocked both doors, giving the drug lord access to the relative safety of the Caddy.

"Get out of here," Ortega said to Gabriel.

The kid seemed confused. He had been told to watch the car under penalty of death for him and his family. Now he was suddenly being told to get lost.

"Go, take off," Ortega said again.

"We're safe," Estévez said. "I had this thing armor-plated."

Ortega backed the car away from the curb, and then shifted into drive as he floored the accelerator, taking the car over the curb. He drove straight for the entrance to Hoppity's building.

As he closed the distance, Jimmy came out of the doorway, casually carrying his .38 in his right hand. He opened the right-front passenger door as soon as Ortega stopped the car and climbed in.

"It's over. Let's get out of here," he said.

CHAPTER *Sixteen*

Ortega drove back to The Oasis, and the trio entered the club through the rear of the building, out of sight of patrons. Once they were in the office, Estévez flopped onto the sofa. Ortega took one of the chairs opposite Estévez, and Jimmy sat on the corner of his boss's desk. He picked up the phone.

"Boss?"

"Scotch and soda," Estévez said.

Jimmy looked at Ortega, who shook his head.

The enforcer punched the phone buttons. "Two scotch and sodas to Mr. Estévez's office."

Ortega was nauseated. During the ride back to the club, Jimmy told them he had waited for Hoppity's partner to exhaust his second magazine of ammo. Then he'd opened the door and fired two slugs into the dealer's head. Although Hoppity's partner was a pusher and responsible for ruining the lives of others, he was still a kid. And now he was a dead kid.

Estévez opened the humidor on the coffee table and extracted one of the thin cigars. He lit it with a lighter designed to look like a dolphin. After several puffs, he eased back onto the sofa and crossed his legs.

"You handled yourself well, Ron," Estévez said. "Quick thinking."

Ortega thanked Estévez for the compliment, not sure he sounded convincing.

"Very well," Jimmy added, still sitting on the desk.

Estévez took a long drag on the cigar, before tossing his head back and exhaling upward. "Was that the first time you've found yourself under fire?" he asked.

Ortega nodded, still nauseated by the kid's death.

"No wonder he's so quiet," Jimmy said.

Estévez took another long drag, before studying Ortega through narrowed eyes. "You okay?"

Ortega gave the drug lord a throaty, "Yes."

"First time in a situation like that can be unnerving for anyone," Jimmy said.

"You sure we can't get you a drink? It'll help you unwind," Estévez said.

Ortega shook his head and was about to speak, when he was cut short by a soft knock at the door. Chipper entered carrying a tray with the two drinks.

"Here," Jimmy said, motioning for Chipper as he slid off the desk and took the drinks from the waitress. He went to the sofa where Estévez was still sitting and gave one of the drinks to him.

"Hello again," Chipper said to Ortega with a smile.

He gave her a weak smile.

"You look a little pale," the girl said, frowning. "You sure you don't want a drink?"

Ortega nodded. "Yeah, I'm okay. Just tired."

She smiled again before giving Jimmy a questioning glance.

"We're fine, Chipper," Jimmy said.

She left the room, glancing again at Ortega before she closed the door.

"Like her?" Estévez asked.

"Yeah. She's fine," Ortega said.

"She sure noticed you," Jimmy said. "See the way she looked at you when she left?"

Ortega felt slimy.

"Jimmy," Estévez said, "pay the man."

Jimmy opened the lower left drawer of Estévez's desk. From where Ortega sat he could see a lockbox. The enforcer extracted a key from his pocket, opened the box. The money was held together by a paper seal, and he paused long enough to thumb through the stack before tossing it to Ortega.

"There's a thousand there," Estévez said. "If you still need work, I can use you again. Interested?"

Ortega should have been pleased with the turn of events. He had successfully persuaded his superiors to ignore his deliberate bungling of the arrest in the Everglades and give him the chance to penetrate Estévez's inner circle. He was in the process of accomplishing the latter task in short order. Yet a death had occurred, as well as two beatings he had failed to stop.

"Yeah, I'm interested," he said.

"I'd like for you to work the bar. Can you mix drinks?"

"Yes."

"Excellent. You will begin in a couple of days. You will work the shift Chipper assigns you, and you'll be available for special assignments as the need arises." Estevez paused to take a puff on the cigar. "I often need a driver, and I can certainly use someone who can think on his feet as well as you do."

"I'll be here. Thanks," Ortega said.

Estévez exhaled again before picking an invisible piece of lint off his pants leg. "I'm having a little get-together at my house tomorrow evening. I'd like for you to come. It will give you a chance to meet some of my associates."

"I'd like that," Ortega said, feeling his strength returning. "What time should I come?"

Estévez uncrossed his legs, rose from the sofa, and flicked ash into the ashtray on the coffee table. "Why don't we say eight o'clock? Most everyone will be arriving a little before that, so you'll have a chance to meet everyone at one time."

"I'm looking forward to it."

"Jimmy can tell you how to get to my house," Estévez said. "I'll be pleased to have you working for me."

Ortega wasn't sure exactly what kind of work the Cuban had in mind, but if he was doing anything like he saw Jimmy doing tonight, he could have no part in it and still call himself a law-enforcement officer.

"Besides," Jimmy added, sliding off the desk and coming around to the sofa. "Chipper will be there. Give you a chance to get to know her better."

Ortega smiled.

"So what do you say?" Estévez said.

Ortega smiled. "I say, thank you."

Estévez smiled the broad smile Ortega had seen earlier when the club was empty. "Excellent. It is good to have you aboard."

CHAPTER *Seventeen*

Ortega didn't sleep well that night. The interrogation Mario had endured, the beating Hoppity had suffered, and the subsequent murder of Hoppity's partner settled over Ortega like six feet of earth. By the time the sun was up he had already brewed a pot of less-than-stellar coffee and was dropping two slices of bread into the toaster. He called Meryl O'Connor while he waited for the toast to pop into view.

"Yeah?" the Boston accent said, responding to the first ring.

"Sounds like you slept better than I did."

"I was doing fine until you called."

"I'm in."

"You're in? That quick?"

"Estévez wants me to attend a party at his house tonight. He's offered me a job."

O'Connor cleared his throat. "Did you say tonight?"

"Yeah. Why?"

"We know something's in the works, but we're not sure exactly what. Any idea who'll be at this party?"

"He said that there would be people at the party I should meet. His associates, I think."

The lever on the toaster popped the bread up. Ortega cradled the phone on his shoulder as he slid the hot pieces of bread from the toaster and dropped them on a plate.

"What kind of job are we talking about here?" O'Connor asked.

"Driving," Ortega said. "Driving what, or whom, he didn't say. Just driving."

"No enforcing? No strong-arming?"

"I stuck with our cover story. The one we used to set up the original sting. I told him I drive. That's it. I'm not playing the hero. I don't want to do anything other than drive."

O'Connor coughed. Ortega could hear the clack of a cigarette lighter being closed. The lifeline puffed before speaking again. "Okay, we've got to get you wired."

"No."

There was a pause on O'Connor's end of the line. "You got to be wired, Ron."

"No."

"It's not up to you."

"It is."

O'Connor sighed. "You want to tell me why you're willing to gamble the whole operation? Just when you get your foot in the door?"

Ortega opened the refrigerator and looked for the jelly. There wasn't any.

"This guy trusts me. At least for now. He's bringing me in on some low-level stuff. If I can build on that trust, I can get the information we'll need if we plan on scoring some major damage. *Then* I can be wired."

"We don't want just the big stuff," O'Connor said. "We want it all. If we lose Estévez on the large deals, we can still smoke him on the smaller ones. Conspiracy, possession...I don't even care if we have to hang him on mail fraud. Anything will do and nothing is too small."

Ortega opened the cupboard in search of anything to add flavor to the toast. "That's exactly what I'm trying to tell you. What if he sees the wire? What if this is a pool party and they invite me to swim? No, Meryl, a wire now is more of a chance to blow the whole thing."

"You can be creative." O'Connor exhaled.

"Being creative is what got me this far. Why don't you guys cut me a little slack and let me do my job?"

"If we give you too much slack and someone on Estévez's end discovers you doing your job, you'll get all the cutting you can handle."

Ortega settled for butter. "Look, I'm in, but barely. They're still checking me out. The whole idea behind me going out with them last night was to see how I'd handle the—"

"Going out? Going out where?"

Ortega smoothed the butter over the toast. "Santiago discovered two local cops on the take. They shook him down 'cause he wasn't paying them. Apparently, while they're slapping him around, they let it slip that no one else is paying them. That got Estévez very upset."

"Sure. The lifeblood of these guys' operations is money. It needs to flow in, but it also needs to flow out. If they don't pay for protection—the cops, judges, politicians, whoever—they can't stay in business."

"So Estévez asked for me to go along…as driver."

There was silence on O'Connor's end of the line as he mulled over the information he had just been given. Ortega poured some coffee and bit into the toast.

"I agree. He's testing you. Probably already having some of his people checking your story."

"Which is airtight. Right?"

"Don't worry. We've got you covered on that. Your concern is going to be building a case against this guy. And staying alive while you do it."

"Will serving as a witness to a couple of interrogations help?"

"Yes. So long as you didn't participate."

"I didn't, but I also couldn't stop them." He told O'Connor about the interrogation of Mario and Hoppity, and about the murder of the dealer.

"I had already gotten Estévez out of the apartment," Ortega added. "When Jimmy came out of the building, he didn't seem to be in a hurry. He told us what happened on our way back to the club."

"Okay," O'Connor said. "I'll look into it with the locals. If we can match Caltabiano's gun to the slugs we take from the dealer, we can put him away for murder on top of everything else."

"How did you know his name?" Ortega asked, finishing his piece of toast.

"It's not rocket science. I've been in this business a long time," O'Connor said. "Caltabiano is an ex-New York cop. He was fired for bribery and he's been on the take ever since. He's worked with Estévez since Estévez began his rise through the ranks. The man is a leg-breaker, nothing more. To the best of our knowledge he's never been on the inside. Never a deal-maker, never a thought leader. He's there to enforce and to protect Estévez's back. But we also know the man has no family and he has a heart condition that will ultimately kill him, so there's nothing he won't do."

"He has nothing to lose," Ortega commented.

"Exactly. And that makes him dangerous." O'Connor paused to inhale on the cigarette. "And second," he said, exhaling, "he is intensely loyal to Estévez. He'll do anything for the man. And has."

Ortega started on the second piece of toast. "I can bear witness to that."

"You may have to."

"By the way," Ortega said, "Estévez paid me last night."

"Keep it. I'll come by and get it later. We'll need to log it."

"Anything else?" Ortega said.

"We can't force you to wear the wire," O'Connor said. "But you'd be a lot better off with it."

The younger agent couldn't argue. But given the fact that Estévez might be testing the waters, Ortega saw nothing to gain in testing Estévez.

CHAPTER *Eighteen*

Like all cities, Miami has two faces. There is the public face, the one touted on the Travel Channel, the vacation ads, and the chamber of commerce brochures. The family-friendly face. The city that offers the American dream in spades. A place where opportunity abounds and the chance at a better life is within the grasp of anyone. It's that face of Miami the average American sees. The sun, the surf, the beautiful people—these are the things that make the city appealing to those who live there, and inviting to those who wish they did.

But there's another face to Miami, one that doesn't appear in the travel ads. This is the city that exists in the shadows, that dwells in the dark places. It's this Miami that comes alive at night and whose children ply their trade in the secret recesses where no one sees and no one cares. It's in this Miami that men like Jimmy Caltabiano work, and it was in this Miami, on this night, that his time had been well-spent.

By the time the sun was up, he had all the information he needed, even if he didn't have all the rest he required. Estévez would be waiting for this information and Jimmy knew the Cuban didn't like to be kept waiting.

As he had done on so many occasions, Caltabiano drove along the winding driveway to the mansion secluded from public view by a stone wall and a shroud of palms. And as he and Estévez had arranged the night before, minutes after Acuna left and their talk had turned to more urgent matters, he did not enter the house through the front door, but instead walked around the building to the veranda, where he would find his employer.

Clearing the house, he was struck with the beauty of the view. The sun had just risen above the horizon, swathing the sky and the ocean beyond in a peach-red glow. The view was breathtaking. Especially to a battle-worn ex-New York City cop.

Estévez was sitting on a chaise dressed in a bathrobe, enjoying his coffee and the best sunrise money could buy. Though he was clearly aware Jimmy had arrived, he said nothing for a few moments, before finally breaking the silence. "It's beautiful, Jimmy."

"Yes, sir."

"There isn't a woman in the world that can compete against that."

"No, sir."

Estévez raised his cup to his lips, blew, and drank before returning the cup to the table. "Except for my Maria, of course."

"Yes, sir. She's a beautiful woman, Mr. Estévez. You are a lucky man."

The Cuban scanned the view. "That I am, Jimmy."

"I have the information you wanted," the enforcer said. "I have numbers, locations, and men…all of it."

Estévez gestured to a chair next to his own. "Have a seat, Jimmy, and tell me all about it."

Caltabiano sat. Too large in the middle to cross his legs, he opted to fold his hands across his ample frame.

"Kingman is moving his junk through a warehouse."

Estévez grinned. "That's not exactly original, is it?"

Caltabiano shook his head. He was too tired to smile. "I followed two of his guys to a citrus warehouse and I saw guys working there all night long. It looked like they were loading crates of oranges, except they were tossing them around like they were full of air."

"Too light to be thirty pounds of fruit," Estévez said, filling in the details for himself.

The ex-cop nodded. "That's what I was thinking. Too light to be oranges."

"So Kingman is using citrus warehousing to ship his stuff."

"I saw trucks moving in all night long. They pulled into the bays and then shipped out again loaded with the crates."

"He's buying from the Colombians, storing in warehouses, then moving it from there to the citrus plant, where he ships. If the plant gets hit, he's clean.

If the warehouse gets hit, he's clean and he can absorb the loss by spreading his risk around."

Jimmy agreed. "And I think he's expanding, moving his stuff to other parts of the country. I saw out-of-state tags on several of the trucks."

Estévez drained his cup and refilled it from a copper carafe. "He's building a base in the country so that when he moves into Cuba he will face little competition." He drank more coffee. "He's probably been building it for years. We've been asleep while he's been at work."

"How do you want me to handle it?" Jimmy asked.

"I want you to get some of our guys together…use Guerrera and Stoneman, and have them keep an eye on Kingman's place."

"Okay," Jimmy said, rubbing his eyes with the heel of his hands. "For how long?"

"Until I say otherwise. After you've got our guys in position, I want you to personally torch one of our places. I don't care which."

Caltabiano raised an eyebrow.

"Just be sure," Estévez said, "you get the stuff out first. Got it? Get the junk out first, then torch the place."

"Did you say you want me to torch one of our places?"

"One of our warehouses, Jimmy. Burn the place to the ground."

The big man rubbed his reddened eyes again. "Okay. Any preference?"

"No. Just be sure you have our stuff out, and that the fire gets pegged for arson."

"I don't understand. Isn't that going to bring a lot of cops looking in on us?"

"Yes, Jimmy. That's exactly what it's going to do. I want lots of cops looking at our place. I want lots of attention."

"You want Guerrera and Stoneman to burn Kingman's place too?"

Estévez shook his head. "Just the opposite. I want them to be sure that nothing happens to Kingman."

"You want this guy to take the heat for torching our place?"

Estévez smiled. "I want him to take the right kind of heat, Jimmy."

Caltabiano didn't need to ask more questions. Thirty years with the NYPD had given him a sixth sense, a sense that told him there was a story behind the story. And those years had given him the enviable ability to do a job without the burden of moral parameters.

This had not always been the case. When he had joined the NYPD, he had been as proud as any of the cadets in his class. His commitment to the job and to the ideals of his badge was exemplary. But time and reality had altered the prism of youth.

Politicians made decisions for expediency. The brass made policy to please the politicians. And the beat cop was sacrificed on the altar of political correctness while the city sank in a morass of prostitution, theft, muggings, and murder. Even worse, this decline seemed accepted as inevitable.

After a while, Jimmy's motivation to enforce the laws became a motivation to go home alive. And the decline in the city became the decline in the man. Eventually it became no longer acceptable to just go home alive, with feet that ached and legs that were tired. That had been replaced by the desire to live well. To live as well as those who preyed on the innocents—the thieves, the muggers, the politicians, and their cronies on the force.

And so he began to take a little here, a little there. And the line between right and wrong began to erode. And moral ambiguity became his savior. No longer did he need to fight the battle of the streets. He needed only to fight the battle within. And that battle had been lost a long time ago.

"I understand, Mr. Estévez," he said. "I'll take care of it."

"Thank you, Jimmy," Estévez said, raising his cup to his lips. "I know I can count on you."

CHAPTER *Nineteen*

According to Santiago, Dowd and Hurst usually began their day with breakfast at the Sunshine Diner, a popular place located far west of Hokey's and that was bounded on both sides by empty storefronts badly in need of repair. One of the buildings had once housed a coin-operated laundry, while another had been a liquor store. Neither looked likely to provide space to anyone anytime soon.

Ron Ortega's entrance drew little attention. Although his face was new in a crowd where new faces stood out like black skin at a neo-Nazi rally, his Cuban descent made him okay with the other Cubans, Hispanics, and Colombians who patronized the restaurant. The two officers, both Caucasian, gave Ortega only a passing glance before returning to their breakfast and their conversation. Both men were sitting in the last booth on the left, across from the breakfast counter. Ortega took a seat on a stool not more than ten feet from the two policemen and pulled one of the laminated menu cards from a metal clamp attached to the counter.

Dowd and Hurst had full plates, which meant they would be in their booth for a while. That would give Ortega a chance to assess each man before he approached them with Mikey's payout.

A waitress in a pink uniform and with no name tag approached Ortega. Like everyone else in the place, except for Dowd and Hurst, the woman was Hispanic. Ortega placed her in her mid-forties, five-feet-four and two hundred pounds. She wasn't wearing a wedding band.

"Coffee?" she asked.

"Black."

She pulled a white ceramic cup from underneath the counter and flipped it right side up before splashing coffee into it. "Ready to order?"

"Two eggs, scrambled, with toast."

She didn't write it down. She walked to an opening in the wall and repeated the order to the Hispanic kid working the grill.

Ortega tried hard to listen for snippets of the conversation between Dowd and Hurst, but the level of chatter, the clinking dishes, and the noise of passing traffic made it difficult. The small pieces he did manage to pick up centered on "the boss," "my old lady," "I told him that report was the best I could do," and "I want my pension and then I'm hangin' it up." By the time the waitress brought his breakfast, Ortega had downed one cup of the toxic coffee already and was extending his mug for more.

With his cup refilled, he glanced casually over his shoulder at the two officers directly behind him. They were nearing the end of their breakfast.

Ortega began to eat, trying to keep pace with the two men. As he finished the first of his two slices of toast, he heard Dowd and Hurst begin to slide out of their booth. Ortega called to the waitress. "Hey, you got any beef sausage in here?"

She was talking to a man who sat at the other end of the counter and ignored Ortega.

"Hey," he called, loudly this time, "have you got any beef sausage in here?"

She turned to look at him with a scowl. "If you wanted sausage, why didn't you say so?"

"I want beef sausage. I don't like *pig.*"

He could hear Dowd and Hurst pause behind him. The other diners paused in their chatter, looking at the officers standing behind Ortega.

"'Cause pig *stinks.* It's inferior meat. Like this inferior coffee."

"Hey, buddy," the battle-hardened waitress said, coming to his end of the counter. "If you don't like what we got, just pay your bill and move on."

Ortega pulled a crumpled ten out of his pocket and tossed the bill on the counter. "I ain't coming back to this dump as long as you serve pig meat to pigs." He turned on his stool and gave Dowd and Hurst a direct stare. "You do know what I'm talking about, don't you, you graft-suckin' hogs?"

Dowd reacted first by grabbing Ortega's shirt collar and pulling him off the stool. The young agent was about to strike the older, much bigger officer when Hurst stepped in between them.

"Hold it," he said, to his partner. "We don't want a brawl in here. Let's just take him outside and see what his beef is."

"That's the problem," Ortega said. "There ain't no beef in this dump. Just a lot of pig."

Hurst groaned as Dowd half-pulled, half-dragged the young Cuban through the dining room and out the door.

Hurst followed, telling everyone in the restaurant that there was nothing to see and urging them to return to their breakfast.

Once the officers and their new subject were outside, Dowd slammed Ortega against the patrol car and began his frisk. Hurst stood to one side, keeping an eye on the younger Cuban in order to react to any sudden attacks.

"You got a smart mouth," Dowd said, patting Ortega down. "I don't know you. You must be new around here."

"I know you, Officer Dowd," Ortega said. "Or are you Hurst?"

Dowd finished his search and whipped the Cuban around. The officer kept his hand on the younger man's chest so that he remained pinned against the car. "Like I said, I don't know you."

Hurst stepped closer to his partner. "But he knows us."

"Of course I know you. Everyone on the street knows you two. And if you want what I got for you, you better back off."

Dowd glanced at Hurst. "What do you mean, 'What I got for you'?" Dowd said.

"Mikey sent me."

Ortega saw the exchange of glances between the two men again.

"Hand it over," Dowd said. "Real slow."

"No," Hurst said. "In the alley."

Dowd pulled Ortega away from the squad car by the shirt front, and dragged the Cuban into the alley that ran alongside the former liquor store and another building. Hurst followed, glancing over his shoulder for any stragglers or onlookers who might be nosey enough to want to see what was happening.

Once in the alley, Ortega counted out the money that Mikey owed the two officers and tossed it to broken pavement.

"Pick it up," Dowd said.

Ortega stooped to pick up the money but tackled Dowd instead, grabbing him around the knees.

The officer fell and Ortega climbed on top of him, pounding him with an avalanche of blows.

Hurst closed in on Ortega and punched the younger man solidly in the left kidney, sending a searing shock into his left flank.

Ortega rolled off of Dowd and kicked the pursuing Hurst in the groin. The officer groaned and doubled over.

Dowd rose to his feet before Ortega could stand and came at the Cuban with unleashed fury.

Jumping on the agent, the officer began to deliver the same blows he had just taken.

Ortega wrapped his arms around the officer's waist and attempted to roll him over on his side, but Dowd was too big and had leveraged himself by spreading his feet apart. The officer, like the Cuban underneath him, was a street brawler and had learned how to fight the hard way.

Ortega pulled a can of pepper spray from the officer's belt and began to spray the blinding fluid at Dowd. The corrupt cop winced and yelled for Hurst, who was beginning to climb to his feet with his own canister in hand.

As Hurst approached, Dowd continued to fight with Ortega for control of the spray. With each reach for the canister, however, the officer had to release his grip on Ortega's left hand, which he then used to punch at Dowd.

Ortega put up the fight he had intended and didn't roll over for the officers as they had expected. But two cans of pepper spray are better than one, and as Hurst forced the stream of toxic fluid into the Cuban's eyes, all desire to fight left him.

Dowd and Hurst were presented with the dilemma that police officers on the take often confront—forfeit the graft, arrest the suspect, and have their illicit deeds uncovered, or take the money and the attack that comes with it. Once Ortega was cuffed and the subsequent beating from Dowd was over, the two officers weighed their options.

"If we take him in, we're done," Dowd said. "I say we take him somewhere and snuff him."

Hurst leaned against the alley wall, breathing hard from the struggle and the blow to his groin. He considered Dowd's suggestion. "If we ice this guy, Mikey will know."

"So?"

"So that could be a problem for us. On the other hand, if we take him in, we forfeit the graft and word gets out. That could be a problem too."

"You mean that the others might not pay and take their chances?"

Hurst nodded as he remained leaning against the wall, doubled over. "Yeah, that's one possible problem. The other is that we get accused of taking the money and then we fight it, but some of the other people we've been dealing with are rounded up and support the charges."

Dowd sighed and placed both hands on his hips as he looked at the cuffed and subdued Ortega lying on the pavement. "I still say we kill the dude. The word gets out from Mikey that we mean business and he takes it back to Kingman and the others, it will eliminate a lot of problems in the future."

Hurst straightened from his crouched position and breathed deeply, slowly. "There's no smooth way out of this."

"Kill him."

Hurst shook his head. "No. We're not going to do that. I have a better idea." He eased away from the wall and knelt next to Ortega, speaking directly to him. "We're going to keep what Mikey owes us and we're going to let you go. But you tell Mikey this little stunt has cost him. We want another two-fifty apiece, and we want it by the end of next week. Got it?"

"I do," Ortega said barely raising his head, "but he doesn't."

Hurst grabbed a handful of the Cuban's hair. "If he doesn't have it by Friday next week, right here, we take him out and take our chances."

To underscore his point, Hurst slammed the Cuban's head into the pavement and Dowd kicked him one more time.

CHAPTER *Twenty*

Ortega stood in front of the mirror as he removed his shirt. He gingerly placed his hand on one of the ribs he had thought might be broken from the beating. Although the area was sore and bruised, the pain wasn't bad enough to indicate a broken bone.

He studied his face. Like his upper body it too was swollen. A large bruise had developed under his right eye. Although he was in pain, the wounds were welcome. They would serve their purpose by giving the Cuban the credentials with Estévez he didn't yet fully possess.

After showering, and redressing, he sat at the kitchen table and began to write a brief report on the events with Dowd and Hurst. He would leave these with O'Connor at their next meeting.

Although his specific task was to build a case against Estévez and his crew, the Cuban would undoubtedly run into peripheral suspects and issues that would not necessarily be of interest to federal agents, but which could be added to the government's overall case. Any information along those lines would be passed on to the Miami PD. From the DEA's end, Ortega's report would be submitted to the United States attorney, who would decide which federal laws had been broken and how best to go after those responsible for breaking them. It was a politician's job to decide those things and Ortega wasn't a politician. He was a federal agent—a cop. And he would do the good cop thing by collecting as much evidence as possible.

There would, of course, be the inevitable score of meetings, briefings and debriefings, depositions, discovery, and testimonies at trial. But those events were so far in the future that they seemed like a distant storm. One for which there was time to prepare.

Tonight, he would enjoy himself. He would attend Estévez's party and try to fit in as much as possible. But he would also keep in mind that his patrolling of Estévez's veranda was no less dangerous than patrolling the dark alleys of Chicago, or Miami for that matter.

The Cuban finished his report, sealed it in the government envelope provided by O'Connor, and then called Libby. He had been instructed to make all personal calls, limited though they were, on his cell phone. His apartment phone could be bugged by the very men he was seeking to put into prison, and any discovery of inconsistencies would spell almost certain annihilation.

Libby answered on the second ring.

The baby had shifted slightly, she told him. The doctor said everything else was fine.

"Are you feeling okay?" he asked.

"I'm tired and I'm tired of being pregnant, but otherwise I'm okay."

He wished her parents had been able to visit and to help her through this time, especially while he was absent. But neither of them was in shape to travel. Her father had been diagnosed with multiple sclerosis not long after Libby had graduated high school, and the ravages of the disease had reached the final stages. He breathed by way of a ventilator and required near constant attention. It was that requirement that kept her mother from being near her.

Ortega's mother had died while he was young, and his father had been an alcoholic, who ultimately succumbed to cirrhosis not long after his only son had married.

A few weeks after his father's death, Ortega and his wife had been transferred to the Chicago office and hadn't had enough time to develop close friends. Although the DEA was indeed a family and many of the other agents' wives would help her any way they could, they were not blood. And they were not him.

"I wish I could be there," he said.

"I know. I'll be okay. You just be careful."

"I will." He fingered the swollen area under his right eye. "Is everything else okay?"

He had sensed some hesitancy in her speech. She finally told him that the car had given out and the washing machine had leaked, running water into the living room.

"But I'm okay," she quickly added. "God has taken care of us. The insurance company is sending a claims adjuster."

Ortega sighed.

"Really, Ron, it's okay. The carpeting in the living room will probably need to be replaced but I caught the leak before it got too bad."

"We can't replace *some* of the carpeting, Libby. It's either all or none."

Despite the strain he knew she was under, she remained calm, soothing. He knew she was doing it for him.

"The Lord takes care of us, Ron. We'll be fine. You just be careful and come home as soon as you can."

"If the water was that deep, what about the flooring?"

Again she was hesitant before answering. "It's going to need replacing too."

Ortega groaned. "How much?"

She sighed. "The adjuster said he can't tell for sure until he sees it, but he's estimating close to five thousand dollars."

"Five thousand—"

"But that's for the carpeting *and* the flooring."

"Are we covered?"

She sighed again. "Ron, why don't you—"

"Libby, is it covered? Is the insurance company going to—"

"He said they might cover some of it. That they'd pay for the cost of clean up."

"Clean up? That's still going to leave us with nearly the whole cost."

She didn't answer.

"It's that old machine," he said, referring to the washer. "It was old and used when we bought it."

"We're fine."

"You deserve better."

"I'm okay."

Maybe, but that didn't lessen his resentment over the fact that he wasn't with her. He loved her and wanted her to have the things she needed, like washing machines and cars that ran, but that meant he would have to spend more time on the job than with her. And since his career was only beginning to blossom, time away from her could extend for months—possibly years at a time. But what he resented most was that their needs would compel him to be an absentee father, much like his own.

"I don't want to be a bad father," he said, abruptly

"Why would you say a thing like that? You won't be a bad father—you'll be a great father."

"I'm a little down, I guess."

She was silent for a while, a signal that she too was down but wouldn't let him know it. "We'll be fine," she said. "You just get this thing over with. I want you home."

And that was exactly where he longed to be.

CHAPTER *Twenty-One*

Ortega arrived at Estévez's mansion at precisely eight o'clock. As instructed, he pushed the call button on the gate. Immediately, it swung open and he drove onto the plush estate. Eyeing the ornate home he couldn't help but wonder if Estévez's washing machine had ever leaked.

Several valets, all of them dressed in white shirts, black pants, and black bow ties, were waiting to park cars and direct their occupants toward the back of the house. Nearly all of the men who were attending the party were casually dressed, with most wearing short-sleeved cotton shirts and light-colored pants. The few women all seemed much younger than the men with whom they arrived, and most seemed to be dressed far more fashionably.

"I can park this for you, sir," one of the young men said, suddenly appearing at Ortega's window.

Ortega slid out of the car and the valet directed the agent to follow the sidewalk to the rear of the house, where the party was underway.

As he rounded the corner of the mansion, he came up on the breathtaking view of the Atlantic Ocean, cast in the violet-pink glow of the setting sun. A live band was playing softly from the corner of the large patio at the foot of the veranda, and the pleasant sounds of a party in full swing filled the air.

Ortega made a brief count and estimated there were probably a hundred people on the veranda. But he knew there were more in the house, judging from the laughter coming from there. Off to his right, he saw a bar, and behind the bar was Chipper. She smiled as soon as his eyes settled on her.

"Hey," she said. "Glad you could make it."

He walked to the bar and sat on a stool. She frowned briefly when she saw his bruised and swollen cheek.

"What would you like?" she asked.

"Coke."

She glanced at his swollen cheek again. "Coke?"

He shrugged. "I don't drink."

"And you're going to be tending bar with me?"

"I had a bit of a problem with it once," he said. "No reason to ask for trouble."

The news didn't seem to affect her. She pulled a glass from an overhead rack, iced it, and filled it with the beverage from a nozzle attached to a tank underneath the bar.

"Try not to drink all of it at once," she teased. "I wouldn't want you to slide under the table."

He grinned. "You'd kid a man about his drinking problem?"

She brushed a lock of hair from her forehead. "Listen, I've been around booze all my life. My father was an…"

"Alcoholic?"

She nodded. "Yes. He was an alcoholic. But he quit. And he hasn't had a drink in years. I figure you must be doing the same."

"Four years clean," he said.

She smiled. "Takes a lot of fortitude to quit. Maybe even more than it takes to not start."

Ortega nodded. "For some of us—guys like your father and me—once it gets its foot in the door, you've got a battle on your hands." He sipped the Coke.

"Where are you from?" Chipper asked, leaning on the bar and glancing at his battered face again.

"Chicago. I moved here a few weeks ago."

"Did the Windy City get boring? People usually don't just up and move for no reason."

He shook his head and set the glass down on the bar. "No, I just needed to get out of town. So what's your story?"

"My story?"

"You said 'hey,' not 'hi,' and you have an accent you're trying hard to hide."

She laughed. "You're good. I'm from Louisville. I moved here a couple of years ago."

"Like it?"

"Sure. Mr. Estévez is good to me, and gives me free rein to run the bar the way I see fit. I started out tending it, but he eventually asked me if I could take over. He has his hands full running the club. So I said, 'Sure, why not?' "

"And just like that, you've got the power?" He grinned.

"Just like that." She then focused on his face again. "What happened?" she asked.

"I fell in the shower." He smiled.

"You must've fallen pretty hard."

He rubbed his cheek. "Does it look that bad?"

She smiled, inched closer, and shook her head. "No. It fits you."

"Fits me?"

She nodded. "Some guys look better with wrinkles, bruises, things like that. Gives their face character."

He grinned. "I'm one of those guys?"

"You have character." She smiled. "It might as well show."

He raised his glass. "Here's to character."

She gave him a teasing smile. "Starting tomorrow, I'm going to be your boss. How do you like that?"

"I've had worse."

She smiled. Her hair brushed his shoulder.

"So tell me," he said, "how did you get a name like Chipper?"

"My name is Carol Ann. But when I was a kid I was always in a good mood. Always upbeat, you know? So my daddy would come home drunk, and he would talk to me about his job and why he hated it so much. Probably more than a kid should hear. And one night he said, 'Darlin,' you're a chipper little thing. Don't ever change.' So it kind of stuck."

"He's right. Don't ever change, Chipper."

She smiled and was about to say something, when her expression suddenly grew serious and she pulled away from the bar.

From behind him, Ortega could hear the familiar voice of his host. "Ron, I'm so glad you could make it." Estévez was smoking one of the thin cigars that the agent was beginning to recognize as the drug lord's trademark.

"Thanks for the invitation," Ortega said.

"Chipper taking care of you?"

Ortega glanced back at the blonde who seemed very professional, yet very comfortable in Estévez's presence.

"Yes, she is."

"Well, come with me," Estévez said, wrapping an arm around his guest as he guided him off the stool. "I've got some important people I'd like for you to meet."

CHAPTER *Twenty-Two*

Estevez steered Ortega along the veranda. A mix of older and younger guests—heavily Cuban—were laughing, drinking, and having an all-around good time. Estévez directed the young agent away from the people on the veranda, however, and toward the house.

"What happened to your face?" Estévez asked.

"I ran into the cops who rousted Mikey. Or rather, their fists ran into me."

"When?"

"This morning. Mikey was pretty shook up, so I offered to take his payment to them. I don't think they like me much."

Estévez focused on Ortega's cheek. "Look's like it's going to be there for a while."

"It won't be the first."

Estévez smiled. "Neither will it be the last."

They entered through French-style doors into a kitchen that was bigger than the house Ortega shared with his wife. White cabinets lined three sides of the room, above and below a marble countertop. A large center island with matching marble top stood in the center of the room. At one end of the kitchen a brick wall was fitted with an oven and a microwave. At the other end was a fireplace, through which the living room could be seen.

"Imported from Greece," Estévez said, running his hand over the countertop. "It came from the discovered ruins of an ancient temple. Set me back a few." He grinned. "Now, I'd like you to meet my family."

The drug lord led Ortega into the lavish living room. In front of the fireplace that looked into the kitchen were two matching white sofas facing each other, with a large cherry coffee table in the center. A bouquet of fresh-cut flowers sat on the table in a obviously expensive crystal vase.

"Maria?" Estévez said.

A tall, darkly complected woman with thick black hair pulled tightly back acknowledged Estévez with a smile. She was wearing a form-fitting, sleeveless white dress accented by a tasteful, ruby necklace. She held a drink in her hand.

"I have someone I would like for you to meet," Estévez said. "Maria, this is Ron Acuna. He is a new associate at the club and a friend of mine."

The woman smiled gracefully and extended a hand. "I am pleased to meet you." Her accent was thick and definitely Cuban. She didn't seem to notice the bruises on Ortega's face.

"The pleasure is mine," Ortega said. "You have a beautiful home."

She thanked him for the compliment.

"Where are the children?" Estévez said. "I want him to meet the girls."

"I believe they are upstairs," Maria said.

Estévez took Ortega by the arm and steered him toward the staircase that swept into the living room in one, graceful spiral.

Once upstairs, Estévez led the agent down a hallway that was wide enough to accommodate the car on which Ortega still owed forty-eight payments, and which no longer ran. Several doors lined the passage, as well as several pieces of clearly expensive fine art. At the end of the hallway, the men turned right and passed through a large entryway. Inside were two young girls, twins, who Ortega guessed to be no more than four or five. A heavy-set Hispanic woman was on the floor with them, playing with a large set of plastic blocks.

"This is a friend of mine," Estévez said to the woman. "I want him to meet the children."

Estévez sat on the floor and crossed his legs. Ortega joined him as the woman rose from the floor and left the room, closing the door behind her.

"This one," Estévez said, pointing to one of the girls, "is Dominga and this little rat right there," he said, pointing to the other girl, "is Carmen."

"Nooo, Daddy," Carmen said, "I'm Dominga. *That's* Carmen." The girl giggled and pointed to her sister who was looking at Ortega with her head downcast. A smile was on her face.

"She's the shy one," Estévez said, picking Carmen up and setting her on his lap.

"But *I'm* not shy," Dominga said.

"No, you are definitely not shy," Estévez said. "Is Mrs. Cortez taking good care of you?"

Carmen nodded.

Dominga said, "We've been playing games. I won."

"Family is everything," Estévez said to Ortega. "It is a man's greatest accomplishment if he can have his children look forward to seeing him. Don't you agree?"

"Yes, I do."

"Although I never knew my father," Estévez said, "that has not stopped me from having a family of my own and being a good father to my children."

"You have a beautiful family," Ortega said.

"Thank you." He kissed Carmen on the cheek. "My own father was no man at all. But I will not be like him. The children will come first."

Ortega nodded his understanding.

"They are the reason I work so hard. A man who will not take care of his family is no man at all. The Bible tells us this, does it not?"

Ortega fought to stifle his astonishment. This man who sat on the throne of one of Miami's most vicious criminal gangs, who was reaching for the brass ring in an effort to consolidate his power and, by extension, his hold on the city, had read the Bible?

The young agent shrugged. "I guess so."

Estevez hugged his daughter. "You should read the Bible, my friend. I do not always do what I should, but I always put my family first. It is the right thing to do. A man should always put the needs of his family above all else. Always."

CHAPTER *Twenty-Three*

After a few minutes Mrs. Cortez returned. Estévez kissed his two daughters goodnight and the two men made their exit. As they descended the stairs, Estévez continued to recount various aspects of the house—another acquisition of which he was clearly proud.

As the men stepped back onto the veranda, Estévez picked a drink off a passing tray. Ahead of them, Ortega saw two couples sitting at an umbrella-covered table. All four of them were considerably older than their host, and all seemed fixed on Estévez's every movement.

"Nice party, Ricardo," one of the men said as the club owner and his new friend approached. "Thank you for inviting us."

The man was dressed far more formally than anyone else at the villa. His thinning hair was slicked straight back, accenting his round face. The woman next to him was dressed in an evening gown that would have been more appropriate for a White House dinner than an evening with Miami's aspiring power broker.

"Thank you, David," Estevez said. "I am so glad that you could make it." He leaned forward to kiss the man's wife on the cheek. "And I am so very pleased Mrs. Salter could come."

The woman smiled.

"It looks like the weather is cooperating as well. Eh, Ricardo?" the second man said.

Unlike Salter, the other man appeared to be far more relaxed. He was of

Hispanic descent and dressed more casually, wearing a polo shirt and shorts. The woman with him was also of Hispanic descent, stunningly beautiful, and much younger than the man she accompanied.

Estévez smiled and extended his hand across the table. "So good to see you too, Julio, and your beautiful wife."

"Join us?" Salter asked.

"Perhaps for a minute," Estévez said, gesturing for Ortega to pull two nearby chairs to the table. As soon as both men sat, Estévez introduced the agent to the others.

"Are you from Miami?" Salter asked, sipping a daiquiri.

"Chicago," Ortega replied. "I've been in the city a few weeks."

"I see," Salter said, eyeing the agent.

"You have family in Miami?" Julio Lopez's wife asked. Her smile was far too warm and her gaze far too penetrating to go with the small talk she was making. Ortega shifted uncomfortably in his seat.

It was Estévez who picked up on the situation first. He gave Salter a knowing glance. Salter responded.

"Ladies," the older man said, setting his drink on the table, "I don't think that Ricardo would mind if you toured the house. Maria is here, yes?"

Estévez smiled. "She would love to show you the house. I believe you'll find her in the kitchen. She has worked with the caterers all week, and still it continues."

The women took the hint, well aware from experience that business was to be conducted and their presence was no longer required. Lopez's wife gave Ortega a smile as she left the table.

"Gentlemen," Estévez said, moving forward after the women had left, "we have encountered a serious problem."

Lopez and Salter glanced at each other, then at Ortega before leaning forward to hear what Estévez had to say.

"I have heard through my sources that Kingman may be planning a strike at our assets." He paused to gauge their reaction. "I don't know whose, and I don't know when. But my source says he will hit soon and hard."

"Who is this source?" Salter asked.

"A reliable source, David," Estévez said.

"That all you got?" Lopez said. "All you know is that Kingman is planning an assault on one of us and you don't know when, who, or even what?"

A hurt look crossed the Cuban's face. He spread his hands on the table.

"What do you want from me, Julio? I give you the best I have got, and it isn't good enough for you?"

Lopez sighed and turned to Ortega before continuing. "And who are you?"

"I told you a minute ago," Estévez said.

"You told us his name," Lopez said, "but you didn't tell us what he's doing here."

Civility would normally have required Ortega to excuse himself from any family quarrel in which he found himself. But he wasn't here to be civil. He was here to gather evidence and build a case against the men who were sitting around the table. He was about to answer when Estévez cut him off.

"Ron may be a nice asset to my operation. Who I hire is my business," Estévez said, revealing, for the first time, a hint of anger. "I discovered," he continued, "that some of my people, and probably some of yours as well, were not making their payments. I don't need to tell you how serious that can be. Ron made rounds with us on a couple of them and came in very handy."

Salter frowned at Ortega. "Sorry. Nothing personal."

Ortega smiled and dismissively waved off the man's earlier comment.

Lopez remained silent.

"My suggestion," Estévez said, "is to beef up your security and keep your heads low. If I hear anything more, I'll let you know as quickly as I can."

The two men glanced at each other before looking again at Estévez.

"Okay?" the Cuban repeated. "I will let you know if I hear anything else. Right now that is all I have."

There was another moment's hesitancy before Salter broke the tension.

"Okay," he said. "Okay. But you let us know the moment you hear anything."

"I will. And of course it goes without saying, you will do the same."

Lopez snorted. "Of course, Ricardo. We are all in this together."

CHAPTER *Twenty-Four*

The rest of the evening passed quickly as the guests took full advantage of their host's reputation for a good time. By the time the partygoers were ready to leave, some of them had to be helped into their vehicles—or cabs. Ortega was exhausted, but he had managed to meet two of the most dangerous men in Miami and that alone had made the evening worthwhile.

"You look tired."

It was Chipper. She was packing cases of unopened liquor.

"A little," Ortega said. "But then I didn't stand behind a bar all night feeding hooch to a bunch of rich drunks."

She smiled. "Goes with the territory."

The woman was gorgeous. Not just physically, but there was something else attractive about her that Ortega liked. Something deeper.

"You have a ride home?" he asked.

She glanced to a couple of the young men who had been parking cars but who were now packing liquor. "Actually, yes." She nodded toward the men. "We have to go back to the club. Unload this stuff." She smiled.

"Okay," he said. "Just thought I'd offer."

"Well, don't." It was Estévez. "Sorry, Chipper, but he's mine for a bit."

Chipper acknowledged her boss's first dibs, smiled again, and watched as Estévez steered Ortega away from the bar, and the girl, for the second time that evening.

"I want you to take a ride with me," Estevez said. "I've got something I want to show you and some work for you to do. Are you up to it?"

"Sure."

"You look beat," Estévez said. "Maybe we should wait."

"No," Ortega said. "Now's fine."

"Okay then," the Cuban said, handing the agent a set of keys. "Bring the car around. It's in the garage."

After bringing the car to the front of the house, Ortega drove Estévez to a rural location in Broward County. Although the two a.m. traffic was light, the drive took almost an hour. Estévez spoke very little during the drive, and Ortega sensed tension in the man.

They were coming up to what appeared to be a hardware store when the drug lord said, "Here. Pull in here."

Ortega steered the Cadillac onto the small gravel lot of the store and killed the engine.

"We'll just sit here," Estévez said.

Ortega glanced in the rearview mirror. There was no other traffic, and the town seemed to have rolled in the sidewalks a few hours ago.

Estévez reached across Ortega and turned the ignition key to "on" before pushing the window button. He pulled a packet of matches and a cigar from a small leather case he took from the glove box. He lit up and sighed deeply.

The hair on Ortega's neck began to rise. The light, fun-loving Estévez of the party had vanished. The dark Estévez of commerce and enterprise had risen up in his place.

"Are we waiting on something?" Ortega asked.

The Cuban looked into the mirror attached to his door. "Not something," he said. *"Someone."*

Ortega turned in the direction in which Estévez was looking. A dark SUV was coming down the same road he had just driven. As the vehicle approached, its headlights went out and it turned into the lot. The gravel crunched under its tires as it came to rest next to the Caddy.

"Come on," Estévez said, getting out of the car.

Ortega followed.

Four men got out of the vehicle. One of them was Jimmy. Ortega had seen the other three men parking cars at the house. Before any of them could say a word, Estévez motioned for Jimmy to come closer.

"Ron is going to help us tonight," the Cuban said, under his breath. "I told Lopez and Salter about the information we had on the possible attack from Kingman."

Jimmy nodded. The other men stood around the car. Two of them were watching the road, each looking in different directions. The other was watching Ortega.

"If I was Kingman and I wanted to hit one of my assets, this is the one that would send the clearest message."

"Right," Caltabiano said. "It's isolated. Rural. It would show others that he could hit them anywhere."

The Cuban agreed. "If he were to hit us, it would happen here."

"Then we hit him?" Jimmy asked.

Estévez shook his head. "No. We go back to the others. If we stand united, there is less chance of a war."

"Why wait?" Jimmy asked. "Why not take this thing to him and get it over with on our terms?"

"It's the wrong way to go. Why start a war when we can ease him out?"

The big man paused to think. "Yeah. Sure."

Estévez smiled and patted Jimmy on the arm.

"We better get our stuff out of here," Jimmy said. He turned to the other men and motioned for them to follow him.

Estévez led Ortega, Caltabiano, and the others to the storefront. Jimmy used his key and entered the store first, choosing a flashlight instead of using the light switch to navigate the darkened interior of the store.

No one said a word as the big man led the others down an aisle flanked with wheelbarrows, rakes, weed trimmers, and garden hoses, past a table that held trays of screws, nuts, and bolts of various types and sizes, and through a door that opened into a large stockroom. Caltabiano turned off the flashlight and flicked on the light switch in the windowless room.

The room was filled floor-to-ceiling with shelves full of hardware stock. The concrete floor sloped to the center, where a large drainage grate was located. Caltabiano nodded to two of the men. One of them selected a crowbar off one of the nearby shelves and handed it to the other, who began prying the grate up. As soon as it was loosened from its position in the floor, the two men lifted it free and carried it out of the way.

The other man took the flashlight from Jimmy and lowered himself into the hole. Ortega could see the glow of the flashlight coming from below the floor. After a moment, the hole was awash in light.

"Okay," the man said, his voice echoing.

The other two men were next to go down. Estévez followed and motioned for Ortega. From what the agent could tell, Jimmy was too big to fit, so by default he became the one to remain behind and serve as lookout.

Ortega was the last man down the ladder. Once in, he saw that two of the men had already begun bagging kilos of cocaine in gym bags that had been stored in the room. They were leaving a few smaller packages of the drug on the cutting table.

The process went quickly, though the two storage tables held what Ortega figured were a hundred kilos of coke. Estévez tossed one of the zippered gym bags to Ortega.

"Let's get this stuff out of here, my friend."

Ortega loaded plastic bags of cocaine. The others were moving more rapidly than he and seemed familiar with the mechanics of moving large quantities of the stuff under duress.

"Be sure to leave the weighing and cutting supplies. I want the law to know there was a drug operation here," Estévez said. "And leave the grate off when we torch the place. I want the cops to find everything."

"This is a lot of money to go up in smoke," Ortega said.

"It won't go up in smoke. Most of it we're moving out of here. The building fire will attract the fire department long before it is completely destroyed. Then the law will begin looking at the arson. That's when they will find the destroyed cocaine operation, and it will make news." He smiled. "They will find what appears to be a drug operation and a fire that was started in this room."

Ortega shook his head. "Do you ever wonder if the risk is worth it?"

Estévez looked at the agent as though he had asked if life was worth living.

"Did you see my family?"

"Yes, of course. But—"

"No 'buts,' my friend. I have a family I love. I will take risks for them." He held a bag of the white powder in his hand for Ortega to see. "People have needs. This helps to fill those needs." His voice took on an ecclesiastical tone. "People deal with problems every day that are beyond their capacity to solve. Poverty and hopelessness and despair will always be with us. But this stuff," he tossed the bag lightly in his hand, "is the great benefactor for all of that."

Behind Estévez, the others were busy packing the coke and replacing it with decoy bags of sugar. Estévez continued, his eyes alive with jihad intensity.

"For those who can rise above their circumstances, this is the gateway to the good life. For those who cannot, it is their avenue of escape. In many cases, it is their *only* way of escape. It brightens their darkest corners and eases their unbearable burdens. It fills the hole in their being." He grinned. "It fills their need, dulls their pain. It cleanses them. It touches their soul." He smiled and tossed the bag lightly again. "White soul, my friend. People die for it."

Ortega took the bag of coke and placed it in his bag.

Estévez grinned and put an arm around Ortega's shoulders. "They get what they need and I get what I want. My family is cared for properly, and the people who cannot cope can escape what would otherwise be, for them, inescapable."

"There is still risk," Ortega said.

Estévez nodded. "Yes. But life is a series of risks. The question, my friend, is not whether there is risk, but how acceptable that risk is." He turned slightly to wave an arm at the stash. "And as you can see, this risk is very acceptable."

CHAPTER *Twenty-Five*

It took the men less than half an hour to load the cellar stash of drugs into Jimmy's SUV for transport to one of Estévez's other locations. Estévez didn't reveal where the coke was going or how long it would be there. But that information wasn't important. What was important was that Ortega now had a firsthand view of how extensive an operation Estévez ran. If the man could store over a hundred kilos of coke in just one location, how much more did he have put away elsewhere? It could be worth tens of millions—more than enough to feed a battalion of graft-hungry politicians, cops, and judges—and enough to trigger a war that city officials would never be able to contain. Estévez's organization was far more operational than anyone in Miami or the DEA had thought.

After returning home, Ortega slept fitfully, as he had the night before, and was up with the sun. It didn't take long for the local news to mention the hardware store fire.

Ortega was astonished at how accurate Estévez's predictions of an assault on his remote warehouse were. The place had been torched before sunrise, but because it was found to house a cocaine operation, it made news, which meant his intended targets would hear about it soon.

The undercover agent finished his coffee, rinsed his cup, and set it in the sink before using his cell phone to call his lifeline. "We need to talk."

"So talk," O'Connor said.

"Then let's have breakfast," Ortega said. "There's nothing to eat in this dump."

"Meet me at the IHOP on West Sunset," O'Connor said. "I'll even pick up the tab."

Ortega was showered, shaved, and sitting in the back of the booth when O'Connor arrived. As soon as the men placed their orders, Ortega began to fill him in on the events of the past two days. O'Connor didn't seem as concerned about the interrogations as Ortega had anticipated.

"You seem okay with all of this," the younger agent said.

The lifeline shrugged. "This isn't the academy, kid. Sometimes you get your hands dirty." He looked Ortega in the face again. "Have you managed to rub someone the wrong way?"

"A couple of cops."

"Cops?"

"Miami PD," Ortega said. "They're on the take and they rousted Mikey. He was supposed to pay off and didn't. When he agreed to meet their demands, I offered to take it to them."

"And?"

"I got a little snippy with them. We tangled."

"Is that what happened to your face?"

"That's the part you see. There's more."

"You write your report?"

"Yes."

"Has anyone else raised suspicion about you?" O'Connor asked.

Ortega shook his head.

"Any problems with the Mexican?"

Again, Ortega shook his head. "I haven't seen him in a while, but during my confrontation with one of the cops, he mentioned something about Kingman."

"Kingman?" O'Connor said, pausing as the server set their breakfast before them. "Isn't Santiago working with Estévez?"

"Part of the time. But he's hustling. Could be he's working both sides of the street."

O'Connor frowned as he picked up a strip of bacon.

"If he's working both sides of the fence and he's mentioned you to Kingman's crew," he shrugged, "you may be approached by them."

"Maybe. At this point, I haven't had any problems and Estévez seems to be impressed with me. When he found out about my tussle with the cops, the door opened a bit more."

O'Connor nodded thoughtfully as he chewed the strip of bacon. "That's going to put you in good stead. You'll hear more than we thought. Like, for example, what he's planning against Kingman."

"How come I didn't know about all of that beforehand?" Ortega asked, drinking the coffee.

"Need to know," O'Connor said.

Ortega glanced around the restaurant, before leaning across the table and lowering his voice. "I'm in an undercover position that could wipe Estévez and his crew off the map, and you guys didn't think I needed to know?"

O'Connor forked some of the scrambled eggs into his mouth and shrugged. "Sorry. I don't make the rules, I just live by them."

"Anything else I need to know about?" Ortega asked, angry that he was being left in the dark, especially when the dark could become permanent.

"No. How about for me?"

The agent sighed as he set the cup down. "I helped Estévez, Caltabiano, and three bartenders at the club move a whole bunch of coke last night."

O'Connor had been stirring cream into his coffee when he stopped. "How much?"

"A hundred kilos or more."

O'Connor let out a long whistle before he began stirring again. "That's a lot of dope."

"Estévez met with a couple of guys at his party last night. He told them he had a tip from a source that someone's assets, somewhere, were going to be attacked. He said he felt like it was coming from Kingman and the attack would most likely be on one of their warehouses."

"Who were the other two?" O'Connor asked.

"Their names were David Salter and Julio Lopez." Ortega bit into his omelet.

"Where was the coke?" O'Connor asked.

"At a hardware store in northern Broward County." Ortega gave the senior agent the address. "They use it as a warehouse. The store is operational, but underneath the floor, through the storm drain in the stockroom, there's a cellar where they keep the stuff hidden. They torched it last night. It's on the news."

O'Connor took time to eat another forkful of eggs and mull over the information that Ortega had given him. "So maybe we have a gang war brewing."

Ortega shook his head. "I don't think so. I don't think it'll get that far. When we got to the warehouse last night, Jimmy wanted to hit Kingman first. Take the fight to him." He ate another bite of the omelet.

"Really?" O'Connor said, a bit surprised. "Kingman is bigger. Better connected."

"Nevertheless," Ortega said, "that came up. But Estévez nixed the idea. Said the best thing to do was to prevent any damage to Kingman, do business as usual, and when the time is right, present a united front." He drank some coffee, winced, and drank some more.

"It could be, too, that Estévez is setting this whole thing up to take advantage of the situation. Knock off Kingman as a player then condense his operation into Estévez's own. It would be a snap at that point to take over Lopez, Salter, Torres, and Garcia." O'Connor ate another strip of bacon. "You got a tiger by the tail, Ron. Whatever you do, don't let go."

CHAPTER *Twenty-Six*

As news of the fire broke, Estévez called Lopez and Salter for a meeting. The three men met that morning at Salter's home, a modest two-story located in a working-class neighborhood. Most of Salter's neighbors were already at work and most of their children were already in school. A postal delivery truck was making its rounds.

"I got hit last night," Estévez said. "And one of you could be next."

News of the cocaine facility's torching had already reached Lopez and Salter, but hearing it directly from Estévez put a color on it that Eyewitness News couldn't muster.

"You think Kingman's behind it?" Salter asked.

"I do."

"So why you?" Lopez asked. "Why not one of us?"

"You mean 'again'?" Estévez asked. "Has he not already taken a healthy bite out of your backsides?"

The men acknowledged that he had.

"So why wouldn't he come after me?" Estévez said.

"You're larger than the four of us…and younger," Lopez said. "You're a threat to his son's future, while we," he gestured around the room, "we are a threat to no one. With you, he risks an all-out war."

Estévez steered Lopez back to the business at hand. "Jimmy discovered Kingman is moving stock across the country. By taking his territory national he's increasing sales for the Colombians. He's also working to build alliances with the Italians, the Asians...everyone." He sat forward on the couch to emphasize his point. "He's gotten bold. Too bold. His connections have increased his desire for more. He doesn't fear a war, he wants one."

Salter's face creased in concern as he crossed his legs.

Estévez continued. "He expects me to do exactly what you have said, my friend. But starting a war will only serve to further alienate the public and deepen the commitment of the law. That's what he wants. He wants us to become entangled with each other and with the police while he moves in, cleans up, and closes the deal he is making with Havana." Estévez sat back on the couch and studied the men as they mulled over the situation. It was Lopez who spoke first.

"It's got to be him. We've all been hit and he hasn't."

"Ricardo," Salter said, "this source of yours, the one who told you that Kingman has been visiting Havana, is this the same source that you mentioned last night? The one who said that something bad was about to go down?"

"No," Estévez said.

"And yet, something did go down last night. Two separate sources saying the same thing."

"That Kingman can't be trusted," Lopez said, completing Salter's logic.

Estévez pulled an envelope from his back pocket and tossed it onto the coffee table.

"What's this?" Salter asked.

"Open it, my friend. Maybe it will convince you of what I say."

Salter opened the envelope and unfolded the paper inside. He frowned as he read.

Lopez took the paper from him and read it.

"That is a photocopy," Estévez said. "As you can see from his itinerary, Kingman flew from here to Venezuela and from there directly into Havana." He paused as he watched Salter rise from his chair and begin to pace the room.

"I can't believe it," Salter said, again. "I just can't believe it."

"He's double-crossing all of us," Lopez said, refolding the paper and tossing it back onto the coffee table.

"Gentlemen, I need your help," Estévez said. "I believe we can take him out without a war. But it will take a united front. I want you to talk to the others. We must all pull together for our common interests."

Salter was standing in the middle of the room, still trying to make sense of it.

Estévez went to him and gently put an arm around the man's shoulders. "I am sorry to have to bear this news to you, my friend. I truly am. I know Kingman was your mentor."

"Okay, Ricardo," Lopez said, "What do you think we should do? How do we handle this without a war?"

Estevez smiled. "We must meet somewhere else. Somewhere offshore, where we don't need to worry about the government prying."

Salter turned toward them, seeming to have come out of his funk. "I have a friend who has a yacht. There was a time when we owned some horses, but we sold them to him. He's active in racing, and away most of the time."

Estévez smiled. "Racehorses?"

"Yes. Why not? A man can't work all the time. There have to be some diversions in life."

Estévez turned to Lopez. He shrugged. "Sure, why not?"

"Okay then," Estévez said, smacking his hands together. "Now all we need to do is to get the others to agree to a meeting."

"That shouldn't be difficult," Lopez said. "I think everyone recognizes the need to come together."

"Don't tell them why we're meeting, Julio. Let them think it is because of the government. Once we have them together, I can present them with the same information I've given to you."

Salter moved closer to Estévez. "That won't be easy. Even with the information you've presented here today. For most of them, Kingman has been a mentor. Like me, they have an affinity for the man. They won't be easily persuaded."

Estévez's tone turned somber. "Let us hope you are wrong. Let us hope they are able to put aside their love for the man to see the evidence as clearly as you have."

"I can reach some of the others today," Lopez said. "The sooner we address this thing, the better."

"Okay with me," Salter said. "I can call some too."

"And you will secure the boat?" Estévez asked. "Perhaps now? We do not want to have everything in place and have nowhere to meet."

Salter glanced at his watch. "I can try."

"Excelente," Estévez said.

CHAPTER *Twenty-Seven*

Lopez helped himself to a beer from Salter's refrigerator while Salter made the call to his friend. Estévez excused himself to find the bathroom.

Lopez and Estévez returned to the living room as Salter was ending his call.

"Okay," Salter said to the others. "We've got the boat."

"Now all we've got to do is to get everyone to agree to meet," Lopez said, before tipping the bottle.

"That's where you come in," Estévez said. "Both of you have been around a lot longer than I have and you both carry weight. The others will listen to you."

"Maybe that is the problem," Salter said. "They have been listening and we haven't been telling them the right things."

"We are not young men, Ricardo," Lopez said. "Our time in the sun has come and gone. But if you think we can be helpful in this situation, then you tell us what we should do and we'll do it."

Estevez was ready with advice. "It will be best if we can get everyone on the yacht for a couple of days, let them have a good time and loosen up a bit. Tell them anything you want to get them on board. After everyone has relaxed, we can talk."

"It will take a lot more than a cruise on a yacht to convince them," Salter said. He nodded to the travel itinerary on the table. "If you have any more evidence to corroborate your assertions it would be wise to bring it along."

"Most everyone else has been hit with something," Lopez said. "Everyone except Kingman. That should be enough."

Estévez looked at Salter. He shrugged. "It won't," he said. "You'll need something more than circumstantial evidence. Just as you did with us."

"So then what?" Lopez broke in. "Suppose everyone shows and everyone believes you. What then?"

"Then I tell them that the best way to fight this thing with Kingman is to unite. All of us coming together under one tent." He paused. "Do you understand?"

Lopez said, "You're suggesting a merger? Ricardo, are you crazy?"

"No, I am not crazy," Estevez said, clearly amused.

"It sounds like you've taken leave of your senses," Salter added. "Working together is one thing, but merging is an entirely different matter."

"I can assure you I haven't taken leave of my senses," Estévez said. "My intent would be to function under one corporate structure. If Kingman hits us, we each help the other to recover and continue business as usual."

"And how will that get rid of Kingman?" Salter asked. "What's to keep him from coming after us?"

"We take his business."

The two men began to grumble.

Estévez held up a hand. "Hear me out. We take his business by using our combined resources to overrun his routes. We deliver better product, faster—and cheaper. Our betting tables start paying higher, and more often. And we support the loss by taking swag from anywhere we can find it, including Kingman. In other words, we take losses in the short run, using the leverage we can have with each other, to protect ourselves while we make efforts to expand into new areas of revenue."

Lopez grinned. "We Wal-Mart him to death. Is that it?"

Estévez spread his hands. "In a sense, yes. We'll syndicate him to death. It's much better than a war."

Salter shook his head. "I can't speak for the others of course, but before I completely sign on to this, I'd like to know more about how you see this developing."

"Me too," Lopez said. "What sounds good in theory can fall apart in practice. I'm going to need more."

Estévez was silent. Then he said, "Bring me a deck of cards."

Salter rose from his chair and went into another room. He returned a moment later with a packet of playing cards. Estévez took the pack from his host, opened them, and spread the cards out on the table. He selected a card and held it out for the men to see.

"Four of clubs," Lopez said.

The Cuban selected another card and held it in his hand.

"King of spades," Salter said.

Estévez held up a third card.

"Five of diamonds," Lopez said.

The Cuban held up two more cards in quick succession, a two of hearts and a three of diamonds.

"What do I have here?" Estévez said.

"Nothing," Lopez replied.

Estévez picked up the four of clubs, rifled through the deck and selected four more cards. After choosing them, he spread the hand on the table.

"I have a four of clubs, five of clubs, six of clubs, seven of clubs, and an eight of clubs."

"Straight flush," Lopez said.

Estévez picked up the king of spades he had drawn earlier and added a queen of spades, three of hearts, four of diamonds, and two of clubs.

"Now what do I have?"

Salter sighed. "A pair."

"And a straight flush beats a pair, agreed?"

Both men nodded.

"Gentlemen," Estévez said, "we have been fighting among ourselves for too long." He picked up the king of spades and the four of clubs. "We are all trying to be the king," he tossed the card onto the table, "because none of us wants to be the little guy." He held up the four of clubs for both men to clearly see. "But when the little guys work together, each playing his role," he tossed the card onto the other clubs, "we all end up as a straight flush. Winners."

Lopez shook his head. "That's it?"

"It's a simple strategy, but powerfully effective," Estévez said. "If we can get everyone to work together—to form a syndicate—we can each have a piece of the pie by sticking to what we know best. Some of us can handle the junk, some of us can handle gambling—we each can do well by doing what we do best."

Salter ran a hand over his thinning hair. "On the surface it sounds workable."

"But?" Estévez said.

"But what about the guys who are making more in coke than in anything else? How're they supposed to recoup their losses if they agree to get out of that and go into, say, women? We aren't the Italians, Ricardo. We aren't organized the same way they are."

"But we can be smarter than the Italians, David," Estévez said. "That's the power of unity. We pool our income, share our expenses, and then dole out the profits based on the percentage of input. Of course, we will need some way of calculating for inherent losses, but that can be done and it can be done equitably."

"Who oversees all of this?" Lopez asked. "Who runs the operation and settles disputes? Because it's going to happen. There will be disputes."

"I will," Estevez said without blinking. "It is the one thing I ask. It is my plan and I will make it succeed."

"Alone?" Salter asked.

"No. I will need…shall we call them 'advisors'? They can be selected from among all of you. We'll need legal, accounting…that sort of thing. And we'll need someone who can run the laundering operations as well. That would be perfect for you gentlemen who say of yourselves that you are no longer young men. Later, as the others get older we could transition others out of their specialized areas into the front operations. Dry cleaners, movie theaters, hardware stores—"

"Nightclubs," Salter said.

Estévez grinned. "Yes, my friend, nightclubs too."

Salter ran a hand over his hair again. Lopez finished his beer.

"Well?" Estévez asked.

"I will make the calls," Lopez said.

"Me too," Salter agreed. "I will call as many as I know. But this won't be an easy sell. For Julio and myself it is no problem. But for some of the others, especially the younger ones who are trying to make a name for themselves," he wiggled his hand, "maybe it will not be such an easy thing."

Lopez agreed. "They are assuming the strikes are coming from overzealous officers or one of the others. Because of this, their level of paranoia is up. But at least one of them is beginning to suspect Kingman, since, as you have pointed out, Ricardo, he is the only one who hasn't been hurt."

"Who is the one who's suspecting Kingman?" Estévez asked.

"Garcia."

Estévez leaned back onto the couch and threw one arm across the back. "Talk to him, my friend. Get to him before he does something stupid."

"I will try, Ricardo. But if he or any of the others can pin their losses on a specific target, there will be a war," Lopez said. "In order for them to agree to your plan, they will have to see it in terms of their interest. Something must happen to cause them to see your plan as the solution to their problems."

"That may yet happen, my friend," Estévez said. "That may yet happen."

CHAPTER *Twenty-Eight*

Ricardo Estévez was a happy man. He had succeeded in laying the foundation for his plan. Next came part two of the scheme. In the early hours of the following morning, the drug lord dispatched Jimmy Caltabiano and Frankie Gatto to the Salter home. The men parked a block north and walked carefully along the street, avoiding the security lights that seemed to line every corner.

After they reached the back of the Salter home, Gatto found and disabled the sophisticated alarm system that secured the house where Salter had lived with his wife for the past five years. Then Caltabiano motioned for the more athletic Gatto to climb through the bathroom window. Once inside, the younger man would open the rear door for the bigger, burlier enforcer.

This wasn't Gatto's first hit and he had made no secret of his resentment of Caltabiano's presence. But Caltabiano had insisted on coming along. There was, after all, a great deal at stake, including his own neck. Ex-cops didn't fare well in prison, which meant that Jimmy could never afford to be taken alive. So if the younger man's resentment was the price to pay to ensure a job well done, so be it.

Once Gatto was inside the kitchen he opened the door for his older counterpart.

The two men moved cautiously through the house, following the plan Estévez had devised. He had mentally sketched the general floor plan during his trip to Salter's bathroom, passing it on to the two men as soon as he had returned from his meeting.

Their orders were specific. Kill Salter quickly, quietly, and while his wife was still away. Estévez was himself a devoted family man, and he would not sanction a hit on a man's family nor even a hit on a man in the presence of his family. It was one of the standards of conduct by which he had come to respect the Italians.

The hallway along which the two assassins moved was well-carpeted. Several nightlights lined the corridor, helping the men navigate the unfamiliar area. But they did not have to search far. Salter's snoring could be heard from the last room on the right.

The method for killing Salter would be strangulation. Although Jimmy was more powerful, it was Gatto's stronger heart and love of the task that made him the better choice. Caltabiano couldn't help but notice that the younger man already had the garrote in hand.

The two slid into the darkened room like boas on the hunt. The nightlights that had lined the hallway were not present in Salter's bedroom, but that made little difference. His snores provided all the direction Gatto needed.

Jimmy took a position near the door. When Gatto was finished, the ex-cop would check to make sure the job had been done right. After a moment poised over the bed of his victim, Gatto made his move. He pounced on the unsuspecting Salter like a ravenous wolf on a lost sheep. Within a second, he had the garrote around Salter's throat and began to pull with all his strength on the ends of the cord.

Gatto preferred the cross-hand technique. Although it didn't provide the sheer force of a straight-handed pull, it did make it easier to subdue the victim by forcing the crossed hands deeper into the airway.

Salter woke, gasped, and then gurgled before beginning to fight. He thrashed right to left, raised his legs, and pushed with his hands, but the stronger and more agile Gatto continued to pull. Caltabiano stepped into the hallway to look at his watch in the glow of the nightlights.

"What's going on..."

He was startled by Salter's wife stepping from the bedroom across the hall. The one that Jimmy had assumed was empty, based on the information Estévez had given him.

At once the woman began to scream, setting in motion two events that would turn the night inside out.

Caltabiano jumped and stumbled backward into the open doorway of Salter's bedroom, landing on the floor.

Gatto turned at the scream and, unsure if someone had shot or stabbed his partner, loosened his grip. This gave Salter a brief chance to push the killer off him and reach for the nightstand drawer.

Gatto struggled to get to his feet. Caltabiano rolled over and tried to climb to all fours, but Salter's wife pounced on his back and began pounding him with her fists as she pulled his hair. Jimmy knew if he didn't quickly get the situation under control, the screaming would alert a nearby neighbor, which would bring the law on them.

On the other side of the room, Gatto rose to his feet just as Salter pulled a gun from the drawer. The younger man slammed the drawer onto Salter's hand, but the older man kept a firm grip on his weapon.

"Finish him," Caltabiano yelled. "Do it and let's get out of here."

Gatto pounced again on the older man, who had transferred the gun to his uninjured hand. He slapped the weapon away and punched Salter several times. As the resistance weakened, Gatto fished through the bed covers with his other hand, trying to find the garrote.

Salter's wife continued to scream as she fought with Jimmy. Her weight on top of his own kept him from getting up.

Gatto at last found the cord and reached for it, when Salter suddenly found the strength to hit the younger man hard enough to knock the wind out of him. Gatto rolled off and onto the bed to his victim's right.

Gasping, Salter jumped out from under the covers and began to feel along the floor.

"Get him," Jimmy yelled. "He's going for the gun."

Gatto slid from the bed, landing on Salter's back just as the older man grasped the pistol. Gatto punched the older man, pushed his head to the floor, and tried to pry the gun from his grasp, but Salter was fighting for his life and that gave him the edge he needed.

On the other side of the room, Caltabiano was gaining the upper hand by rolling over and pinning Salter's wife under his back. Still, she desperately continued her hair-pulling and random punching.

Gatto hit Salter again and again, but the older man held tightly to the gun. "Enough of this," Gatto finally growled. He leaned forward and bit Salter's ear. Salter loosened his grip, and Gatto quickly got hold of the weapon. He put the barrel behind Salter's right ear and fired. Then fired again.

Salter gasped and the struggle ceased.

The gunshots had now raised the stakes considerably. Caltabiano had turned to see what happened, and this freed Salter's wife from where he'd pinned her. She shot to her feet and ran down the hall screaming.

"Get her," Caltabiano yelled.

Gatto took off after her with Salter's gun in hand. Jimmy got to his feet, took a long, deep breath, and followed. By the time he was outside, Salter's wife had already exited the house and was running down the driveway, screaming.

Gatto ran after her, stopped in front of the garage door, and fired.

The first shot hit her in the back and knocked her into the street. She landed face down. She continued to scream as she struggled to rise.

Gatto fired again. Again she was knocked to the ground. Still the screaming didn't stop.

He fired again. Then again and again.

The screaming stopped. The woman lay motionless in the street at the end of her driveway.

Jimmy had reached Gatto by the time the last shot was fired. He wiped sweat from his forehead with a handkerchief and noticed lights coming on in several homes along the street. He grabbed the pistol from Gatto's hand and wiped it down with the handkerchief he had been using. Then he dropped the pistol onto the driveway, where it landed with a clatter.

"Let's go," Jimmy said.

And the two men left the way they came.

CHAPTER *Twenty-Nine*

The news of the murder of David Michael Salter and his wife reached Estévez by a prearranged phone signal from Caltabiano. Long ago, Estévez and his enforcer had set up a code. If an assignment went well, Caltabiano would ring once. If things went poorly, he would ring twice. If the situation had swung out of control, he would ring three times. Estévez made it a practice to never discuss business over the phone. Although his sources in the government had assured him that the courts had long ago dropped their taps from his line, he felt it was wiser to assume such measures were still in place.

But no one called Julio Lopez, by code or otherwise. He received the news of his colleague's murder by way of the channel six news. His response was a hasty trip to Ricardo Estévez's estate.

When he arrived and was shown in, Estévez was sitting at his dining table. A plate of scrambled eggs, lightly covered in hot sauce, and bacon with toast sat before him. A carafe of coffee was within reach.

"Have you had breakfast?" the drug lord offered.

Lopez sat down opposite Estévez. Ignoring the question, he said, "You heard what happened?"

Estevez tasted his eggs, then said, "Yes, I have heard. I am so sorry to hear about our friend. I was shocked. Profoundly shocked."

Lopez leaned forward on the table. "I will ask you straight up, Ricardo. Did you know there was going to be a hit?"

"No, of course not," the Cuban answered. "How could you accuse me of such a thing?"

"I'm not accusing you, Ricardo," Lopez said. "I'm asking. Did you know?"

"And again I am answering you with the truth. No, I did not know of this. How could I?"

"You knew of the attempt on our assets. That alone causes me to ask, could your source have known of this too?"

"If my sources had known of this atrocity they would have warned me. David and I were not the closest of friends. But I do believe he understood the viciousness of our common enemy. I could work with him, even if it were for no other reason than he could help pull our plan together. His death is a loss for me too, Julio." Estévez took a sip of orange juice and continued. "His death is a blow to our plans. But it is not a deterrent." He reached for the coffee carafe and gestured toward Lopez. "Are you sure you would not like some coffee?"

"Yes. I'm sure."

"My friend," Estévez said, pouring some coffee, "have you ever known me to be anything other than fully devoted to my family? Have I not preached this to all of you? Family first? First before business? Have you ever known me to even berate a man in the presence of his family? I certainly would not destroy a man and his wife."

Lopez sighed briefly, then rose from his chair. "I hope you can understand why I had to ask."

Estévez rose to meet him. "I do, my friend. But we must not let this tragedy derail our plans to unite. We will face more such events if we do not work together. It is our only salvation."

Lopez nodded somberly as Estévez escorted him to the door.

As the older man was leaving, Caltabiano entered. The two exchanged greetings before the enforcer was led through the house and onto the veranda.

"What happened?" Estévez asked, out of earshot of his waking family.

Jimmy was apologetic. "I didn't want to call you last night, but I also didn't want you hearing it on the TV."

"I appreciate that, Jimmy. But I ask you again, what happened?" Estévez was standing near the seawall with his arms folded.

"The best information we had said that his wife was out of town." Jimmy shrugged. "So we followed your directions and when we got to the house, I had Frankie disable the alarm. He let me in and we found Salter alone in bed. Gatto got to work and then next thing I know is this…crazy woman is screaming her head off."

An expression of compassion flashed across Estévez's face. "She wasn't a crazy woman, Jimmy. She was his wife. His family."

Caltabiano nodded.

"Go on."

"So I fall back into Salter's bedroom and the wife jumps on me and starts fighting with me. Meanwhile, Gatto's got his hands full and Salter gets a gun out of the nightstand. So we got this woman screaming, and Gatto's trying to whack the old man, and everything is just falling apart." He shook his head. "In the interest of time, Gatto grabs Salter's gun and ices him right there on the floor. Then the wife jumps off me and takes off. Next thing I know, she's running screaming down the driveway." He paused to shrug again. "Frankie had no choice. He had to take her out so we could get out of there."

Estévez sighed.

"I took the gun from him," Jimmy said, "wiped it clean and left it there."

"Okay, Jimmy," Estévez said, running a hand through his hair. "Where's Frankie now?"

"Home."

"Do you think the two of you were seen?"

Caltabiano shook his head. "No. It was early and everyone was still asleep. Some lights had started to come on as we ended it, but by then we were on our way out of there."

Estévez nodded. "Okay. Just have Frankie stay in for a couple of days. If the heat turns up, I'll get you two out of town."

"You want me to take someone else out on deliveries today?"

Estévez frowned. "I'd forgotten about that. Frankie was supposed to go with you, wasn't he?"

"Yes, sir."

"Call Acuna. He's been okay and driving is what he does best."

Jimmy nodded. "Okay. And I'm really sorry about all of this."

"I am too," Estévez said. "I don't like that a man's family took the rap with him. But the purpose can still be served. In fact, as much as I hate to admit it, we can actually reap from this a whole lot more than we've sown."

"How so?"

"I had hoped the hit on Salter would drive everyone into our camp against Kingman. And that can still happen. But Garcia is already looking at Kingman and that may be something we can use. After all, if Garcia is convinced Kingman took out Salter, then maybe we can spin Garcia in the right direction."

"You want Kingman hit?"

"No, Jimmy," Estévez said. "I want him dethroned. If he loses, so does his son. And that, my friend, will throw all of Miami our way."

CHAPTER *Thirty*

Santiago had been lying low after the rousting from Dowd and Hurst, preferring to stay out of the spotlight in what was getting to be a spotlight kind of world. Since the pressure had been on, most of the city's other vices, the ones the Mexican preferred, had begun to dry up along with the drug trade. Several gambling joints had been closed, some of the local houses and their madams had been rounded up, and a lot of dealers, mostly small-timers, had been arrested. Even some of the fences were feeling the heat, which hurt Santiago's pocket in a big way. No one wanted to move his merchandise, and that left him with such a load of items that he was beginning to have a hard time moving through his already tiny apartment.

"Man, this thing has got to break," he said to Caltabiano over lunch at Hokey's. "It's killing me."

Caltabiano nodded understandingly. "Things are tough all over, Mikey," he said. "The cops aren't getting paid and that means the politicians aren't getting paid, and the whole thing starts to snowball into one giant mess. You know what I'm saying?"

Santiago nodded. He had a cigarette between the first two fingers of his right hand and the plastic fork in his left. He was scooping the beans from his meal into a neat pile for the final assault.

"By the way," Jimmy said, "Mr. Estévez says he wants you to know how much he appreciates what you did for him."

The Mexican stopped scooping and looked up from his plate.

"Really," Caltabiano said. "I'm not pulling your leg here."

"Did he say that?" the Mexican asked with a seriousness that made the burly bouncer want to laugh.

"Absolutely. No question about it, Mikey. I was there."

Caltabiano watched as the Mexican hustler's face brightened and he scooped the last of the beans into his mouth.

"I was beginning to wonder, you know? I wasn't sure if he was still mad at me for blowing it with the sale."

Caltabiano wiggled one hand back and forth while he ate a forkful of salad. "He wasn't none too happy about that deal, let's face it. And when he had the gun in your ear, I really thought he was going to do you in."

"Me too," the Mexican said, with a shake of his head. "Me too."

"But in the end, would he actually do it?" Jimmy shrugged. "Who's to say? Maybe. He takes his business very seriously."

Santiago nodded as he cut into his enchilada. "And I knew you was covering for me in there, Jimmy. You know? When Mr. Estévez wanted to blow my brains out on the bar and you said, 'No, waste him in the office'?"

Caltabiano nodded and grinned. "Yeah. Sorry about that, Mikey, but I needed time for Mr. Estévez to cool down. You understand?"

"Yeah. Exactly. That's what I'm getting at. If it wasn't for you, I'd probably be dead by now."

The enforcer looked at the Mexican's plate. "You want more? It looks like you're drying up there."

Santiago was flabbergasted. "I can have more?"

Caltabiano rose from the booth and went to the register. He ordered another number 2, paid the girl, and came back to the table.

"She's going to bring you another one. Or would you like something else?"

"Maybe another Corona," Santiago said, taking advantage of the situation.

Jimmy got up again and ordered a bottle of Corona to go with the number 2.

"And an extra packet of hot sauce," Santiago yelled to the big enforcer as he was about to leave the window.

Jimmy told the girl he wanted a couple of extra hot sauces before going back to the booth. He ate a bite of the salad before continuing the conversation.

"I think you're probably right, Mikey. Mr. Estévez would probably have killed you right there on the bar if I hadn't been there."

Santiago finished the last of the enchilada just as the girl brought him another plate and a bottle of Corona.

"I think so too," he said.

"I think he would have regretted it though," the enforcer said, finishing what was left of his salad. "That bar is hand-cut, and it would have been destroyed."

The Mexican swallowed hard as he poured two packets of extra-hot hot sauce on the enchilada.

"But of course, I was thinking of you too, Mikey. I wasn't thinking so much about the bar."

Santiago nodded as he opened the bottle of Corona. His hand was shaking, a fact Jimmy didn't miss.

"Thinking about it makes you nervous, doesn't it?"

"Yeah."

"You came kind of close that night, Mikey. I'm glad I could help."

"Thank you."

"You don't need to think bad of Mr. Estévez. He was just mad. I think he maybe would've stopped himself, but I just didn't want to take the chance." Jimmy pushed the tray containing the shell of the taco salad to the kid who came to collect it. "You've been a big help to him and I know he would have a hard time replacing you."

The Mexican's hand still shook, but a thin smile began to form across his face.

"He values your information. He knows he can rely on you. You've always come through. So maybe it wasn't just the bar he was worried about destroying. Maybe it was his relationship with you."

The Mexican had forked up some more beans from his plate, but paused. "He say that?"

Caltabiano nodded. "Oh yeah. Absolutely, he said that. That's why I'm here. He wanted me to tell you how sorry he is and that he even has a job for you to do. If you want it. No pressure."

Santiago ate the beans. "How come he didn't come himself?"

The big enforcer looked out the window at the passing traffic and sighed. "He's a busy man, Mikey. You know that. Things are happening. We lost a warehouse the other night and a good friend was killed."

"Salter?"

Jimmy continued his stare out the window. "Yeah. Someone hit Salter. But worse yet, someone hit his wife too. And Mr. Estévez is taking the heat for it."

Santiago grew serious. "Who did it, Jimmy?"

The enforcer fixed his gaze on the diminutive man. "Kingman. We know it was him."

"Why?"

Caltabiano shrugged. "There's some speculation he's trying to take over. Consolidate his power. He's got a lot of people up in arms. Salter was well-liked."

"He was always good to me," Santiago said.

Jimmy nodded.

The Mexican put his fork down. "What does Mr. Estévez want me to do?"

Caltabiano looked out the window again. "He wants you to get word to Garcia. He wants you to let Garcia know that you heard it was Kingman."

"On the sly?" Santiago asked.

"On the sly," the enforcer said.

CHAPTER *Thirty-One*

Ortega reported for work two hours before the club opened and was greeted by Chipper. She handed him the requisite emerald vest before taking him on the employee's tour of the club, culminating with an oral history of the crystal bar.

"Hand-cut," she said. "Every square inch of it. It's beautiful, don't you think?"

Ortega ran a hand along the top of the bar. "Yes, it is. Must have cost a fortune."

"Listen," she said, lowering her voice, "he's making it. I've tended bar in a lot of nice places, and some that maybe weren't so nice, you know? And this place rocks."

"What do you want me to do?" Ortega asked, cutting to the chase.

"I want you to mix drinks, smile pretty, and do the heavy lifting. Okay?"

"Sure. But it looked like you had plenty of hired muscle at the party the other night."

She gave Ortega a puzzled look.

"The other night at the party," he said. "You had some guys helping you pack, remember? The same guys who helped park cars."

"Oh, them," she said. "They only help out when we have an outside gig. Mr. Estévez arranges it."

"So I'm going to be doing the heavy lifting most of the time."

She put an arm around his shoulder, standing close enough to allow her hair to fall on his chest.

"You're the big strong man here, Mr. Acuna," she said in mock flattery. "Why, I'm just a weak little ol' Southern belle."

Corny but effective. Ortega couldn't help but be aware of Chipper's attraction to him. And her scent, the smoothness of her skin, her upbeat demeanor, they were having an effect on him that went beyond what he knew he should allow.

"Okay," he said. "What needs lifting?"

She stepped away and pointed to a shelf underneath the bar. "See those empty boxes?"

"Empty? You need me to lift empty boxes?"

"No, silly, I need you to go to the storeroom and get *full* boxes to replace the empty ones."

She reached underneath the bar, grabbed a key off a hook, and tossed it to the agent.

"Now?" he asked.

"Now."

Ortega left the bar and crossed the dance floor to the hallway that accessed Estévez's office. According to Chipper, the door on the left was the liquor storeroom. As Ortega entered the short hall, he noticed Jimmy coming into the club from the main entrance. Another man, one that Ortega recognized by the tattoo on his arm, was accompanying the enforcer.

Ortega inserted the key into the lock and opened the storeroom. Both men passed by the open door on their way to Estévez's office without saying a word.

Once the men were inside, it wasn't long before Ortega could hear a muffled conversation. He eased out of the storeroom with a case of Seagram's in his arms and stood near the door. Jimmy was talking.

"It's all set. He's going to take care of it."

"Excellent," Estévez could be heard saying. "That means that as soon as he takes care of his end, we can set things up and get ready for the boat show."

Boat show?

"When do you want me to stop Garcia?" Ortega didn't recognize the voice. He assumed it was the man with the tattoo.

"Before he can do any damage," Estévez said.

"Nothing happens to the other party?" the man asked.

"Of course not. We can't let anything happen to our friend. It's much better to let things take their course naturally. Don't you think?"

Ortega peered around the mouth of the hallway to the bar. Chipper was still there, going over receipts. When Ortega went back to his position at the door he heard Jimmy speaking.

"Once this is set in motion, what's next?"

"We take the boat out and have fun. If we can't get our ducks in a row there, after all of this happens, then we didn't have a chance anyway and we can take care of the situation some other way."

"It's always quicker," the man said.

"And messier," Estévez said. "This isn't the eighties. The Colombians were shooting this town to pieces. That isn't the way we're going to do things." There was a long pause. "Unless we have to. I'm not above doing what needs to be done to come out on top. I just happen to prefer the thinking man's route." Another pause. "Much easier on everyone, Frankie."

Frankie. The man's name was Frankie. Ortega ran through his mental Rolodex but couldn't come up with a record to match. He made a note to run the name by O'Connor.

"Jimmy," Estévez said, "you be sure and take Acuna on rounds today."

"Okay."

"He did a good job the other night, and he didn't let those two cops push him around either." There was a brief silence. "It wasn't the smartest way of dealing with them, but all-in-all not bad."

"Okay," Jimmy said again.

"Frankie, you get out of here. Lay low for a while. If something turns up, I'll call you."

Ortega heard steps moving toward the door. He pulled away and bolted from the hallway, where he nearly ran into Chipper.

"You okay?" she asked. "I was wondering if you got lost."

"No, I'm fine," he said. "I thought I saw a mouse."

"A mouse?"

"Yeah."

She gave him the once-over. "You afraid of a mouse?"

"Well, no, but he kind of caught me off guard and I thought I was going to drop this." He raised the case of Seagram's for emphasis. "This stuff ain't cheap."

"No, it's not. Good thing you didn't drop it." She gave him a budgeted smile and told him to set the case down on the bar. As he began to move, the door to Estévez's office opened. Jimmy came out first.

"Hey, Acuna," he said. "Put that thing down and come with me."

Chipper put her hands on her hips. "He's supposed to be working for me."

"Yeah," Jimmy said, "but Mr. Estévez wants me to run a few errands and I need him. You can have him back when we're done."

Estévez appeared in the doorway, smoking one of his thin cigars. Ortega tried to look past the drug lord and see if Frankie was coming out too, but there was no sign of him.

"It's okay, Chipper," Estévez said. "Jimmy's going to the shelters and he'll need some help."

Chipper smiled. "Oh, okay." She put her hand on Ortega's arm. "You'll like the shelters."

CHAPTER *Thirty-Two*

After leaving the club, Jimmy and Ortega took a van bearing The Oasis logo to the near west side. Ortega drove, and the only time Jimmy spoke was to give the directions, or to follow the line of small talk Ortega tried to keep going. After twenty minutes of idle banter, Jimmy told Ortega to turn into what appeared to be a warehouse district.

As he drove on, the area became increasingly isolated. Most of the warehouses appeared to be vacant, with little traffic of any kind on the streets. As they neared what appeared to be a dead-end, Ortega began to get a sour feeling.

"What are we doing here, Jimmy?" he asked.

Jimmy didn't say anything until the van neared an isolated warehouse at the end of the row. "Turn in here."

Ortega pulled the van into the parking lot of a small, yellow brick building. Unlike the others, this one seemed to be operational. Ortega counted five delivery docks, all but one of which was occupied by small yellow trucks that bore the same name as the sign over the building: *CROWN MEATS.*

Ortega followed Jimmy's directions and parked the van in front of the building's main entrance.

The enforcer didn't say a word as he rolled out of the van. Ortega followed.

Jimmy paused to wipe his forehead with a handkerchief as he glanced toward the eastern sky. The sun was still climbing, as was the humidity, and the man sighed as he lumbered up the wood-plank staircase to the warehouse's office. Once inside, they were met by a young man at the desk. The undercover agent recognized him as one of the parking-lot attendants at Estévez's party.

"Donnie, Mr. Estévez needs a little extra this month," Jimmy said. "About a hundred pounds."

The kid nodded. "Sure, Jimmy. Will there be anything else?"

Jimmy paused. "Yeah, would you wrap up some sausages for me? I want to make some sauce tonight and the sausage always makes it better."

The kid grinned. "Yeah, sure, Jimmy. I can do that."

He rose from his desk and went to a door that separated the office from the warehouse. "You want me to load it for you?" he asked, pausing with his hand on the door's handle.

Jimmy shook his head. "I got this fellow. He can help," he said, gesturing to Ortega.

The agent obeyed Jimmy's nod and followed the kid through the door. Sides of beef were suspended on hooks that spun around the room on an automated conveyor belt. Each time a side would roll by, a man dressed in a bloody white coat and hard hat would push a red button to stop the conveyor. Two other men, similarly dressed, would then hoist the meat off the hook and drop it onto a table, where it would be divided by a power saw. The saw ran all the time, and the kid had to yell to be heard.

"This way," he said, gesturing toward an immense door.

Ortega followed the kid into a walk-in freezer that was as large as the house he had lived in as a child.

"We got to wrap up some sausages for Jimmy," Donnie said, lowering his voice in the relative quiet of the freezer. "Then we'll get some of the beef. I'll help you load the van."

Ortega nodded and waited as the kid placed several large sausages into a white, tray-like carton and wrapped them with salmon-colored paper. He handed the package to Ortega.

"Here. Hang onto this until we talk to the guys about the beef." He opened the freezer door and the noise of the floor again drowned out any chance at conversation.

The work area was busy and the floor was covered with blood, fat, and bits of bone, which made it extremely slick. "Mr. Estévez needs an extra hundred pounds," the kid yelled over the buzz of the saw.

The foreman nodded and turned to yell the number to the man working the saw. Donnie led Ortega outside. Jimmy remained in the air-conditioned office, reading a magazine.

"Pull the van over to the first dock," the kid said, pointing to the only empty bay. "We've got the usual order cut so we can go ahead and load up. By then, the extra meat will be ready for loading."

Ortega pulled around to the loading dock, where he began to back in. Once the van was in place, the kid held up his hand, and Ortega stopped. The kid opened the rear doors and motioned Ortega to join him in the warehouse again.

As soon as they were inside, the foreman rolled a skid full of large white cartons toward the loading dock. Some were labeled *hamburger,* some *steaks,* and some just *beef.* After they got the skid at the van, the kid pitched in, and within a few minutes, they had the van loaded, including the extra poundage. Jimmy joined them as they closed the doors.

"Thanks," Jimmy said to the kid, taking the sausages off the front seat where Ortega had left them.

The warehouse manager waved them off as Ortega pulled the van away from the warehouse.

"Where to?" he asked.

"Downtown," Jimmy said. "Mr. Estévez likes to deliver fresh meat to the homeless shelters. We're going to hit all of them."

Ortega glanced at the enforcer, who was lazily looking out the window. "Estévez does that?"

Caltabiano shot the young Cuban a sharp look.

"*Mr.* Estévez," he said. "And yes. He tries to take care of the less fortunate."

"Okay," Ortega said. "I didn't mean any disrespect."

The big man shifted the package on his lap. "He's been a true friend. Took me in when I had nowhere else to go."

Ortega didn't comment, preferring instead to let Jimmy talk.

"The man takes care of people," the enforcer said. "Took me in, gave Chipper work when she couldn't find it anywhere else, even took in that kid you just met. Got him cleaned up and gave him work. There's been a lot of people like that. People who had no hope, no future—and then they meet Mr. Estévez and he helps them to get on their feet. Gives them back their dignity."

"I didn't know," Ortega said.

"A lot of people don't. But that's the way he wants it. Take that warehouse back there," he said. "He owns that for one reason only. To feed the hungry.

He doesn't need the money. Doesn't need the profit. He got into the business because he was hungry as a child and didn't want others to feel that kind of pain."

"Sounds like quite a man," Ortega said.

"He is," the big enforcer said, his voice becoming softer, respectful. "He truly is."

CHAPTER *Thirty-Three*

Making the rounds of the city's various homeless shelters and other outreach centers took the better part of the day. But Ortega had been truly moved by what he saw. Many of the shelters provided housing for single mothers, battered wives, and their children. Others offered a place of solace for the homeless or those who were otherwise disposed. But in all cases, the food that Estévez provided was sorely needed. And those he fed, sang his praises. By the time Ortega and the enforcer returned, the nightclub was in full throttle serving as a stark contrast between the "haves" and the "have-nots." The music was thumping, people were dancing, and Chipper was as active behind the bar as Ortega had ever seen. She motioned for him, and Jimmy followed.

"Were you guys expecting visitors?" she asked, nearly yelling over the music.

Ortega shot a glance at Jimmy. The Italian shook his head.

"Three guys I've never seen insisted on meeting with Mr. Estévez. When I told them he was out, they said they'd wait. They went into his office." She paused to pour a couple of drinks and put them on a tray that a waitress immediately scooped up. "Frankie isn't here and I wasn't sure if I should have one of the other guys toss them out or not."

"They still in the office?" Jimmy asked.

She nodded. "And so is Mr. Estévez. He came in about a half hour after they got here. He didn't seem too happy." She accepted an empty tray from another waitress. "I thought you'd want to know."

Jimmy gestured for Ortega to follow him as he left the bar and headed for the office. The crowd in the club was dense and the two had to weave their way through thick clusters of dancers and other revelers. When they reached the office, Jimmy paused to listen, putting his ear directly against the door.

"This guy has to be dealt with and dealt with now," a voice said. "I'm tired of the talking. I'm tired of your games. In fact, Ricardo, I'm tired of you."

"Follow me," Jimmy ordered, drawing his gun and opening the door.

The two entered and saw Eduardo Garcia leaning over Estévez's desk. The club owner was sitting with his feet planted firmly on the floor, smoking one of his trademark slim cigars. His right hand was resting casually on his right knee, just inches from the top desk drawer. Standing behind Garcia were two other men, both tall and lean, in their late thirties, both wearing tank tops and jeans. One man had a line of tattoos that ran from his shoulder to his wrist. The other had earrings in both ears. As soon as the man with the tattoos saw Jimmy's gun, he drew his own.

"Don't," Jimmy said.

"Everybody just calm down," Estévez said, easing forward in his chair. "There is no need for anyone to get riled up."

Ortega closed the door, blunting the driving beat of the music outside.

"Take his gun," Jimmy told Ortega.

The agent took the pistol and ejected the magazine into his hand. After opening the chamber and removing a round, he handed it, the gun, and the magazine to Jimmy. The second man glared at Ortega.

"Now everyone just do what Mr. Estévez said and stay calm," Jimmy said.

Garcia was unperturbed. He began jabbing his index finger at the club owner like a dagger.

"If we wait like you want, Kingman will pick us off one man at a time."

"If we work like I am suggesting, Eduardo," Estévez said, "there will be no Kingman."

Garcia was breathing heavily. His face was red and large beads of sweat had formed on his brow.

"You're not running the show," Garcia said. "I've got my own interests to protect."

"That's what I'm trying to do, my friend," Estévez said, patiently. "I'm trying to—"

Garcia cursed. Estévez sighed. The man with the earring continued to glare at Ortega.

"Look," Estévez said, stubbing what was left of the cigar into an ashtray, "why don't I have some drinks sent in and we can sit and talk. That is much better than all of this yelling and screaming."

Garcia spit on the Cuban's desk. The man in the earrings took advantage of the diversion and reached for the small of his back. Ortega stepped forward and punched the man on the side of the head. A gun fell to the floor and the agent kicked it over to where Jimmy was standing. The enforcer knelt to pick up the gun and tossed it onto his employer's desk.

"You come in here with guns when I asked you to meet with me this weekend as my friend?" Estévez said, rising from his chair. "I treat you with respect, and you repay me with insults and threats?" He moved from behind his desk so he stood toe to toe with the much older Garcia.

"You don't intimidate me, Ricardo," Eduardo said. "If I suffer any more losses, I will personally go after Kingman. And I will do it regardless of what you say."

Estévez moved to put an arm around his nemesis. The gesture was friendly, but a mistake in the tension-filled room. The man with the tattoos grabbed Estévez.

Ortega reacted for the second time that evening by getting between them and stopping the man with a right hook. As the man went down, Ortega felt a sharp slice across the back of his left arm. Garcia, red-faced and breathing hard, was holding a knife with a retractable blade.

Estévez grabbed the older man by the wrist and twisted his arm behind him. The knife fell to the carpet and Jimmy knelt to pick it up, keeping his gun trained on the other two.

"You okay?" Estévez asked Ortega, still forcing Garcia's arm behind him.

The wound was superficial, but could have been a lot worse if Estévez hadn't acted in time.

"I'm fine," Ortega said, dabbing at the cut with the tail of his shirt.

Estévez released the older man, slapped him across the face twice, and told him to sit down. Garcia's men moved to react, but hesitated after Jimmy cocked the revolver.

"Now I will say again, Eduardo, you may do anything you like. And you are correct when you say that I do not run the show, as you put it. But I am trying to do what is best for all of us. Kingman is strong. But he cannot stand against a united front. It is what I am trying to build." Estévez sat on the end of his desk. "I would like for you to be a part of that united front."

Garcia was breathing heavily and although his face bore the handprint of his host, the tenseness of his expression had softened a bit.

"He killed Salter."

Estévez nodded.

"He killed Salter and his wife."

"Yes," Estévez said, softly, "I know."

Garcia sighed and ran a hand across his face.

"Give me a little more time," Estévez said. "We are scheduled to meet this weekend. Pass the word. Bring in some of the others who are facing the same threat and let's talk. We will have a good time. No wives. Just us." He smiled. "Okay?"

Garcia sighed again. He glanced at his men, then at Jimmy and Ortega.

"Okay," he said. "But I will not sit idly by if I am attacked again."

"If all goes as planned, you will not be attacked again. Ever."

CHAPTER *Thirty-Four*

Like many men in his business, Eduardo Garcia found his line of work rewarding. He had, after all, survived many years in his trade—a trade that did not often offer longevity as a reward. And the financial gains were immense. Life was good.

But on occasion, men like Kingman would arise and raise the stakes far beyond anything the law was empowered to accomplish, and that would cloud a business that otherwise offered a clear road to profit. Garcia had seen it before and had endured. Now that it had come again, he would surely endure again.

Like his colleagues, Garcia knew his customers wanted the product in which he dealt, but only if they didn't have to see behind the curtain. Like watching a magician and his bag of tricks, they preferred to not know how things were done. But of course they did know. And occasionally, when the ugly hit the proverbial fan, they became indignant, enraged. Having been exposed to the seedy side of their desires, to the cost of their sins, they would suddenly find a need to assuage their guilt. Their rage would turn into action, and action would turn into a witch hunt. The resulting witch hunt always had one effect—it would decrease the source of their supply until their need cooled their rage and they would turn against the law again. It was the inevitable cycle. In his many years in the business, Garcia had seen it before. If he lived, he would see it again.

For most law-enforcement officers, the law was a thing of honor. It was the glue that held society together. These men and women were sworn to uphold the law—to defend it and, if necessary, die for it.

The law, after all, was the voice of the people. And the people wanted what they wanted when they wanted it. And what they wanted for the moment was to remove the guilt they felt for the vice they enjoyed.

But the tide would change and the people would demand their vice once more, and the police would have to respect their wishes. Such things were cyclical. It wasn't the law that had kept Garcia from sleeping most of the previous night, it was Kingman and the threat he posed.

Garcia turned the burner on his stove to high and set the kettle over the flame. He sat at the breakfast table and began to cough. It seemed to be getting worse. For months it had been his companion—finally sending him reluctantly to the doctor. The diagnosis of cancer was not a surprise. Not even the news that his days on earth were few.

But he knew he had much to do before he left this world for the hell that surely awaited him. He hadn't worked this long and this hard to have it end this way—with someone like Kingman stepping in and profiting from all those years of building.

He sighed heavily. *Kingman.* The tension of a war he did not want, but which he was convinced was being thrust on him, was taking a toll. Even though he had come to expect this sort of thing, it still wore on him.

Most of the wars he'd seen had been fought over a tightening market. Sometimes over a tightening supply. In all cases, greed was at their root.

The kettle whistled, and he rose and poured himself a cup of Earl Grey tea. He dropped a lemon wedge in and sipped as he moved to his recliner in the living room and watched out the window as the sun rose in the eastern sky.

The neighborhood in which he lived, like the one in which his friend Salter had lived, was solidly blue-collar. Most of the families on his street were young. In a few minutes, children would be leaving their homes for school. The mail would be delivered and the garbage trucks would begin their route. All things were new each day. Except for the problems of a man under duress. They rode with him into the netherlands of sleep, and woke with him in the morning. And always their solution was just as elusive. Just as hopeless as they had been when the sun had dropped below the horizon and darkness had settled over the earth.

He sighed again, but the tension remained. He stirred the lemon in his tea and drained the cup.

He would listen as Ricardo recounted his plan. But if it were not feasible, he would strike Kingman alone and strike him hard. While there was still a business to be had and a base from which to defend it.

He looked out the window again. The sun was ascending rapidly now, and he rose from his recliner, dressed in pajamas and robe, to get the morning paper.

Outside, the air was warm but not yet humid. Across the street, Mrs. Norman waved as her children walked along the sidewalk in front of her home on their way to the bus stop. Two doors down, the garbage truck was already on its route.

Eduardo Garcia waved back as he walked toward the street to retrieve his paper. As always, the delivery boy had left it at the end of the driveway. No matter, Garcia needed the exercise. In his advancing years, in a world that seemed to change with each passing minute, the dependability of his morning routine provided him a measure of stability.

He stooped to pick up the paper and scanned the headlines. The garbage truck stopped, ready to empty the overflowing cans he had set out the previous evening.

The market was down, Congress was vowing to override the president's veto, and a senate hearing was underway into a bribery charge that involved a White House aide. Garcia smiled a wry smile. His war, if there was to be one, would be only one of many in the country.

He shook his head. The news never changed. Always negative. Always hopeless.

He tucked the paper under his arm and glanced at the men who had jumped from the garbage truck. The cans they were supposed to empty were still standing. Instead, each of them held a gun in his hand.

At that moment Eduardo Garcia knew he would never see another war.

CHAPTER *Thirty-Five*

The gathering was to be held on *The Funny Bone,* a six-and-a-half-million-dollar yacht built by Diaship. The vessel held five well-outfitted passenger cabins, in addition to a deluxe cabin located on the upper deck just behind the bridge.

The meeting was planned to be a relaxing time for the men involved. But as Ortega stood in the bow of the boat watching the others board, he knew Garcia's murder would cast a dark shadow over the otherwise sunny afternoon.

The entire complement of guests and crew were on board by four p.m. Estévez took the main cabin on the upper deck, while Torres and Lopez shared one of the passenger cabins on the lower deck. Next to them, two other men that Jimmy had identified as Manuel Delahoy and Carmine Jiménez shared another, and the two men who had accompanied Garcia to Estévez's office shared yet another. Jimmy told Ortega that the men's names were Oscar Highsmith and Delbert Deets. It was Deets who wore the earrings. Both men had been with Garcia for a long time.

But there was another guest. One that Estevez had not mentioned. Chipper came aboard carrying the club's signature vest over her arm. The woman was wearing jeans and a T-shirt and her blonde hair caught the wind in a way the best sail never could. She was stunning. And as she passed Ortega, she smiled before kissing him lightly on the cheek.

Jimmy and Ortega took the last two cabins. Chipper boarded in one of the two spare crew cabins.

At ten minutes past four, the hired crew guided *The Funny Bone* away from port toward the open sea. The weather cooperated, providing a warm breeze and an ocean that was calm. By the time the yacht was at sea, some of the despair that Estévez's guests had brought with them began to lift. When they all gathered for dinner outside on the upper deck, Ortega even heard some lighthearted bantering.

"You like to sail?" Chipper asked.

Ortega had been concentrating on the others from the upper deck. He hadn't heard her approaching.

"Love it."

She leaned on the guard rail, next to him. Her emerald eyes squinted against the sunlight as it reflected off the Atlantic. "Me too. But there isn't this kind of sailing in Louisville."

He grinned. "You mean the Ohio River isn't the same?"

She laughed and dropped her head on Ortega's shoulder. His heart jumped.

"Hardly," she said.

"You working?" He heard the guttural sound of his own voice.

"Yes. You?"

"I think so. Just not tending bar."

"Doesn't matter," she said, raising her head and looking directly into his eyes. "You're here."

She leaned forward and kissed him.

He resisted.

"I have to join the boss," he said, following their embrace.

"I know, silly." She grabbed his collar with both hands. "I'm serving."

She kissed him again and he went to the lower deck to join the others.

They were seated at a large round table shielded from the sun by an equally large umbrella.

"Gentleman," Estévez said, standing. "I am so very glad that you could come. It is a sad time when we lose one of our own. Our gathering will seem incomplete without the presence of Eduardo. However, I am especially honored to have two of Eduardo's closest associates join us." He raised his glass. "A toast to the memory of Eduardo Garcia."

The others concurred and drinks were lifted. Ortega sat motionless, next to Jimmy, who kept an eye on Highsmith and Deets.

After the toast, a dinner of roast chicken, roasted potatoes, asparagus, and a fine white wine, was served. Dessert followed in the form of rich chocolate cake and Colombian coffee Estévez had specially blended for the occasion. Chipper ran a hand over Ortega's shoulders as she passed him.

The agent, like the men around him, thoroughly enjoyed the open air, the sea, and the conversation. The fact that some of the best coffee in the world was also being served added to the flawless day. But his mind was on the girl.

"My friends," Estévez said, capturing the group's attention again, "I hope you enjoy being free of the encumbrances that often come with the life we have chosen. It is my wish that you enjoy the next couple of days and that you feel refreshed when we return to land. I have, as a special treat, arranged for all of you to do a little fishing while we are at sea." The men were clearly surprised and delighted at the announcement, and Lopez offered a toast to their host. Deets and Highsmith remained silent.

"But as you know, we also have work to do," Estévez said, his demeanor growing serious. "And our meeting here is all the more pressing with the death of Eduardo at the hands of Kingman. Therefore, in order to enjoy our brief voyage to the fullest, I propose that we talk business this evening. Let us discuss the work ahead of us fully, so that we can spend the rest of our time enjoying what God has designed for us." He gestured to the open sea with his glass.

His declaration was met with agreement. Then Estévez returned to the subject on everyone's minds.

"Our dear friend Eduardo was gunned down in his driveway as he read the morning paper. David Salter and his lovely wife were murdered after being roused from a peaceful sleep in their own beds." He paused to gauge each man's reaction to the seriousness with which he spoke. "We have had our differences, to be sure. But today we face a common enemy. And we know who that enemy is, don't we?"

A couple of the men said "Kingman." Deets and Highsmith remained silent.

"This man will stop at nothing in his push to be the only player in the new Cuba." Estévez leaned forward in his chair. His dark eyes penetrated each of the men sitting across from him. "His ambition is laudable. I too, have such ambitions. But I have them for all of us. Cuba is too big for any one man to inhabit all of it. But together, all of us," his eyes were alive with excitement, "*we* can manage the new Cuba. But we can only do that, gentlemen, if we work together."

"And what about Kingman?" Lopez asked. "He must be eradicated first."

Estévez nodded. "Exactly, my friend. If we are to be in a position of dominance, we must be in place *before* anyone else. And I can tell you, from my own sources, that Kingman has already begun his initial preparations for a takeover of the island."

Ortega glanced around the table. The men seemed eager to hear more.

"How far has he advanced?" Jiménez asked. He was a bit younger than the others, but still older than Estévez.

"I don't know," Estévez said, settling back into his seat. "Unfortunately, my sources only go so far. I have none in Cuba. But I do know he has made several trips there already and he is the only one of us to not suffer any type of internal advance."

"And he killed Eduardo," Deets said, finally breaking his silence.

"Gentlemen," Estévez said, with a look of genuine concern on his face, "recently I had the misfortune of finding myself at odds with the two men you see sitting to my left. Their employer, your friend, Eduardo, wanted desperately to go on the offense against our formidable enemy." Estévez lowered his voice. "I talked him out of it...and he is now dead."

The others were silent as each man looked to his feet, his hands, or the top of the table.

"It is true. I underestimated Kingman's viciousness. But I did not underestimate the method which works best. Kingman is an old man. His time is short. Killing him will ignite a war no one can win. I've seen these things before and so have you." He looked around the table. "You were all here during the eighties. You remember Reagan's 'War on Drugs' and the money it cost us." He waved a dismissive hand. "We spent more time fighting each other than the government. And we ended up hitting civilians in the process." He shook his head in disgust.

"I am telling you, gentlemen, if we let ourselves become engaged in another war, a war that hits civilians again, especially in the current climate, we are all but dead in the water. The demand for our product will remain, but someone else will fill the need because none of us will be here." He was quiet long enough to allow all that he said to sink into each man. "During the government's drug war, we lost our share of the trade, and the Colombian government went after her own people. When Escobar was killed, the business fragmented into what we have today. Now we have an oversupply—and a stable demand." He studied each of the faces around the table. "If we are going to *grow* our market share, we must move into Cuba and we must move when the time is ripe. Ahead of Kingman."

"What are you proposing, Ricardo?" Delahoy asked.

"I am suggesting we band together and shut off the pipeline. Dry Kingman up. If we kill him, we have only cut off the snake's tail. The head will remain in place."

"His son?" Jiménez asked.

"Yes," Estévez said. "But if we can eliminate his business, dry up his supply, cut off his ability to pay protection—what does he have?"

"So how do we do this?" Torres asked.

"Each of us will need to put something into the pot," Estévez said. "For example, Julio," he said to Lopez, "no one handles the gaming better than you. No one. Let us say that in the future, games are all you do." He turned to Jiménez. "And you, Carmine, who runs protection as well as you?" He looked around the table. "Certainly none of us. Suppose you weren't restricted to the North Beach? What if you had all of Dade County? And Broward?"

Jiménez paused to think. "But I should give up the dope? The gaming?"

Estévez threw himself back into his seat and spread his hands. "Why not? Why take on the extra risk and incur the extra cost? Let me do that. I'm already equipped to handle it." He studied the others. "See what I'm getting at? It's nothing new. But it is a different way of thinking for us. If we work together, each man doing what he does best, we can pour all of our efforts into one pot and divvy up as we need. By protecting each other, we can spread our individual losses over the spectrum of time and organization."

Torres frowned.

"What, my friend? What is it?"

He scratched his head and looked around the table at the others.

"This all seems a little too...simple." He shook his head. "I don't know. Maybe it's just me, but Kingman shouldn't want a war either. In this current climate, no one should." He shook his head again. "And if we move on his territory I don't think that Kingman is going to roll over so easy. Any way we slice it, there's going to be some shooting."

Estévez pushed his chair back from the table to give himself ample room to cross his legs. The yacht turned into the western sky, forcing the drug lord to slip on a pair of sunglasses as the warm breeze ruffled his hair.

"Perhaps. And if it comes to that, we can address it better unified than as several individuals that he can pick off one at a time. But I believe if we do it right, if we buy his protection from under him, if we pay off his law and his politicians at rates above what he's paying now, we can let the good police officers of Miami do what they do best. With the way things are now, if he loses his protection, the judicial system will take him out for us."

"Why not just whack him and his son now and be done with it?" Deets said. "We got no problem with that."

"Because it would leave his organization intact. And an organization that is that large and that powerful will have the means to retaliate, regardless of who heads it." Estévez shook his head. "No, gentlemen. We must hit Kingman where it will do the most good. And the sooner we move, the sooner our problem is solved."

The others glanced around the table, before Lopez said, "Where do we go from here?"

Estévez smiled. "For now, we sail. Tomorrow we fish. Then we will settle the details." He rose from the table. "By the time we return to Miami, gentlemen, we will be one united force."

CHAPTER *Thirty-Six*

The remainder of the trip was as relaxing as Estévez had promised. Nearly everyone caught a fish, including Ortega, and nearly everyone was able to let his hair down and enjoy a satisfying day at sea free from the prying eyes of the law. Even Chipper was able to take a break. She spent most of her free time with Ortega. Only Estevez managed to work.

By the time *The Funny Bone* sailed into port, Estévez had managed to work out an agreeable plan with the others. The lone dissenter was Torres. His mistrust of Estévez, and his concern that the events of the past several weeks seemed entirely too packaged, caused him to decide to opt out. While the others were disappointed at his decision, no one seemed upset by it.

As the guests disembarked, Estévez awarded each man a Rolex Yacht Master. Each watch had the name of the recipient, along with the dates of the meeting, inscribed on the back. Ortega received one as well.

After the rest of the men were gone, Estévez, Jimmy, and Ortega met in Estévez's stateroom.

"We're going to have a problem with Torres," Estévez said, settling in a chair next to the bed on which Jimmy and Ortega sat.

"He raised a point that some of the others were probably thinking," Jimmy said.

"Ron," Estévez said, looking at Ortega. "what do you think?"

"I agree with Jimmy," the agent said. "I think Torres mentioned what the others were thinking. And if we don't address his concern sooner than later, the others will be persuaded to his point of view and we'll see the alliance begin to fall apart."

We? He couldn't believe his own ears.

"I agree," Estévez said. "The question, is what do we do about it?"

Jimmy said, "We could always take him out."

Ortega shook his head. "Not after Garcia. That would be too obvious."

"Everything is on the table," Estévez said. "Whether it's obvious, costly, or just plain stupid, everything is open for discussion. Right now, I want options."

"We could cut into his territory," Jimmy said. "Set it up to look like Kingman is behind it."

"How?" Estévez asked. "Putting Kingman on the spot for the hits, the arson, and the hijacking is easy. How do we make it look like he's cutting into Torres's turf?"

"We could buy off some of Torres's mules," Jimmy said. "Make sure the word gets passed to him that Kingman is engineering it."

Estévez considered this. "Maybe."

"We could front an operation and use Kingman tactics," the Italian added. "Maybe even doctor some trucks to look like his."

Estévez laughed. "When I said 'stupid,' Jimmy, I didn't mean it literally. Using Kingman's fronts in Torres's territory would start the war I'm trying to avoid. It would take Kingman about two seconds to see what's going on. As it is, he thinks we're all turning on each other, which he is more than willing to let happen."

Ortega spoke next. "We could set Torres up for a fall. Feed him to the law."

"How would that make it look like Kingman was involved?" Estévez asked.

"It wouldn't," Ortega said. "But it would get Torres out of the way, and that's our goal after all, isn't it?"

Estévez glanced at Jimmy. The enforcer was slow to come around. When he did, he nodded. "It could work. It would get Torres away from the others. It wouldn't put the finger on Kingman, though."

"But that may not be such a bad idea," Ortega said. "Think about it." He leaned forward to reinforce his point. "If we let the law take him out, that gets him out of the way, and it also eliminates the possibility that everyone is going to be wondering why Torres was hit by Kingman. Especially since he was the only one to not sign on to the pact."

Jimmy agreed. "It does seem to tie things up. There'd be less suspicion from the others if it was the law that took Torres out."

Estévez weighed his options. "There could be some repercussions for the rest of us."

"They'd be minimal," Ortega said.

"I agree," Jimmy said. "Whatever we do, there will be risk."

"How do we do it?" Estévez asked. "An anonymous tip is going to look too much like a setup. It'll look like Torres's competition is trying to get him out of the way, which will only deepen the other's suspicions."

Ortega stood and began to pace the stateroom. The eyes of the other two followed him.

"We'll need an incident. Some type of inciting action the police can't ignore, but which won't endanger any civilians. We want to take Torres out of the picture without fueling the fervor that already exists." He continued to pace about the room.

Estévez turned to Jimmy. "Any ideas?"

Jimmy shrugged. "Lots of ideas. No answers."

"Let's hear them," Estévez said. "We're brainstorming here, Jimmy. You got something to say, say it."

The enforcer said, "We could hit a cop. Leave a trail to Torres. It would keep the civilians out and bring the law in without leaving a trail to us or the others. It would be strictly a Torres action."

Estévez shook his head. "Hitting a cop in these times would bring the entire Miami PD down on us, and maybe the DEA."

"But it might work," Ortega said, "if we could find someone with whom Torres has had a beef. Someone he is known to have a problem with..."

"There's no love lost with Deets and Highsmith," Estévez said. "They were loyal to Garcia, and since it appears that Kingman was behind the hit and Torres is reluctant to work against Kingman, we may have an ally there."

"Strange bedfellows," Ortega said.

Jimmy shook his head. "It'd be even better if we could show that the cop is on the take. You know, maybe he wanted more and Torres refused to pay. So the whole thing is settled the hard way. Only Torres gets caught, or one of his men gets caught, and the whole thing hits the fan."

Estévez nodded. "He's paying somebody—we all are." The Cuban turned to Ortega who was still pacing. "Hey, how about those two guys you had the run-in with?"

"Dowd and Hurst," Ortega said.

"Yeah, that's right. Mikey had a run-in with them too. They said that no one was paying them so they slapped him around a little," Estévez said. "Maybe we could even get Mikey to set it up. There's no love lost between them."

Jimmy shrugged. "Sure. We can arrange to have the guys meet Mikey somewhere, whack them, and leave something on the scene to lead the cops back to Torres. That shouldn't be too hard."

Estévez grinned. "It might be better if we can include Deets and Highsmith in the arrangement."

"Too many mouths involved," Jimmy said.

"Spread the risk around," Estévez countered. "Better to have them with us than against us."

Ortega shrugged. "Okay with me, but let me set it up. No offense, but Jimmy is too well-known and I've developed a trust with Mikey."

Estévez and the enforcer cast a wary glance at each other. "You sure you can handle it?" Estévez asked.

"Sure. I'll run the plan by Jimmy as soon as I come up with one, and if he signs off, I'll get it done."

Estévez turned to his chief enforcer. "Okay with you, Jimmy?"

The big man paused to think. "Okay, I can go along with it," he said, clearly reluctant. "But only if he checks with me first and I sign off on it. I don't trust Mikey."

Estévez smiled. "Okay," he said to Ortega. "You've got the green light. Bring a plan to Jimmy he can live with, and do it in the next twenty-four hours."

Ortega nodded. In twenty-four hours he would set aside his goal of bringing these men to justice as he devised a plan to do away with their nemesis—and take the life of two police officers.

CHAPTER *Thirty-Seven*

Ortega contacted O'Connor by cell phone. At the lifeline's suggestion, the two men met at a seafood restaurant in Broward County. Given the level of penetration Ortega had achieved, it was reasonable to assume that anyone from Estévez's organization could stop by Ortega's apartment at any time. That meant the two federal agents would need to meet in places they were unlikely to be seen.

The restaurant they chose was decidedly upscale—the government was paying, after all—and once they were seated, Ortega handed his lifeline the recording from his meeting on the yacht.

"It's all there," he said. "I'll have my report completed by tomorrow evening."

O'Connor quietly slid the disc into his pocket. "Is there any mention of Kingman's activities?"

Ortega shook his head. "No, but there's a lot of discussion about the need to eliminate him. In a business sort of way," the agent said, sarcastically. "Working with these guys is like watching Enron with guns."

Both men paused as a server handed them a menu. She poured glasses of water before setting a basket of bread sticks in front of them.

"If they eliminate Kingman," O'Connor said after the server was out of earshot, "it'll clear the way for Estévez to pull Battles's old organization together."

"He's trying to pull something together. Whether it's The Corporation or some kind of facsimile is anybody's guess," Ortega said, opening his menu. "What's good here?"

"The snapper is excellent," O'Connor said. "The mahi-mahi isn't bad either."

Ortega flipped through the pages. O'Connor already knew what he wanted. When the server returned, they placed their orders and then resumed their conversation.

"If he wants Kingman," O'Connor said, biting into a bread stick, "he'll have to pull something together beforehand. Estévez isn't powerful enough to do it himself."

Ortega grinned. "Listen to the tape. You might be surprised."

O'Connor's face darkened. He leaned forward and got as close to Ortega as he could. "Listen," he said, tapping his forefinger on the table, "if you know of something about to go down, you tell me now. I don't have time to listen to the tape."

The younger agent acknowledged his mistake. "Estévez is pulling some of the lesser guys together," he said, listing them for his lifeline. "We all met on *The Funny Bone* and—"

"The what?"

Ortega cleared his throat. "*The Funny Bone.* It's a yacht Estévez borrowed. We met and discussed the plan to dethrone Kingman. Everyone signed on to the idea except Torres."

"Dethrone?" O'Connor asked, settling back into his own side of the booth. "You mean *decapitate?*"

"No," Ortega said, shaking his head, "I mean dethrone. The plan is to render him useless. To remove him and his family from a position of power by removing the source of the power."

Ortega and O'Connor paused as the dinner was set before them. When the server left, O'Connor, with a hint of desperation, asked, "So there's no hit planned?"

"No hit."

The lifeline picked a stalk of asparagus off his plate and ate it. "Taking Kingman's organization away isn't going to be easy. He won't go down without a fight."

"Funny," Ortega said, "but that's exactly what Torres said."

"Torres? He's small potatoes."

"He is when he's alone," Ortega said, "but if he stands with Kingman, he's not so small."

"So let me get this straight," O'Connor said. "Estévez is putting together an ad hoc syndicate that will attempt to pull Kingman down, slowly, while advancing their own agenda."

"Something like that. Except for the 'slowly' part. I'd say his plan to dethrone his rival is more on the fast track than the slow."

O'Connor seemed genuinely puzzled. "Why? Why not just hit Kingman?"

Ortega shrugged. "Personally, it's the way I would have gone. But Estévez's opinion is that it would start a war that would involve all the other groups in town, of necessity. Then the war would inevitably spill over and civilians would get hurt." He paused to fork a bite of buttered, baked potato. "Given the current climate, his feeling is that civilian casualties would spell more law-enforcement trouble, and that would lead to more crackdowns with fewer deliveries and more graft being paid, which all leads to a diminished profit margin."

"So he's *committed* to avoiding a war," O'Connor said, with a grin that told Ortega he now understood.

"Absolutely."

O'Connor said nothing for the next couple of minutes as he ate and reasoned through the situation. When he spoke, he nodded toward Ortega's wrist. "Where'd you get the watch?"

"It was a gift from Estévez. Everyone who attended the meeting got one as they disembarked."

"Nice."

"Yes."

"Don't get used to it."

"I won't."

"It'll have to be turned in for evidence when this thing is over."

"Yep."

Ortega couldn't help but notice O'Connor's fixation on the watch.

"So," the lifeline said, breaking the silence, "if Estévez and his followers are going to take Kingman off the map without firing a shot, how do they plan to do it?"

"They don't."

O'Connor gave Ortega a puzzled look.

"They plan on letting you do it," Ortega said. "They want a cop hit and they want it to look like Kingman drove the process."

O'Connor smiled. "Let the law do their dirty work for them. But that'll require finding a dirty cop, one who can easily be exposed, and then tying him to Kingman."

"Exactly. Which isn't, by the way, a particular problem."

"I suppose you have someone in mind?"

"I do," Ortega said. "Especially since I'm the one they expect to carry out the hit."

CHAPTER *Thirty-Eight*

The plan to take out Dowd or Hurst was going to involve Santiago. He was the only person who Ortega knew had personal experience with the dirty cops, which meant he would have to be recruited.

The morning after Ortega's meeting with O'Connor, the agent met with the Mexican street hustler in the back room of Hokey's. Bets were being placed and Mikey was at the center of the action.

"Apprentice Run is not your best bet," the Mexican said to a Hispanic man who spoke broken English. "Put your money on Taylor's Delight. The odds are better and the payoff is still substantial." He glanced around the room before dropping his voice and leaning closer to the man. "Trust me on this. I wouldn't steer you wrong."

The man, who Ortega guessed to be no more than thirty, hesitated before licking his lips and glancing about the room. He looked at the betting board Santiago had laid open before him on a card table. The man hesitated a moment longer before nodding his agreement with a nervous smile. After the bet was placed, Ortega pulled his friend aside.

"That horse is a long shot, twenty to one. He doesn't have a chance."

The Mexican shrugged. "So?"

Ortega looked at Mikey in disbelief. "What's wrong with you, man? How do you sleep at night?"

"I sleep just fine." He glanced over his shoulder at the man who was leaving the room by a door that went to the outside. The man smiled. Santiago smiled back before facing Ortega again. "You don't think he'd be doing it to me if things were the other way around?"

"First of all," Ortega said, "things aren't the other way around. Second, it doesn't matter."

Santiago recoiled like a man slapped across the face. "And what are you, a preacher? Who made you my guardian?"

Ortega sighed. "Okay, you're right. I didn't come here to argue, I came to ask for your help."

Santiago looked around the room. "I'm kind of busy. Some other time, maybe."

"No," Ortega said. "Now. This is important. And big. Very big."

The Mexican studied Ortega's face before scratching his head and saying, "Okay, but outside."

The two men left the room through the same door the Hispanic bettor had taken. Once outside, the dazzling sun reflected off the agent's watch.

"Hey, man, where did you get that?"

"Estévez," Ortega said. "It's part of—"

"He gave you that?" Santiago pulled Ortega's wrist toward him. "Is it real?"

The agent nodded.

"No fooling?"

"No fooling."

He released the Cuban's wrist. "It must be hot."

Ortega shrugged. "I don't think so, but I don't care either. He gave me the watch during a big meeting and that's what I want to talk to you about."

"Big meeting? *You?* Wow, that was fast."

Ortega sighed. "Do you want to hear this or not?"

The two men were standing in an alley that ran alongside the restaurant. After glancing toward the open end, the Mexican told the Cuban he was listening.

"Estévez is going after Kingman."

Santiago's eyes widened. "You kidding?"

"No. I'm not kidding."

The street hustler rolled his eyes and let out a long, low whistle.

"There isn't going to be a hit, so to speak. At least not on Kingman or anyone in his immediate crew."

"But?"

"But there will be a hit. And that's where I need your help."

Santiago held up a hand. "Hold on. I don't do no hits. I may hustle but I'm not a killer."

"I'm not asking you to kill anyone. I'm asking you to set it up."

"That's the same thing, man. It ain't no different. And—"

"We're going to take out one of the cops who rousted you."

Santiago wilted as the news sunk in. He leaned his back against the wall of the restaurant. "Which one?"

"It doesn't matter which one," Ortega said. "Just as long as it's one of them."

The wiry hustler ran a hand across his face. "Man, oh, man. Why did you have to tell me that? Why couldn't you just leave me alone?"

"Because you know them, Mikey," Ortega said. "You know what they're doing and so do I. But they know you better. They don't like you, but they know you better than they know me."

The Mexican sighed. "I don't know, man. Like I said, it's the wrong thing to do."

"You want them off your back, don't you?" Ortega said.

"Yeah, but not like this. You're talking murder, man. Killing someone. Killing a cop."

"If things were the other way around," Ortega said, echoing the Mexican's earlier comments, "don't you think they'd do it to you?"

"Didn't you just ask me how I can sleep at night because some dude loses a few dollars on a horse?"

"That guy is innocent. The only thing he's guilty of is being dumb. He's a civilian. Dowd and Hurst aren't. They're players, and they're players by choice. And they're not dumb. They're corrupt. And they got themselves into a mess that good cops shouldn't get into. They know the score."

Santiago slid down the wall until he was fully seated on the pavement. "Who?"

"I don't care."

"When?"

"Tomorrow evening. Tell him you got something for him. Tell him to meet you at your apartment."

Santiago buried his face in his hands and groaned. "Man, do you know what you're doing to me?"

"From what I've seen," Ortega said, "I may be saving your life."

CHAPTER *Thirty-Nine*

Once Santiago agreed to set up one of the cops, and once the plan was cleared through Jimmy, Ortega passed the word on to Estévez. The drug lord was relaxing on the veranda of his home with a cigar and a Corona. Ortega was sitting on a chaise lounge next to Estévez, enjoying the view.

"This is beautiful," the agent said. "Absolutely stunning."

Estévez nodded as he sipped from the bottle with one hand, before sliding the cigar between his lips with the other. "I knew I would have to live here one day. And now I am."

"You chose this place?"

"Yes," he said, through teeth that clenched the cigar. "A long time ago, when I was still a child."

Ortega turned to his boss. "You know a lot about me, but I know next to nothing about you."

Estévez grinned. "What would you like to know, my friend?"

"More. It wasn't too long ago you told me you didn't have a mother."

"Yes." He pulled the cigar from his mouth and exhaled slowly. "My mother was no good."

"I'm sorry."

"Yours too?"

Ortega nodded. "Yes. Mine too."

"She was no mother at all. She left me to wander the streets while she visited the bars and the hotels. And I never knew my father," Estévez continued, flicking ash off the cigar, "so I had no man to show me how to be a man."

"You've done fine despite that."

Estévez gazed at the Atlantic. The sea was calm and the waves lapped gently. "I've done okay. But I was raised on the streets. My influence came from others like me. Kids who had nowhere to go and no one to guide them." He inhaled on the cigar. "I took whatever job I could find to make extra money," he said, as smoke escaped his nostrils. "Of course, extra money is just another way of saying beyond what my mother brought in by doing what she did best."

"You're still young. Things must have turned around for you very quickly," Ortega said.

"Yes, very quickly. I came to this house to rob the man who lived here. My friends and I broke in while he was gone. We came to take what we could find. Instead, it was here I left my heart." He drew on the cigar again and threw his head back to blow the smoke upward. "You ever have anything happen to you in your life that you knew was going to set you on a different course?"

"Everyone has," Ortega said. "Sometimes they know it, sometimes they don't. We're all faced with choices at critical times. And there are times when it doesn't come down to a black-and-white choice, but a shade of gray. Do the right thing or do the desired thing."

"I did the desired thing, which I also believe was the right thing for me." He gazed across the ocean again. "I decided I would one day live here. So I began to work, really work, to make it happen. I had no chance at college, no chance at becoming a doctor or lawyer or astronaut, but I knew the streets and I knew I could learn how to work them. So I did. I worked hard and I worked smart, and I made the decision I would let nothing stand in my way. I would have this home, I would have enough money to live well, and I would have the family I never had as a little boy. And now," he swept an arm around the panoramic view of the ocean, "I have it all."

Ortega followed Estévez's gesture. The drug lord did indeed seem to have it all. A vast view of the Atlantic and access to yachts in which to sail it. Great food, and a mansion that dwarfed anything Ortega would ever call home. And though it was true there were men who would kill Estévez if they could, he also could afford protection from the men who coveted his power and position. The law was after him, true, but both men knew the public's heated demand for justice would eventually cool and the law would throttle down its efforts. And the status quo would continue.

Ortega knew that even if he succeeded in bringing Estévez to trial, there were a million ways he could walk. And if that happened, the agent would be looking over his shoulder for years to come. And without the means to hire personal protection. He might even be forced to take himself, his wife, and their new baby into the witness protection program. All of this risk, Ortega thought—so his wife could bear their child alone in a house that was flooded because he couldn't afford a decent washing machine.

He glanced at the watch on his wrist. It alone would buy a hundred washing machines with dryers to match. And Estévez was able to hand them out like inexpensive baubles.

"I have nothing," Ortega said, hearing the words as though they had been spoken by someone else.

Estévez turned toward the Cuban agent. "Stay with me, Ron. Stay with me and learn. And one day you too will have everything you want. I'll teach you, my friend. I'll teach you the rules of the game and how to work them to your advantage." He gestured again to the glittering, sapphire sea. "I can put all of this in your hands. All I ask is your loyalty and your commitment."

Ortega squinted against the horizon.

Do the right thing? Or do the desired thing? Like the blue sea, which merged seamlessly into the sky beyond, the lines had suddenly become blurred.

CHAPTER *Forty*

The hit would happen at three-thirty in the afternoon. When Ron Ortega first presented the plan to Jimmy, Dowd was marked for the slaying. But Jimmy immediately expressed his concern with the setup.

"Leaving Hurst alive will send a message that the rules have changed. Other cops on the take, or those we will need to buy to work with the new syndicate, might opt to leave the graft alone and begin to pursue us with renewed vigor. But knocking over a couple of dirty cops, dirty partners no less, will send only the signal we want sent. That Dowd and Hurst got into bed with Torres and couldn't get out."

Ortega agreed and decided that the best course of action was to get both men to agree to meet with Santiago at an isolated place, preferably while they were off duty and without access to a police radio. It was ultimately Santiago, however, who came up with the best solution.

He arranged for the officers to meet him at the same location in the Everglades where he and Acuna had tossed the coke. The premise for the meeting was that the Mexican had confiscated a couple kilos and wanted to buy out of his arrangement with the officers while being allowed to remain in Miami. In exchange for the two kilos, they would leave him alone and he could continue to work as he always had, unmolested. The two officers agreed to the Mexican's proposition for the two reasons Ortega and Jimmy knew they would.

First, in a hundred years of payouts and shakedowns, the pair would never come close to accumulating the estimated six hundred thousand dollars the coke was worth. Second, it would enable both men to retire earlier than planned, and in comfort. Not a bad scenario after spending a couple of decades mopping garbage off the streets, only to see it right back in place before the mop was even dry.

The first part of the plan had been easy. It was the second part that would prove difficult.

Deets and Highsmith declined to participate, a stark reversal from their position when on the yacht. While they made it clear to Ortega they had no love for Torres, given his potential alliance with Kingman, they had greater disdain for Estévez. Neither man wanted anything to do with the club owner, which raised concerns as to where their loyalty would lie when everything was ultimately set in place. That meant Ortega's job of pointing the hit toward Torres had grown more difficult.

Pinning the hit on Torres would require planting something that would give investigating officers a clue. But clues can come in various shapes, colors, and sizes. There are the big ones that bite you on the end of the nose, and then there are the ones that only a Columbo could see. Given the need to direct detectives to Torres and to make it seem at least as credible as any other clue they were likely to get, the two men decided on the former. That type would require some pre-arranging, which would be handled by Jimmy.

It was decided two days before the hit to leak word on the street that Dowd and Hurst were on another rampage because payments weren't coming in like they should. Chief among these offenders would be Torres's crew. Once this disinformation had been fed into the snitch system, the next step involved burgling one of Torres's warehouses and lifting two kilos of coke. The warehouse would then be torched, but only after the fire department had been called to tell them about the fire in progress. If all went well, the fire department would arrive, put out the blaze, and discover some of the remaining cocaine. This would then be dutifully reported to the law.

A couple of days later, the bodies of Dowd and Hurst would turn up in the Everglades, with a single shot to the back of each of their heads, two kilos of coke still missing, but enough residue in their car to finger them for the burglary. It wouldn't take long for astute detectives to discover from their snitches that Torres wasn't paying his freight, and even less time for them to surmise that the two officers had taken things into their own hands. Detectives would deduce that the pair had snatched a couple of kilos they were planning on selling to the highest bidder, only to meet their fate at the hands of Torres, the man they had wronged.

To be sure the proper conclusion would be reached, Jimmy had suggested planting one of Torres's business cards in Dowd's wallet. The card listed American Diamond, a well-known jewelry store and cover for Torres's operation. Jimmy would also write Torres's cell-phone number across the back of the card. The plan wasn't entirely without holes, but it was the plan Ortega presented to Jimmy, and Jimmy eventually agreed to support. But there was another plan too—a plan that would supersede the first one. And this one would involve Meryl O'Connor.

Two days prior to the planned murder of Dowd and Hurst, Ortega met with his lifeline to discuss the arrangement. O'Connor agreed to have a team of DEA agents and local police in place to squelch the murders before they happened. After their arrest, both of the bad cops would be taken into protective custody where they would be held in isolation until the case was resolved. Details of their "demise" would be released to the media, and both men would be given some degree of immunity for their cooperation. Like the first plan, the second plan was not without its deficits either. But on balance it was as good as it was likely to get.

On the morning of the planned hit, Ortega drove to the same remote section of the Everglades where he and Santiago had arranged to meet with the four buyers. The agent settled behind a tree fifty yards from where the two officers were to meet Santiago for the two kilos of coke. Ortega had a loaded rifle on his lap to lend authenticity if anyone should happen to drop by, or if things were to go wrong. But if all went well, there would be no need to use it.

Below him, at the base of the hill, the van was in place, and the coke was inside. Ortega relaxed, confident he had it made, when he heard the sound of a car coming from behind. It parked at the base of the hill, on the side opposite of the van. Ortega groaned as Jimmy and Frankie climbed out of the car.

"This is your first time, kid," Jimmy said, puffing as he came up the hill. "We came to make sure you didn't get cold feet."

Frankie grinned but kept his eyes on the van below them.

In the Italian mobs, especially the Mafia, a hit transformed the perpetrator into a "made man." While there was no such formality in the Cuban groups, the concept was the same. If the man known as Ron Acuna carried out the hit, he would be a made man.

"Jimmy," the agent said, "I can handle this."

"Sure, kid," Caltabiano replied placing a hand on Ortega's shoulder. "We're just here to help. That's all."

"You don't trust me?'

"If we didn't trust you, you wouldn't be here," Jimmy said.

"But we've been in your shoes," Frankie added. "We know how easy it is to bug out."

"And we don't want that to happen here today," Jimmy said.

Ortega sighed. He didn't want to press his opposition too firmly. "Let me handle it, then. Okay?"

"Sure, kid," Caltabiano said, "but we're staying."

For the next hour, the three men sat quietly in their shielded position. Although the sun had yet to reach its zenith, the heat and humidity bore down on them like a steam press. Caltabiano kept dabbing the perspiration from his brow.

"Where are these guys?" he asked, glancing at his watch. "They should've been here by now."

Frankie sat with his back against a tree, his eyes closed. If it weren't for the gum he was chewing, it would be easy to assume he was asleep.

Ortega said nothing. He kept his eye trained on the van as he scoured the scene for signs of O'Connor and the others. Finally, at twelve-fifteen, a late-model Pontiac emerged from the same area where the Broward County deputies had emerged a lifetime ago. Ortega glanced at Jimmy and Frankie. They had also seen the car.

The Pontiac came to a halt behind the van. The engine continued to run as Dowd got out of the passenger's side. He was dressed like everyone else in Miami, wearing a short-sleeved open-tail shirt, light-colored slacks, and tennis shoes. He held a gun in his right hand, hanging loosely by his side.

From where Ortega sat, he could hear the officer call to the van. When there was no answer, Dowd turned nervously to the Pontiac and said something to the driver. The engine quit running and Hurst got out of the car. He was also carrying a gun, but held it in position to fire. Both officers approached the vehicle as though it were a road stop. Dowd walked along the passenger side, while Hurst took the driver's side.

Ortega focused on the nearby cluster of trees and grass. Where were O'Connor and the others?

"Now, Ron," Jimmy muttered from his position behind the agent. "Do them now."

Ortega raised the rifle. His moist palms slipped on the weapon's stock.

"Do them," Frankie said. "Pop them now."

Ortega saw no evidence of O'Connor. Where was he?

"Do it, now," Caltabiano said, more insistent this time. "Right now."

Ortega sighted the rifle—and fired.

CHAPTER *Forty-One*

The shot went wide of the mark and slammed into the Pontiac, less than a foot from where Dowd was standing.

Ortega knew he wouldn't be forgiven for missing a second time and was considering his next move when O'Connor and a crew of men swarmed from their hiding places like angry bees from an assaulted hive. They were all wearing short-sleeved shirts and jeans, and all of them had guns drawn.

"Let's get out of here," Jimmy said, tapping Ortega on the shoulder. "Somebody's tipped off the cops."

Frankie, Ortega, and Jimmy scurried from behind the tree and slid down the backside of the hill, when a sudden shot hit Frankie in the leg, knocking his feet from under him. The shot had come uphill from where they had been sitting. Someone was shooting at *them*.

Jimmy nearly stumbled over his prone friend when another shot flew over the enforcer, barely missing him.

"Get down," Ortega yelled. He grabbed Frankie by the collar and began dragging him down to a position of relative safety in a thick patch of tall grass and weeds.

A third shot was fired and careened off the dirt path less than a yard from where Ortega had entered the grass. Frankie pulled his pistol and returned fire. Jimmy lumbered behind the other two, firing indiscriminately into the thick foliage from where the shots seemed to come. Behind them, at the base of the hill where O'Connor and his men were confronting Dowd and Hurst, gunfire erupted as the agents confronted the two officers.

"Somebody set us up," Jimmy said, puffing as he dropped into the thick thatch. They were far from secure but were at least out of sight of their hidden enemy.

Ortega looked at Frankie's wound. The bullet had hit him in the upper left thigh. He was bleeding badly.

"We've got to get Frankie to the hospital," the Cuban said, removing his shirt. "He's hurt bad."

"I ain't hurt," Frankie said.

Ortega tied his shirt around the man's leg. The bleeding slowed but didn't stop. He didn't want to tell Frankie that pain wasn't necessarily an indicator of the severity of the injury. Blood—bright red blood—pumped from the wound, indicating a large artery had been severed.

Jimmy motioned to his car a few feet away. "Mine's closer. If I lay down some cover, Ron, can you get to the car and get over here?"

Ortega passed the rifle to Caltabiano. "Use this and let me have your gun."

Jimmy took the rifle and passed his revolver, along with his keys, to Ortega. "Here," the enforcer said, digging into his pocket. "There are five more rounds. It's all I've got."

"They're in the brush over that hill," Ortega said, dropping the bullets into the open cylinder. "Keep firing in that direction. And be ready when I get the car around. We won't have a lot of time."

Jimmy aimed the rifle for the thick brush from which the shots came, nodded to Ortega, and began firing. The agent bolted from the foliage and ran for the car. The sound of gunfire could still be heard from the other side of the hill—where O'Connor and his men were—left as Ortega slid into Jimmy's car and started the engine.

He jammed the accelerator and spun the car in a one-eighty, kicking up a cloud of dust as he sped to where Jimmy and Frankie were hiding. The gunfire from Jimmy's rifle was beginning to draw fire from the thatch on the upside of the hill. Several shots struck the car, pinging off the trunk and shattering the back window. Ortega kept his head low as he brought the car to a stop, passenger side facing his two friends.

Jimmy came out of the grass with one arm around Frankie's waist and the other holding the wounded man's left arm. Frankie continued to fire with his free hand while he held the rifle with the other.

Ortega reached across the front seat and opened the front passenger door before rolling down his own window and firing Jimmy's revolver at the unseen gunmen.

Frankie jumped into the front seat aided by Jimmy, who opened the rear door and dove in as Ortega again floored the accelerator. The car took off, trailing dust behind it, with Jimmy's feet hanging out the open door.

Ortega didn't want to follow the path around the curve because that would take them *up* the hill, directly into the gunsights of the men trying to kill them. But neither did he want to take the path *down* the hill. That would take them past where Dowd and Hurst were exchanging shots with the police. But since he had only the two options from which to choose, he decided on the lesser of two threats.

"Keep your heads down," he shouted, as Jimmy pulled his feet into the car and closed the door.

The Cuban aimed the car for an area down the road from where they had started, and that passed between the officers' car and the van that had been left as a decoy. O'Connor and the men with him continued to fire at Hurst as he crouched behind the Pontiac. Dowd was lying faceup beside the car. Ortega could see he was dead.

As the car passed through the gunfire, Ortega lowered his head and drove the vehicle through the open path. Once clear of it, he steered the car around the van and back onto the dirt roadway. As he sped the car down the roadway, he glanced into the rearview mirror. There was something odd about the arrest scene but he couldn't put his finger on it. Something was out of place, something not obvious.

"Step on it, kid," Jimmy said. "Frankie's just lost consciousness."

CHAPTER *Forty-Two*

Ortega had driven this road once before, but that had been in almost total darkness while evading the police. This time he had good visibility and no pursuing cops. Still he fought to recall the direction he had driven, remembering only that he had remained on the dirt roadway until a paved one came into view. That memory, faulty as it was, served him well. Within minutes he was safely on paved road heading out of the Everglades.

"How's he doing?" Ortega asked, trying to drive and keep an eye on Frankie at the same time.

Jimmy was sitting forward with his hand over the front passenger seat to feel for Frankie's pulse. He shook his head.

"Not so well. We got to get him somewhere safe."

"The closest hospital is—"

"No. No hospitals."

Ortega turned briefly to see if Caltabiano was serious. "No hospitals? Are you nuts? If we don't get him some help he'll die."

Caltabiano's expression remained flat as he kept his hand on Frankie's neck. After another moment, he shook his head again. "It don't matter. No hospital can help him now. He's dead."

"He's dead?" Ortega said, glancing back in disbelief.

"As Mussolini," Jimmy said as he settled back in his seat.

"Just like that?" Ortega was incredulous.

"I don't understand?" Jimmy said.

"I mean, 'Just like that'? That's it?"

Caltabiano leaned forward and rested his folded arms on the back of the front seat. "He doesn't have a pulse. He's not breathing. And he lost most of his blood back there in that patch of grass. I'd call that dead, wouldn't you?"

Ortega steered the car off the main highway onto a secondary road. With the back window shot out and several holes in the body of the car, it was a certainty they'd be pulled over if any cops should happen to see them. And with a dead body in the front seat, that would mean another gun battle.

Once they were off the main roadway, Ortega slowed the car and said over his shoulder, "What do we do with him?"

"Take the next left," Jimmy said. "That'll get us to Crown."

"Crown Meats? We're going to take him to the packing plant?"

Jimmy didn't respond.

"Doesn't he have a family?"

"No," Jimmy said. "We got lucky on that. He's a loner, just like me. That'll make this easier." He remained draped over the back of the front seat and lowered his head to get a better view through the windshield. "Take the next right and get into the left lane."

"You said we were set up."

"We were," Jimmy said.

"The law was returning fire on Dowd and Hurst. You think it was someone else gunning at us?"

"I do. Don't you?"

The enforcer was right. Ortega knew the instant the first shot came from behind that someone else was barging in on the game he had arranged. And that someone else wanted them…or him…dead.

"We've got a snitch somewhere."

"Yep." Caltabiano nodded as he kept his eyes on the road. "Next left, two miles, then another right."

Ortega did as he was told and was soon in the warehouse district he and Jimmy had visited a few days before. When they reached the plant, Jimmy told Ortega to steer the car around back.

He drove the car to the rear of the building where another loading dock was located. This one had *DELIVERIES* stenciled in red across its overhead door. When Ortega stopped, Jimmy said, "Wait here."

The agent remained in the car as the big Italian lumbered up the steps and went inside.

As the minutes ticked by, Ortega reviewed the scene in his head. Something was missing. Something he should have seen there in the Everglades but hadn't...something that was gnawing away at the back of his mind. He was replaying the scene in his head when Frankie suddenly moaned.

Ortega jumped up just as Jimmy was approaching the car.

"What's the matter?" he asked.

"He's still alive," Ortega said.

Jimmy frowned, reached in through the open door, and pressed his fingers against the side of Frankie's neck. "There's no pulse."

"He moaned."

Jimmy grinned. "He exhaled. Dead people do that. Haven't you ever seen a guy die?"

Ortega knew about the post-mortem effect but hadn't seen it firsthand. It was unnerving.

"Come on," Jimmy said. "Help me get him out of the car."

Ortega slid from behind the wheel and came around to Jimmy.

"Take his feet," Caltabiano said. "I'll get his shoulders."

Ortega grabbed the dead man by the ankles and began to pull as Jimmy reached into the car and lifted the man's upper body. Frankie's corpse was limp—pure dead weight—and getting him out of the vehicle was a struggle. Caltabiano was breathing heavily and sweating profusely.

The two men carried their lifeless comrade up the steps as his head lolled from side to side. As soon as they reached the top, the dock door slowly rolled up. Once inside, they were met by the same kid who had helped them the other day.

"Bring him this way," he said.

The agent and Jimmy lugged the body along the passageway to a metal skid near an elevator.

"Drop him there," the kid said.

Jimmy mopped his brow with a handkerchief as they waited for the service elevator to rise to the upper level. After what seemed like an eternity, the elevator stopped with a sigh, and the kid stepped forward to raise the vertical sliding doors.

Caltabiano stepped into the elevator and motioned. Ortega pressed the *FORWARD* switch on the handle and the skid rolled effortlessly into the elevator. Once they were all inside, the kid lowered the door and pushed the ground-floor button.

"I'll have Tommy take care of this," he said. "You can tell Mr. Estévez he won't need to worry. No one will ever find anything. Ever."

CHAPTER *Forty-Three*

After Frankie's body was taken care of, Jimmy called Estévez. A half hour later, Chipper pulled up to the dock driving an Oasis van.

"We'll leave the car here," Jimmy said. "Donnie will take care of it too."

Ortega and Caltabiano climbed into the rear seat. Chipper gave the men a pleasant smile but didn't say anything as she drove them back to The Oasis. Once they arrived, she drove to the back of the building and let them out at the rear entrance. They found Estévez seated on the sofa in his office. The club had just opened and the music had already begun.

"You guys okay?" Estévez asked, rising to his feet.

"Better than Frankie," Jimmy said, moving to Estévez's desk and picking up the phone.

"You okay, Ron?" the Cuban asked.

"Yeah, I guess so," Ortega said, not at all sure his boss believed him.

"I'm ordering something from the bar," Jimmy said, holding his hand over the telephone's mouthpiece. "What do you guys want?"

Estévez asked for a scotch and soda. "Ron?"

During his drinking days, Ortega had often sought refuge in the bottle during times of unusual stress or challenge. And for those times, a deluge of alcohol worked well. But then the stress would return with a vengeance when the high wore off, prompting him to repeat his error.

But God had freed him from all of that, hadn't He? There was no sin he need fear now, was there? One drink would do no harm. After all, a man had just died in his presence. And other men had tried to kill him.

"Whiskey sour," he said.

Jimmy placed the order and returned the receiver to its cradle.

"Have a seat, gentlemen," Estévez said, gesturing toward the sofa, his voice filled with compassion. "Tell me what happened."

He was sitting on the opposite sofa and leaned forward as Caltabiano and Ortega related their experience. Chipper entered the room with their drinks. She cast a wary eye on Ortega as he reached for his.

"Will there be anything else?" she asked.

For the second time that day, Ortega noticed something was out of place. But this time he knew what it was. Chipper wasn't smiling—and he knew why.

"No, nothing else," Estévez said, and she left without giving Ortega her usual second glance.

"Now then," Estévez said. "Tell me the rest."

For the next ten minutes the two told their boss what had happened. Each time one of them spoke, the other would round it out by giving his perspective. By the time they had finished, one thing was as clear to Estévez as it had been to Jimmy.

"Someone sold us out," the Cuban club owner said.

"I don't understand it," Ortega said, setting his empty glass on the coffee table. "Who? And why?"

Estévez set his glass on the table next to Ortega's. "There are a lot of whos," he said. "Torres himself, for one. Especially if he got word of the plan. Then there would be Kingman. You see, we've been relying on him to make the assumption that Torres, Lopez, Salter, and all the rest were at war with each other and with us. And we're basing our assumptions on him seeing that all of us are having the kinds of problems he isn't having. But if he gets word we're trying to take him out, things will change."

"In that case," Caltabiano said, still nursing his drink, "we've got the war we've been trying to avoid."

"But why?" Ortega asked. "What's to gain from it?"

"Lots," Estévez said. "Whoever shuts us down will stand to gain from us everything we stand to gain by shutting down Kingman."

"Which gets us back to our original assumption," Jimmy said. "We were set up."

"Which takes us back to who," Ortega added.

Estévez stood and paced the room. "The most obvious name would be Mikey. He knew the plan, knew when and where, and he'd do anything for a buck."

Jimmy shook his head. "I don't know. He may be a weasel, and I have no doubt he'd sell his mother's tongue if he thought he'd get a nickel out of it, but I can't picture him being disloyal to you. That's the one thing he's never done."

"I agree," Ortega said. "Dumb? Maybe. But disloyal? Not Mikey."

"Okay, but we can't scratch him off the list. Not yet," Estévez said, continuing to pace. "So now we start working down the list, starting with the guys who were at the meeting."

"Highsmith and Deets would be my choice," Jimmy said. "They knew we were after Torres, so it wouldn't take a lot for them to put a tail on me or Ron and take us out. After the events of the other night, it's reasonable to assume they don't like Ron or me. And they feel the same way about you."

Estévez shook his head. "I wasn't there this afternoon, Jimmy. You and Ron were. No one was shooting at me."

"Anybody on the boat could be a suspect," Ortega said. "They all knew that Torres is the lone holdout. If Deets and Highsmith said anything to any of them, getting the information to Kingman could put them in a solid position with him and line their pockets at the same time. And they did back out on us."

Jimmy said, "I mean no offense, Mr. Estévez. But this is why I was opposed to approaching those two in the first place."

Estévez acknowledged Jimmy's comment with a nod of his head. "If it was Deets and Highsmith, or one of the others, how did they know where you two would be?"

Neither man could answer the question.

"At the moment," Estévez said, "I'd say it comes down to Highsmith and Deets—or Mikey. And Mikey's not a shooter."

"Which way do you want us to go?" Caltabiano asked.

Estévez drummed his fingers along the upper back of the sofa as he paused to think. "Visit them, Jimmy. Find out what they know."

The enforcer smiled. "Yes, sir. I can do that."

CHAPTER *Forty-Four*

Ortega woke the next morning with a start. Jimmy Caltabiano was sitting beside his bed with an outstretched cup of coffee in his hand.

"It's Colombian," the enforcer said. "Mr. Estévez sent it himself."

Ortega rose to a sitting position and blinked the sleep from his eyes as he took the cup from Jimmy.

"How did you—"

Jimmy recoiled in mock defense. "How did I get in here? Are you kidding me?"

Ortega blew on the coffee and drank. It was the best he had ever tasted.

"I know you two like the same coffee," Jimmy said. "So when I told him you and I were going to talk with Deets this morning, he packaged a couple of pounds of the stuff and told me to bring it to you. He also gave you this." The enforcer tossed a manila envelope on Ortega's bed. The agent opened it.

"All hundreds. There must be…" Ortega paused to estimate the value of the cash. "There must be fifty thousand in here."

Caltabiano grinned. "When he heard that my car got shot up and that yours was left behind, he pulled some cash out of the safe and gave it to me. Told me to buy myself a new one. Something flashy. Then he asked me if you drove a clunker. I said yes, so he gave me another fifty and said for me to be sure you got it and that you buy yourself a really nice car. He wanted to let you also know that Donnie took care of your other one. It'll never surface, so to speak." He grinned.

Ortega was stunned.

"So get out of bed, sunshine," Jimmy said. "We've got to talk to Deets. Then we go car shopping."

Delbert Deets lived with his wife and two sons in a nice upper-scale suburban home, a ranch style that sat on a small lot. The yard was neatly landscaped and a small boat was parked in the driveway, covered by a canvas tarp.

"He's been in the game long enough to know how it works. We tell him we need to talk and he'll come. He knows nothing is going to happen in front of his family, unless he gets mouthy," Jimmy said, as the two of them sat in front of Deets's house in an unmarked Oasis van. "Then if that happens, we come back later and finish the job. Any questions?"

"We're just going to talk to him, right?"

"Yeah," Jimmy said. "We're just going to talk to him."

The two of them got out of the car and walked along a curving sidewalk to the front door. Moments after they knocked, they were greeted by Deets.

"I saw you two sitting out front." He glanced over their shoulders at the van and licked his lips.

"We've got to talk," Jimmy said.

"Who is it, honey?" a feminine voice asked from somewhere in the house.

"Just a couple of friends from work," Deets said. "I'm going to step out. I'll be back in a little while." He was wearing a tank top similar to the one he had worn in Estévez's office, and jeans with no shoes. He turned to go back into the house, closing the door, when Jimmy stepped across the threshold and put his hand on the door.

"Where do you think you're going?"

Deets gave Jimmy and Ortega a nervous look. He was outmatched. "I'm going to get some shoes, okay?"

"You don't need shoes. You're not going to be anywhere where you'll be needing shoes."

The man licked his lips again and said, "I'll be back in a little while, honey. Tell the kids I love them."

"Let's go," Jimmy said, reaching past Deets to close the door.

They walked to the car in a formation meant to instill fear in the man. Jimmy led the way while Ortega walked behind. The signal to Deets was clear. Attempt to flee and you're dead. Play along and you might live.

Ortega climbed behind the wheel. Deets was directed to the right-front passenger seat. Jimmy sat in the rear.

Ortega shifted into drive and pulled away from the curb.

"Take us to where we were yesterday, Ron," Jimmy said.

Ortega didn't say a word as he headed out of the man's neighborhood. For the next hour, the car was silent. When they reached the isolated area where the gun battle had occurred. Ortega parked the van in virtually the same spot Jimmy's car had been sitting when the ambush had occurred.

"Out," Jimmy said, tapping Deets on the shoulder.

The three climbed out.

The enforcer had said he just wanted to talk with Deets—to find out if he had a role in the ambush. But the isolated setting was raising suspicions in the young agent. The tension he felt during the interrogation of Mario was beginning to return—in force.

Ortega cast a wary eye toward Jimmy. The enforcer didn't seem to notice.

Deets moved to the rear of the van and as far away from the two men as possible. He liked his lips before glancing first at Jimmy, then Ortega, and finally back to Jimmy.

"What do you want, man?" Deets asked. "Why did we come all the way out here?"

Jimmy pulled a packet of gum from his pocket and extended it to Ortega. The agent shook his head.

"Gum?" the big Italian said, extending the packet towards Deets.

He shook his head.

"I want to know who shot at us yesterday," Jimmy said, sliding a stick of gum into his mouth.

Deets glanced at Ortega. "You think it was me?"

"Yeah, I think it was you. You don't like me and my friend here. You haven't liked us since we put you and Highsmith in your place. Now I'm beginning to think you blame us for Garcia's death."

"No, man. That ain't right. I don't blame you for nothing."

"Then why the hostility?" Jimmy asked. "How come you shot at us?"

"I didn't man. I didn't," Deets said. "You know that ain't my style."

The tension Ortega had felt internally was now becoming palpable. He didn't like the way things were going. The enforcer nodded thoughtfully as he slid the packet of gum into his pocket. The butt of the snub-nosed revolver protruded as he did.

"Yeah, that's what I thought, too. Initially."

Deets ran the back of his left hand across his mouth. His right hand slid into the pocket of his jeans. "What's that mean? *Initially?*"

Jimmy looked at Deets in disbelief. "I have to explain this to you? It means I don't think you have the moxie to face me. You need my back turned."

"I'll face any man."

"Yeah, that's right. I did hear something like that." Jimmy said. "That you prefer working up close, personal. Unless it's someone you can't handle."

The nervousness that had caused Deets to become defensive now began to embolden him. Like a rat trapped in a cage, the hitter began to change his posture. The nervous glance became a focused glare. The slumped posture became erect. His mouth curled in anger.

"There ain't no man I can't handle. I don't hide behind trees. With me it's always mano a mano."

"You're a real man," Jimmy said, clearly goading his prey.

Deets said nothing. His mouth contorted into a sneer.

"Except you're also a liar," Jimmy added. "You didn't say a word all the way here. You knew why we brought you to this place. You knew and you didn't say a word."

"I wasn't even in town yesterday," Deets said. "You can ask Highsmith. He'll tell you."

Ortega saw Deets tighten his defensive position. He turned his left side to Jimmy. His right hand was still thrust in the pocket of his jeans.

"I did," Jimmy said.

Deets widened his stance. "What'd he say?"

Jimmy gave Deets a mock cry. "No, please, don't," he said. "Or something like that...just before I killed him."

Deets pulled the knife from the right pocket of his jeans and clicked the retractable blade into place. He pivoted his left foot toward Ortega, who was standing less than two feet away.

The agent was unarmed, but not off guard. He began to defend against the attack when he was suddenly cut short by the abrupt report of Jimmy's gun.

The shot drove Deets into the rear of the van. A second shot caused him to drop the knife as he slumped to the ground.

Ortega was still in a defensive posture as he stared at the lifeless Deets.

Jimmy tucked the revolver into his waist band. "Let's go get us a car."

CHAPTER *Forty-Five*

"He didn't do it," Jimmy said, sitting next to Ortega as the two drove back to town.

"Why did you kill him then?" Ortega was angry—and concerned. He had been party to another violent act. And although this one was clearly an act of self-defense, he couldn't help but wonder if Jimmy was hoping to drive Deets into the rage that would get him killed.

"Two reasons," Jimmy said. "First, he had the drop on you and was going to push that knife in your belly. He knew he couldn't reach me in time 'cause I made sure he saw the gun. But he was bent on taking as many of us with him as he could. That means you.

"Second, he'd come after us someday, probably sooner than later, and I didn't see a reason to live life looking over my shoulder watching for Deets."

"I saw him moving," Ortega said. "I can take care of myself."

Jimmy laughed. "The man had a knife. Unless there's something about you I don't know you would have a six-inch piece of steel in you right now."

The two men had left the body lying where it had been shot. It would eventually be found, along with Highsmith's, and the message would be sent.

Ortega drove out of the Everglades the same way he had the day before. Finding his way out, though, had not gotten easier. If anything, finding his way to solid ground seemed more difficult than ever.

"Take us back to town," Jimmy said, "and when we get closer, I'll give you directions."

"Where we going?"

He gave Ortega a quizzical look. "To buy a car. Don't you remember?"

Ortega admitted he had forgotten.

"Mr. Estévez doesn't do this for everyone. He's taken a liking to you. You've proven yourself to him and that doesn't come easy."

Ortega knew that despite the compliment, he would remain under a cloud of suspicion until he could be considered a made man. Even then, loyalty was second only to profit. If he were to fail in either realm, he would be exterminated as easily as the man they had just left lying at the base of a hill.

"You told Deets that Highsmith was dead. How'd you know?"

Jimmy gave Ortega a look of astonishment. "Because I killed him. I talked to him this morning in his apartment and he gave me the same line Deets did, so I popped him." He shifted in his seat. "I had a run-in with those two once before."

"What?" Ortega asked.

"When I first came to work for Mr. Estévez he had me doing some basic security. Checking people out, securing his office, his home, things like that. As I proved myself, he gave me more responsibility. One day, while I was securing his office, I found a couple of bugs. Nothing sophisticated, but still powerful enough that they were able to eavesdrop on conversations. I took the bugs to Mr. Estévez, and he said he thought they might be from Garcia because the man had been able to anticipate every move we were making." He shifted in his seat and rested his elbow on the door frame. "Deets and Highsmith were Garcia's top lieutenants, so they were the ones I went after first. I took along another guy who used to work with us, named Pablo. Pablo and I confronted Deets and Highsmith, and Highsmith pulled a gun and shot Pablo like he was a dog. I was still new then, so they let me go." He glanced at Ortega. "Like I was a civilian or something, you know? So I told Mr. Estévez what had happened. He told me to let it go."

"Let it go?"

Jimmy nodded. "Yeah, just let it go. That's when I learned that the man was able to take the long-range view. He knew he wasn't in any position to do anything about it at the time because Garcia was bigger. He had more influence, more money, more muscle, and more clout. There wasn't a whole lot we could do *then*."

"But things have changed."

Caltabiano grinned. "You could say that. As Mr. Estévez gained ground, there was bad blood between him and Garcia. It wasn't long before Garcia started spreading the word and had everyone up in arms."

"So that's the reason for the bad blood between all of them," Ortega said.

"Yeah. That and money. It always comes down to money." He clucked his tongue. "Like a bunch of lawyers, you know? Anyway, when we started to grow, Mr. Estévez told me we needed to focus on paying off the authorities. But he wanted to do it different than the others. They were all paying off the cops. Street-level cops mostly. But Mr. Estévez wanted to focus on the politicians. The cops' bosses." He shot a brief glance at Ortega. "See what I mean?"

"I'm starting to."

"If you pay off the politicians, you get the judges, the legislators—the guys the cops have to go through if they want to close you down." He told Ortega to take a left turn. "Then as we gained protection, we started paying the news guys. Newspaper reporters mostly, but some TV guys too. They aren't protection but they do sway public opinion."

"They don't seem to be helping much now," Ortega said.

The enforcer shrugged. "No one can help all the time. Besides, we can't buy everyone. Just enough."

"So taking Garcia out was always the plan?"

"No. It was strictly business. Mr. Estévez rarely lets personal feeling get in the way." Jimmy grinned. "But it didn't hurt my feelings any that when it came time to offer someone up as the sacrifice, it was Garcia."

"So old scores got settled."

"With Garcia, Deets, and Highsmith they did. Now we can scratch those three off the list and out of our lives."

"So where do we go next?" Ortega asked.

"We talk to Mikey. Or better yet, *you* talk to Mikey. If you say he's clean that'll be good enough for Mr. Estévez."

"How come it wasn't for Highsmith and Deets?" Ortega asked. "You started on them this morning."

"Those two have had it in for us for a long time. And they're certainly capable of bugging us, even though I didn't find anything on the boat. On the other hand, they couldn't have all the details of the plan, so if they didn't bug us, someone told them. If they knew, they were doing the shooting. It's their style."

"That takes us back to Mikey," Ortega said.

"Yeah. But, like we were saying, he isn't the type to be disloyal."

"No, but we…I…referred to him as dumb."

"Yeah. So?"

"So maybe he wasn't disloyal. Maybe he's just dumb for blabbing about what he knows."

Jimmy thought about the possibility. "Maybe. That would sure explain it. But you got to remember, Mikey knows a lot of stuff. And what he knows makes money for him. If he goes giving stuff away for free, he won't be around long. It's what makes him valuable. He tells what he knows, but he generally works with consistency. He never strays too far from the pen."

"Maybe he didn't," Ortega said. "Maybe someone he talks to did."

From Jimmy's expression it was clear that he hadn't considered that possibility.

"You still want me to talk to Mikey? Or do you want to deal with him?" Ortega asked, aware of the pecking order.

Jimmy continued to think before saying, "No, you go ahead, Ron, and talk to Mikey. Do it tonight so we can clear him off the slate."

"You want me to let you know tonight what he says?"

The enforcer shook his head. "No, I want you to go ahead and waste him."

CHAPTER *Forty-Six*

Ron Ortega chose a black Lexus ES 350 with a bone interior, wood trim, seats that heated *and* cooled. The car also had a navigation system that could probably tell him how to find a restroom in St. Paul if he asked.

It was virtually silent inside. With the windows up and the sunroof closed, he could hear a pin drop. As it was, he wasn't listening to pins dropping. He was listening to a stereo system that rivaled Carnegie Hall.

The car had a substantial, solid feel. Each bump in the road, regardless of how large, seemed like a minor glitch. The horsepower allowed him to glide through traffic like a banana peel on a highway paved with butter.

In the rearview mirror, Ortega could see Jimmy following behind in his own ES 350, differing from Ortega's only in color. They had left the van behind and would send someone to pick it up later.

"If Libby could see this," Ortega said to himself. But his mind quickly moved to the work at hand. He needed to talk to Mikey, but before that, he would need to meet with O'Connor.

As the agent merged into interstate traffic, Jimmy split off in a different direction. Ortega didn't know where the enforcer was going, but considering his orders to find out how much Mikey told of what he knew—before silencing the hustler forever—Jimmy was going to have a better day than Ortega would.

The agent pulled out his cell and dialed the number of his lifeline. He hadn't bothered to call the day before, knowing the man would be tied up all day with the inevitable red tape that came with a shooting. But Ortega had things to say and he needed to talk. O'Connor answered on the third ring.

"Ron?"

"Who did you expect? Your mother-in-law?"

"I don't have a mother-in-law," O'Connor said. "I jettisoned her with the divorce."

"You guys cut it a little close out there yesterday," Ortega said. "They might let me get away with one missed shot, but they weren't going to ignore a second one."

"Yeah, sorry about that," O'Connor said. "We weren't sure where you were."

"Where I was didn't matter. You had Dowd and Hurst and you had the coke."

"How many times in your career...your *limited* career, have you ever seen things go according to plan?"

O'Connor was right, of course, but that didn't do much to assuage Ortega's simmering anger.

"What happened to them?" the Cuban asked, knowing full well that Dowd had been killed.

"They opened fire as soon as we emerged. We returned fire and Dowd went down first. Hurst kept resisting to the end. His end. They're both on a slab at the morgue."

"You got the coke, I assume? We didn't have a chance to..."

"We got it. It'll be tagged for evidence and logged with your reports and recordings as soon as this thing ends."

"I don't get it," Ortega said, glancing into the rearview mirror as he changed lanes. "They knew they didn't have a chance. Why did they resist?"

"Who knows? Maybe they thought they could get away."

"You really believe that?"

"No, but it's possible. I've seen men under stress before and it's amazing what goes through their minds. Do I believe they honestly thought they could somehow escape? No. More likely it was panic brought on by the sudden surprise of seeing so many of us. Their natural instinct was to resist. Or, of course, maybe I'm not giving them the credit they deserve. Maybe they had talked about the possibility of getting caught one day and decided if it happened to them as a team, they would go down fighting. They were cops after all, and there aren't too many places worse for a cop to be than in prison."

"That makes more sense," Ortega said. "But something still nags at me. Something about yesterday that just doesn't seem right. You know?"

"Could be a lot of things. Maybe it's the stress of the gun battle. The stress of being caught in-between. If it's something worth remembering, it'll come back to you."

"Yeah, maybe," Ortega said, not really sure if he believed it.

"So where does Estévez stand at the moment?"

"He's still pushing to unite the others against Kingman. Garcia seemed to hold sway over some of them, so Estévez took him out. Then, earlier today, Jimmy killed Highsmith and Deets."

"Who?"

Ortega repeated the names, telling his lifeline the two men were lieutenants of Garcia and had a history with Estévez that made their demise an inevitability.

"You might want to check out Crown Meats," Ortega added.

"We're already aware that it's a front for Estévez," O'Connor said. "Is there something else I should know about?"

"You could say that. It's also a mortuary. We got caught in a crossfire and someone killed Frankie. We took him to the meat plant and a guy there took care of the body, if you know what I mean."

"I know what you mean, but I don't know about any crossfire."

"We were hiding up the hill from where Dowd and Hurst were sitting. When you guys approached, we tried to leave and we started taking shots from behind."

O'Connor was silent for a moment, then said, "Someone else must've been there. It sounds like you guys got sold out."

"That's what we thought too," Ortega said. "So we began running down the most likely suspects. The feeling was that Deets and Highsmith, seeing as how they had a run-in with Jimmy and me, were probably—"

"Run-in?"

"It's in my report," Ortega said. "But we reasoned they were possible suspects—certainly motivated suspects—so we asked them."

"Sounds like you asked them to death."

"Not me. Jimmy."

Another pause.

"Did he get the right ones?"

"I don't think so and I don't think he thinks so. But he had an old score to settle and this was one way of doing it with Estévez's blessing."

"You have more suspects?"

"Yeah. I'm going right now to talk with Santiago. We figure he might know who ratted us out, but neither Jimmy nor I think he's capable of going against Estévez. He would lose his credibility and maybe his life. It wouldn't make any sense."

"Still, if the evidence is there, it's there. If this guy is taking to ratting on you and Jimmy, he's capable of turning on you in other ways. Correct me if I'm wrong, but isn't he the way you gained access to this group in the first place?"

"Yes."

"Then be careful. If he thinks you're dirty or if he feels a need to remove you, there's a reason."

"Well," Ortega said, "I'll find out soon enough. I'm almost there now."

"Keep me posted," O'Connor said. "I don't want to have to learn about it by reading your obituary."

CHAPTER *Forty-Seven*

Caltabiano arrived at The Oasis a little before noon and found Estévez sitting at the bar drinking a cup of his Colombian brew. Except for a light overhead, the club was dark, and except for Jimmy and Estévez, the building was empty.

"How'd it go?" Estévez asked.

"I took out Highsmith this morning," the ex-cop said. "Acuna didn't quirk when I finished Deets."

Estévez gestured toward the carafe of coffee. Jimmy shook his head and sat on a stool next to Estévez.

"Did Acuna get his car?"

"Lexus ES 350. A black one."

Estévez smiled. "Good choice. I've always preferred Lexus."

"Expensive gift," Caltabiano said. "You think it might rouse some suspicion?"

Estévez shook his head. "No. I think it will buy some loyalty where none may exist and will allay any fears that I'm having doubts."

Caltabiano had dealt on the streets for the better part of his life, long enough to know that shades of gray existed more often than not. Acuna had moved into the circle too quickly and with little testing. But testing was bound to come. And Caltabiano knew that no one tested like Ricardo Estévez.

"Have you seen any problems with him?" the club owner asked.

Jimmy weighed the question. "I don't know. He missed a wide-open shot at Dowd, but when we came under fire, he reacted like a pro. While I was pinned down with Frankie, God rest his soul," Jimmy said, pausing to make the sign of the cross, "Acuna went for my car at considerable risk to himself. When we took off, he drove straight through the shootout between the cops and Dowd, again at risk to himself, and when we finished up at the plant, he watched Tommy take Frankie apart like it was just another day on the job." He shrugged. "I don't know. Why? Something bugging you?"

Estévez paused long enough to take a sip of the coffee, before shaking his head. "I don't know, Jimmy. It's just that something doesn't seem right. We have this good plan to set Torres up for a fall by the cops, a plan that Acuna set up himself—and wanted to execute himself—but then you and Frankie show up and the whole thing crumbles."

"It hasn't crumbled yet," Jimmy said. "The cops showed up and they found Dowd and Hurst with the goods. Goods that any smart detective will discover came out of Torres's stock."

"I'm thinking more along the lines that someone was gunning for you guys. Somebody set you up."

"You think Acuna may be behind it?"

Estévez shrugged. "I don't know. But I've been around long enough to honor my suspicions." He began drumming his fingers on the bar. "If Ron isn't the guy who arranged the shoot, I don't want to rid myself of a good man. On the other hand, if he is the guy, I've got to find out who he's working with before I unload him."

Jimmy rested his back against the bar. "If he's dirty, then it stands to reason he's working with someone and he's a plant. He hasn't been around long enough to have enough knowledge for someone to turn him. And since he was being shot at by the cops just like we were, it's reasonable to assume he isn't with them."

Estévez shook his head. "We don't know it was the law, Jimmy. And either way, it doesn't matter. Cops or someone else, he could be just as dangerous."

Caltabiano leaned forward. "He could be working with Torres."

Estévez drank some more of the coffee. "Maybe. But I approached Torres about the plan to unite against Kingman. Why would he suddenly come after me now, when he's had years to do it?"

"Could be Kingman. Maybe he's figured out what's going on and decided to do you before you do him."

"That'd be more likely," Estévez said. "If Kingman has put his dogs in a row, he may be trying to preempt us."

"Maybe it'd be just as wise to take a wait-and-see attitude. See what develops."

"It's got to happen fast," Estévez said. "If Torres has enough time, he'll undermine our efforts with the others and then Kingman will steal Miami, not to mention Cuba, right out from under us."

"On the other hand," Jimmy said, "if it *is* Kingman and he's planted Acuna, we don't know what damage has been done, which means it could be too late already."

Estévez shook his head. "Never too late, Jimmy. There's always something that can be done."

"You got something you want me to do?" Caltabiano asked.

Estévez finished the coffee and rose from his stool to take the cup to the sink behind the bar. "I think maybe we can kill two birds with one stone. First, we need to have you put Acuna in a position where he can be tested. We've got to know what this guy is made of." He rinsed the cup and set it in the sink. "Second, we need to start cleaning house." Estévez rested with both hands against the bar while he paused to think through the situation. Caltabiano waited patiently until the Cuban said, "Let's start with Mikey. We figured he might be part of the set up on you guys, right?"

Caltabiano nodded.

"Whether he did it or not, Mikey knows too much. With so much at stake it doesn't make a lot of sense for us to let the guy walk around, willing to sell information to the highest bidder."

"After Acuna bought his car, I told him I wanted Mikey checked out."

"Did he hesitate?" Estévez asked.

Caltabiano shook his head. "No. Actually, he seemed pleased to be able to show me he could be trusted. When he asked me what I wanted him to do if Mikey panned out to be responsible for the setup, I told him to waste him."

"Any hesitation?"

"None."

Estévez leaned his full weight against the bar and crossed his arms. "If he takes Mikey out, we'll know he's okay."

"And if he doesn't, what do you want to do?"

The Cuban shrugged. "Then *you* take Mikey out and we'll test Ron with something else. Either way this thing goes, I need to know if Acuna is someone I can trust."

"Okay," Caltabiano said. "If he takes out Mikey, fine. If not, I'll keep an eye on him—and I'll be sure I'm there when the time is right."

"The time may be right sooner than you think. If Torres doesn't go down soon, we may see him and some of the others shift over to Kingman. If that happens, there'll be a war. Acuna will get all the shooting we can give him."

CHAPTER *Forty-Eight*

Ortega found Mikey standing in front of Hokey's, talking to several Hispanic men. None seemed older than twenty-five, and all of them had the wary look that comes from a life on the streets. The men stared at the new Lexus as Ortega pulled to a stop at the curb, but began drifting away as soon as the agent climbed out of the car.

"My, my," Santiago said, in his best white-suburban imitation, "haven't we become one with the man."

"We need to talk, Mikey," Ortega said, not wasting any time.

The Mexican looked around. "You already ran off my customers. Might as well talk here as any place."

"This is a little more serious than that," Ortega said. "Maybe we can go for a ride."

The agent wasn't sure if the Mexican had anything to do with the set-up, but if he did, he'd have to die. Officially. That meant Ortega was going to have to find a way to "kill off" the hustler without putting a bullet in his head. The box in which the Cuban agent was living was growing increasingly smaller by the minute.

Santiago glanced around and ran a thumb along his mustache. "A ride?"

"We really need to talk," Ortega said again.

The Mexican eased himself over to the car and looked inside, before he told the Cuban to pop the trunk.

At first, Ortega didn't understand. But then he realized that for Santiago, the possibility of betrayal by anyone, even those he deemed friends, hung about his neck like a cement block.

Ortega popped the trunk and allowed the Mexican to see that no one was lurking inside. As soon as the lid was closed, the Cuban pulled his T-shirt up to reveal his torso. He carried no weapon and no wire.

Santiago climbed into the car.

Once the Lexus was into the flow of traffic, Santiago glanced in the passenger-door mirror to be sure no one was tailing them. Ortega saw that he now held a gun in his hand.

"What's that for?" the agent asked.

"Can never be too careful," Santiago said. The gun was a .25-caliber automatic—small enough to conceal, but deadly enough to kill.

"You don't need that," Ortega said. "I just want to talk."

The Mexican gave the Cuban a knowing glance. "Just the same, I think I'll hold onto it."

"Dowd and Hurst are dead."

Mikey's jaw went slack.

"Don't act surprised," Ortega said.

"Did you do it?"

Ortega shook his head. "The cops did. And that wasn't part of the original plan."

Santiago's brow furrowed as he gave Ortega a confused look.

"Their bodies were supposed to be found with the coke on them. Torres's coke. Then he goes down for the hit, and Estévez's effort to unite everyone else continues, spelling the end for Kingman."

"What happened?" the Mexican asked, putting the pistol away.

"You tell me."

Santiago shook his head. "I don't know what you're talking about."

"We were set up," Ortega said. "I was to waste both of them, when all of a sudden the cops came out of the brush. Then we started taking fire from behind. Frankie was killed."

"And you think I had something to do with that?"

"Estévez does," Ortega said, easing the new car onto the interstate. "He thinks you talked too much."

The reality of his situation caused the Mexican to run a thumb along his mustache again, betraying his nervousness. "Did he say that?"

"He did." Ortega wasn't being exactly truthful, he knew. In fact, it had been

Jimmy who had directed the agent to uncover Mikey's betrayal. But Caltabiano tended to build on foundations that were first laid by Estévez.

"I didn't tell no one," Mikey said. "No one except Dowd and Hurst. I only told them. That's it. Honest."

"But someone set us up," Ortega said, concerned that if he didn't have something other than the Mexican's denial, Santiago would surely die.

"Then it had to be someone else. Someone else who knew."

"No one else knew, Mikey. No one except Deets and Highsmith, and Jimmy took both of them out this morning."

Beads of sweat formed on the Mexican's brow. "You got to tell them I didn't have nothing to do with it," he said. "Honest."

"I'd like to, Mikey," Ortega said. "I really would. But you've got to give me something to work with."

The Mexican sighed. "Why didn't the cops just arrest them?"

"As soon as they came out of hiding, Dowd and Hurst just opened up. The cops didn't have a choice."

"That doesn't make no sense," Mikey said. "Why would two cops who know they've been caught with stolen coke suddenly open up on the police?"

"You just said it," Ortega said. "They were caught red-handed with over half a million in cocaine."

"Torres's cocaine," Mikey said. "Shooting it out with the police wouldn't free them to do anything other than spend the next few days of their lives looking over their shoulder. And when Torres finally caught up with them, shooting would've been too good. He'd have had them turning over a spit for days."

Ortega didn't know Torres or any of the other locals as well as the street hustler did, but he figured that Santiago was probably right. If Dowd and Hurst had managed to escape the police, their lives would've been worth little. Even though they didn't know it was Torres's cocaine, they knew it belonged to somebody and that Mikey had taken it to protect his own hide.

"These guys would've squeezed you again sooner or later," Ortega said. "They'd take the coke, sell it to the highest bidder, and then when they started feeling heat from whoever they assumed the coke came from, they would have handed you over to them."

"So *you* sacrificed me?"

Ortega ignored the man and continued to reason his way through the fiasco.

"I was supposed to be the only one there," Ortega said. "I was supposed to do Dowd and Hurst and leave everything for the cops to find. Except I came under fire. The fact that Jimmy and Frankie were there was coincidental."

"You step on someone's toes?" Santiago asked.

Ortega hadn't thought so, but it seemed likely someone wanted him dead. "The only people who knew I was going to be there were you, maybe Deets and Highsmith, Jimmy, and Estévez."

The Mexican shrugged. "I didn't tell no one. But how do I prove that?"

"You can't," Ortega said, keeping the Lexus in the flow of traffic.

"I know that Dowd and Hurst could be a couple of hard cases," Santiago said. "But they weren't dumb."

"They weren't smart either," Ortega said, "thinking they could shoot it out with the law, manage to escape, and still remain free to walk around."

"That's what I mean," the Mexican said. "They thought they could get away with anything, because they had. But to shoot it out with the cops? You'd think as soon as they saw it was the law they'd—"

"What did you say?" Ortega interrupted.

"I said, 'You'd think as soon as they saw it was the law they'd—"

"We need to get you somewhere," Ortega said, accelerating the car. "And for both of our sakes, we need to do it quick."

CHAPTER *Forty-Nine*

Ortega was silent despite the Mexican's repeated questions until both men were sitting in a room at the Catalina Hotel on Collins Avenue. They had checked in under an assumed name.

"I've got something to tell you," Ortega said, "and you're not going to like it." The agent was sitting on the edge of the bed. Santiago was in a chair behind a table. The Mexican was on high alert.

"You know who's behind it, don't you?" he asked.

"Yeah," Ortega said. "And I thought they were people I could trust."

"Didn't I tell you to trust no one?" Santiago said. "Even me?"

Ortega was nauseated. "Right now, Mikey, you're one of the few I know who doesn't have a hidden agenda."

"I'm not getting you, man."

"My name is not Ron Acuna. It's Ron Ortega. I'm a DEA agent."

"You're a *cop?*"

Ortega nodded.

"A cop?" the Mexican gasped again, rising off the chair.

"You might as well sit down, Mikey," Ortega said. "Now that I've told you, I can't let you leave. In fact, when I'm finished talking, you might not want to leave." He motioned Santiago back to the seat. The hustler hesitated, hovering over the chair in disbelief before sitting back down with resignation.

"I've been trying to think about what it was that didn't seem right out there," Ortega said. "I kept coming back to why those two clowns would shoot it out with the law. I kept figuring they had panicked. But then when you said they should've recognized it was the law, I knew what was bothering me."

"That two cops didn't recognize other cops when they saw them?"

"Exactly. Dowd and Hurst didn't recognize them as cops because they *weren't* cops."

A frown of confusion creased Santiago's face. "Then who were they?"

"I don't know. But they weren't wearing the blue nylon jackets we're supposed to wear when we move in like they did. No one had a badge, a jacket, or any other identifying symbol. That's what's been bothering me. They were dressed in street clothes with nothing to ID them as cops."

"So you know they weren't cops. So what?"

"They were supposed to be cops," Ortega said. "I was supposed to hit Dowd and Hurst, but obviously I can't do that. So I told my lifeline about the plan, with the understanding he'd have a team of cops and DEA to arrest the two and get them off the street."

"Then your own guys sold you out."

Ortega rose from the edge of the bed and ran a hand through his thick black hair. He began to pace. "That's exactly what must have happened. I've been sold out by my lifeline. It's the only explanation that fits."

"Well, maybe...but I don't see how that's my problem. No offense, but as long as I'm off the hook with Estévez, this doesn't really concern me."

"It concerns you very much, my friend. You see, Jimmy wanted me to find out if you were the one who ratted us out."

"And if I was, you're supposed to take me out?"

"Yes." Ortega said.

The Mexican ran a thumb along his mustache.

"If I don't take you out, Estévez will keep digging until he finds the source of the leak. He'll pin it on someone and, as it stands right now, you're the man."

"Then let him find your lifeline, whatever that is. I'm not going to give up my life."

"What life, Mikey? Running the streets and trying to stay alive?"

Santiago shot off the chair. "Hey man, it's *my* life. *Mine.* Not yours and not your lifeline's. It's nobody's but mine."

Ortega moved to block Santiago's access to the door. "Not anymore, Mikey—not anymore."

The Mexican doubled his fists. His eyes narrowed and fixed hard on Ortega.

"I'm sorry," the Cuban said. "I really am."

The Mexican cursed and kicked a small wastepaper basket across the room. It ricocheted off the wall to Ortega's left.

"So what happens now?" the hustler asked.

"I've got to get you somewhere safe and make it look like you've been taken out."

"And what am I supposed to do in the meantime? I've got a life. And it's *my* life," he repeated, raising his voice.

"You won't have a life at all if you don't let me do this. If I have to throw in the towel now, I may not have enough to put Estévez away. That means he'll walk and you'll get killed."

Santiago sat down. Beads of sweat reformed on his brow. "Man, I knew you was too good to be true. That deal in the Glades. Did you set that up too?"

Ortega stopped pacing. "No. That deal was to go down and you were to be arrested along with the buyers. But when you told me you knew Estévez, I figured if I could get you away from that situation I might have a chance to penetrate the organization."

"You *used* me."

"I'm an undercover cop. Using people and getting used is part of the job."

"Well, I'm not a cop. I was having a nice life until I let you in it." Santiago wasn't nervous anymore. He was angry. Very angry.

"I'm sorry, Mikey. I really am. But you have to die."

CHAPTER *Fifty*

Since becoming a Christian, Ortega had been told repeatedly to beware of Satan for he could appear as an "angel of light." It now became equally clear that the prince of darkness could also appear as a trusted colleague.

After gaining a reluctant commitment from the wary Mexican, Ortega called the SAC and told him everything he knew. At first the boss was highly skeptical that O'Connor had turned, but after hearing Ortega's explanation of the events of the past several days, he began to acquiesce.

"Estévez asked Jimmy and me how Deets and Highsmith, two of Garcia's shooters, could have known the two of us would be in the Everglades. But the fact is, they couldn't. I was the only one who was supposed to be there. Jimmy's coming by was unexpected."

"So whoever was shooting at you two—or three," the SAC said, acknowledging Frankie, "was really gunning for you. The other two just happened to show up at the wrong time."

"And place."

"This makes me sick," Rojas said.

"It's going to make me dead if I don't do something with Santiago," Ortega added.

The Mexican was watching the Home Shopping Network on the TV. He had the sound muted so that Acuna, or Ortega—Santiago said he wasn't sure what to call him anymore—could talk.

"We have to let the USA in on this," Ortega said.

"Of course. But we better be sure O'Connor is as dirty as you say. I don't relish the idea of destroying a man's career unless I can hang my hat on something."

"Who else could it be? Someone set us up. And that someone had to be O'Connor."

"Right now I'd say you're probably right. And unless I can prove otherwise, I'm willing to go along. And I'll keep the U.S. attorney in the loop. But that's all. If you're right and O'Connor has turned, we'll take him down with the rest of them."

Both men were silent. Neither liked considering the possibility that one of their own could have rolled on them. But the evidence was strong. O'Connor didn't show with the police. And a hit had been arranged against Ortega. *Only* O'Connor knew where his agent would be hiding. A fact that Ortega's inexperience had prevented him from seeing earlier.

"I checked in under an assumed name," the agent added, "because I figured it was safer that way. But since I don't know who knows what, or how much, I can't sit here for long."

"Agreed," the boss said. "Let me make a call. I'll get hold of the U.S. attorney and have someone meet you and Santiago. We'll take him into protective custody and arrange a proper…sendoff for him."

"What do I do in the meantime?"

"Sit tight. I'll call you right back."

After ending the call, Ortega sat on the edge of the bed. Santiago turned up the volume.

"Can we get something to eat?" he asked.

Ortega was hungry too, but reluctant to order anything for fear of who might get wind of the order. "Not right now, Mikey. I'd rather not open the door to a stranger."

The Mexican gave Ortega an incredulous look. "Are you for real? You think this guy has people in every hotel kitchen?"

Ortega knew he was probably overreacting and Santiago was probably right. Nevertheless, the stakes were too high to risk for a club sandwich.

"Sorry," he said. "We'll get something soon. I promise."

Santiago cursed. The phone rang and Ortega motioned for the Mexican to turn down the volume. It was Rojas.

"Take Santiago to Arch Park. Know it?"

"I'll find it," Ortega said.

"Northeast 135th. There's a museum there. Take Santiago to the museum and wait. Someone will meet you there."

"Sorry, boss. But I'm going to need someone I recognize."

There was a brief pause before the SAC said, "I'll come. I'll meet you just outside the museum."

After the phone call ended, Ortega told Santiago to turn off the TV. "Let's go," the Cuban said. "I've got to get you killed off."

"Can we eat first?"

"We'll get something on the way."

The two men appeared in front of the park museum after stopping at a McDonald's drive-through. Santiago remained in the car and chewed on the ice that lined his cup. Ortega met with the SAC not twenty feet from the car.

The boss was dressed in jeans, tennis shoes, and a T-shirt that featured a rock band. He was carrying a brown-paper bag and looked more the part of a homeless man than a highly placed government agent.

"Where did the car come from?" he asked.

"Estévez."

"And the watch? Same place?"

Although he had been shuffling through the park like a man on a drunk, the SAC had missed nothing.

"Yes."

"You've got to turn all that in, son."

Ortega was offended. "Of course."

Rojas nodded. "Okay. Just making sure, that's all."

"You want him here or do you want me to drive him in?" Ortega asked.

The SAC grinned. "Relax, Ron. As long as he plays dead, he'll be fine. You're the man of the hour now."

"Where do we go from here?"

"I'm taking Santiago," the boss said. "I'll send a courier by within the hour to provide you with documentation of his demise. Unless Estévez asks for it, don't provide it. It could sound too much like you're trying to put out fires where none exist."

Ortega agreed.

"Otherwise," the SAC said, "stay put until I send the documents."

"Where? If I go back to my apartment, I'm—"

"You have to go back to your apartment, Ron. You can't let anyone know you know what's happened. If O'Connor or Estévez figures out you know something, you're dead no matter where you go."

The agent knew the SAC was correct. If O'Connor figured Ortega knew where everything stood, all bets were off, and the agent would spend the rest of his life, however short, looking over his shoulder.

"It's a cinch O'Connor isn't working for Estévez," the SAC said.

"Yeah, I figured that too. If he was, he could've fed me over early on."

"He's working for someone else. Maybe Torres."

Ortega agreed. "That's when things began to hit the fan."

"You've got to be on your guard. Let me know when and where you go."

Ortega agreed.

"And by the way, it's probably time for you to go armed."

"I've got my Glock at the apartment."

The SAC shook his head. "No good. That's government-issued. If any of these guys are worth the alcohol in their cologne they'll know where the gun came from." He handed the brown paper bag to Ortega. "Take it. It's DEA-issued, but untraceable."

Ortega took the bag.

"Keep it with you at all times, Ron, and trust no one." The SAC glanced around. "There are two extra magazines in the bag. That's forty-five rounds, total. If you get into a firefight and need more than that, you're in a jam."

"It can't get much worse," Ortega quipped. "I'm already in a jam."

CHAPTER *Fifty-One*

Ortega returned to his apartment with a Beretta 9mm pistol tucked under his shirttail. He had the two magazines in his left hip pocket. When he entered, he drew the gun and carried it in his right hand. Except for the gentle hum of the air conditioner, the apartment was quiet. And dark. He had left the window shades drawn when he and Jimmy had left earlier.

He moved through, relying on his senses for any indication an intruder might be lurking inside. Windows, patio door, closets—under the bed—nothing seemed out of place. Even the bag of specially blended Colombian coffee Estévez had sent remained on the counter where the agent had left it earlier that day.

Satisfied his castle had not been violated, but still on edge and unable to relax, he slid the gun into his waistband. He went into the living room and took out his cell phone.

His wife picked up right away.

"How are things?" he asked.

"I'm doing okay," she said.

In the years he had known her, before and during their marriage, he had always found the sound of her voice soothing, a contrast to the vociferous noise of the bullpen in which he functioned. But he also knew when something wasn't right. Her voice was a sure barometer.

"What's wrong?" he asked.

She sighed. "The insurance company is saying we're not covered for the leak. I had to go ahead and call a cleanup crew to dry us out and haul the old machine away."

"How much?"

She told him.

"I can't believe this," he said, teeth grated. "I'm busting my tail for this country and I'm going deeper in the hole with every step."

"We'll be okay," she said. "It's only money."

He couldn't believe his ears.

"Only money?"

"I didn't have a choice, Ron. I couldn't find you when the bill came due, so I—"

"Money doesn't grow on trees, Libby. At least not for guys like me."

"I know it doesn't grow on trees," she said, her voice getting sharper. "I'm not saying it does. But you asked, so I told you. It wiped out our savings and we're still going to need a new washing machine."

He could feel the heat rising. "So what do you want me to do?"

"Nothing. I want you to be safe and come home as soon as—"

"Because there isn't too much I can do, Libby. I'm not a wealthy man. I do the best I can."

"I know."

The apartment was suddenly quiet. And warmer.

"I can't believe this," he said, again. "I really can't."

"Ron, we'll be okay."

"The air conditioner just went out."

"No, it didn't," she said. "It's fine."

"I'm talking about here, Libby," he said. He wanted to lash out. To let her know that her problems weren't the only issues he had to deal with. He felt like a man trapped in a bottle where the air was rapidly disappearing.

"The doctor told me the baby is doing fine," she said, changing the subject. "It may even come a bit early."

Early? He could have done without that bit of information. What was wrong with her? Couldn't she understand he was under intense pressure—risking his life for their future? Why did she keep piling it on?

"I could've done without that, Libby," he said, allowing anger to seep into his voice.

"I thought you'd want to know. That you'd want some good news."

"You thought I'd want to know the baby is coming sooner than expected? That's good news? By what measure of normal human understanding could that be considered good? Don't you know I feel bad enough as it is I can't be there? And now you're telling me I may not be there for the—"

"Ron, calm down—please," she said, her voice beginning to break. "I didn't think that—"

"That's just the point, Libby," he said. "You didn't think. You never think. Your whole world, *everything* in your whole world, is about Libby. I'm sorry, I really am, that you're having such a bad day. That the washing machine conked out, that the savings are gone, that the car isn't working, that you still don't have a new washer, and that the baby is coming so early I can't possibly get there in time. But I'm doing the best I can. And if that isn't good enough, maybe you should've married someone who could provide you with the lifestyle you seem to need."

"Now just a minute," she said, her voice quivering more from anger than hurt. "*You're* the one who volunteered for this job. And you knew when you did it that we had a baby coming. If you can't be here, it certainly is no fault of mine. I can't unring a bell. The baby is coming, and it's coming when God is ready for it to come, regardless of how it interferes with your job."

"Couldn't you have kept it to yourself? Just a little longer?"

"Keep the birth of our baby *to myself?*" He could read her voice clearly.

"Not only that," he continued, "but do you have to tell me about the washing machine, the insurance problems, the—"

"You *asked,* Ron. I didn't offer. *You asked.*"

"I shouldn't have. I shouldn't have called."

"Then why did you?"

He sighed and ran a hand over his face. His own anger had not subsided—had not been erased by the pain he had caused her.

"I don't know," he said. "I really don't."

CHAPTER *Fifty-Two*

Ortega had been given the okay to report to work late. Although Chipper didn't understand it, she knew enough to ignore it, especially when Estévez had approved it himself.

But as the hour came nearer, the agent fidgeted over what he would tell Estévez when he asked how the interrogation of the Mexican had gone. He was reluctant to make up a story if the DEA had already planted news that would cause him to contradict himself, but he also knew Estévez would want to know something and wouldn't wait until Ortega got the right answers from his superiors. His *other* superiors.

He waited another half-hour before deciding he could wait no longer. He dressed and slipped the Beretta into his waistband before standing in front of the mirror. From what he could see, the emerald-green vest adequately covered the butt of the gun. Given the low light in the club, he reasoned the weapon would be virtually invisible.

He grabbed his keys and reached for the door when the phone rang. It was the SAC.

"In your mailbox, " he said and hung up.

The SAC had provided Ortega with a cover story rather than pictures. At first, the young agent was angered. A story was no documentation at all. But after reflection he decided the SAC had been correct.

Doctored photos of a murdered Santiago would, by their very nature, invite requests to see the body. Or at the very least, tell the location of the body. Any such request would lead to more problems. But the SAC's proposed story—that the agent had invited the Mexican to go fishing and had then killed him, tossing his weighted body into the Atlantic—was a far better one. It was impossible to dredge the Atlantic for the body. And when Santiago didn't come around or show up in his usual places, the story would be accepted as the truth without further question. Any challenges to Ortega's standing within the organization, or to his loyalty, would be quelled.

The Cuban drove to The Oasis in his new car, pacing his time by his new watch. His concern over O'Connor's possible defection caused him to consider his friends on the "wrong" side of the law to be more dependable than his friends on the "right" side. On the one hand O'Connor was warning Ortega about the snares of undercover work, honing in on the Rolex as an example, but on the other hand, he was crossing over to the dark side himself. At least with Estévez and his crew, Ortega knew where he stood. They never crossed over. Ever.

The agent parked in the fenced *EMPLOYEES ONLY* lot. A large crowd had already formed in front of The Oasis. As he emerged from the cocoonlike silence of the Lexus, he was immediately enveloped in the white-hot beat of the music wafting out of the club. The place was alive, and Ortega's spirits were instantly lifted. He smiled and waved at Bernie, the big black man who was working the ropes, before going in the side entrance.

Inside, the place was going at full throttle. The mostly young upwardly mobile patrons were having a good time. He had to elbow his way through the room.

Before going to the bar, he punched the time clock in the employees' lounge, off the same hallway as Estévez's office. A quick peek inside revealed that neither Estévez nor Jimmy were at the club yet. Their absence was worrisome. He had wanted to let them know of Mikey's demise and stay as close to them as possible. If there were any chance of discovering who it was that O'Connor had aligned himself with, it would most likely come through Ortega's relationship with Estévez.

After clocking in, he went straight to the bar and began serving the customers, engaging in small talk, bar jokes, the usual banter. Although he said hi to Chipper several times during the busy first hour, she seemed unusually aloof.

"You okay?" he asked as soon as there was a break in the rush.

"Yeah, I'm fine."

Even though he had only known her for a short time, he could tell she wasn't being truthful. It was, after all, the second time in a single day he had clashed with a woman.

"Something's up," he said. "Give."

She had been wiping the glasses clean as she slid them into the rack overhead. She tossed the towel onto the bar and turned to Acuna. Her expression was flat.

"You told me you're an alcoholic," she said.

"I am."

"Then why did you have a drink the other night?"

He started to speak, but stopped. He stifled his excuse with a shrug. "Trying to fit in, I guess."

She studied him. "It just takes one, Ron. One drink and you're off the wagon."

"I'm not off the wagon," he said.

"That's how it starts. That's how it got started in the first place, wasn't it? Trying to fit in? Trying to belong? To be one of the crowd? The boys?"

"So I…was wrong, I guess."

"You guess?" She looked around and leaned forward. "I like you, Ron Acuna. I don't want you to mess up." She leaned close enough to allow her lips to touch his ear. "We could have something together, Ron. But not if you go back to the bottle. Been there, done that. I won't do it again."

He agreed with her. And he was surprised by his reaction. He *could* have something good with Chipper. The woman was stunning. In the low light and the ambiance of people who were free of their cares, he wanted very much to kiss her. To pull her against him. To bury his fight with Libby in the arms of another woman.

CHAPTER *Fifty-Three*

The club closed at three a.m. on a high note. The register was full and, uncharacteristically, no one had been asked to leave.

As the last patron exited, Chipper and her crew were putting away glassware and unused cases of liquor. Ortega was mopping the floor behind the bar and noticed Estévez, Jimmy, and another man he'd never met enter the club. Jimmy hooked a finger at Ortega.

"I think Mr. Estévez wants to see me," he said to Chipper.

"Go ahead. I think we can close it up from here," she said.

He placed a hand on her arm. "Are you sure?"

"I'm sure," she said.

Ortega followed the three men into Estévez's office. The club owner was wearing a tailored, cream-colored suit with brown shoes, a white shirt, and silk tie. He pulled the jacket off and tossed it onto the sofa before sinking into it with a sigh.

The other two, Jimmy and a man he introduced as Tony Guerrera, were dressed in slacks and polo shirts. Jimmy sat behind Estévez's desk while Guerrera sat on the other sofa.

"Have a seat, Ron," Estévez said, motioning to a spot next to him as he loosened his tie.

"Anybody want a drink?" Jimmy asked.

Estévez ordered a scotch and soda and Ortega ordered the same. Guerrera ordered a Bloody Mary. Jimmy placed his order along with the others into the phone.

"How did it go with Mikey?" Estévez asked, crossing his legs.

"Not well," Ortega said.

The Cuban raised an eyebrow. "Oh?"

"Mikey knew the arrangement. He knew the plan and he knew the reason. He knew a lot more than I thought he did." Ortega nodded toward the enforcer. "Jimmy said if I thought Mikey was behind the ambush I should take him out." Ortega crossed his legs and threw one arm over the back of the sofa. "So I did."

Estévez sighed and ran a hand over his face. "The reason for you to interrogate him was to find out who he talked to, Ron. Did you get that information or did you just do him?"

Ortega had become so involved in getting rid of Mikey that he had forgotten the reason for the meeting with the street hustler in the first place.

"He wouldn't talk," Ortega said lamely.

Estévez shook his head. "All men will talk eventually. Didn't you take the time to work him over?"

Ortega admitted he hadn't.

"We didn't send you out on a hit, my friend," Estévez said. "We sent you out to get information."

Ortega's inexperience was beginning to reveal itself. In his haste to secure Mikey and further raise his stock with Estévez, he had dropped the ball.

"He said he didn't talk," Ortega said, feeling the stares of the others. "But he did know enough to make him credible as the leak. Even if we never find who he talked to, we know he knew too much."

Estévez looked at Jimmy. The Italian shrugged.

"Too late now," he said. "What's done is done."

"Where is he?" Estévez asked.

"At the bottom of the Atlantic."

Looks of resignation crossed the faces of the others.

"What's wrong?" the agent asked.

"We don't think Mikey did anything wrong," Jimmy said.

"But now we'll never know for sure," Estévez said.

Ortega was dumbfounded. "He seemed good for it. He set up the—"

"Forget it," Estévez said. "Like Jimmy said, what's done is done."

"How do we know he didn't do anything?"

Estévez was about to speak when the door opened and Chipper entered, carrying a tray with four drinks. She passed the liquor out and left without saying a word and without looking at Ortega.

Guerrera said, "I've been watching Kingman for the past several weeks. Mr. Estévez wanted me to be sure nothing happened to the man."

"I asked Tony here and another guy to watch him, Ron, and be sure he remained untouched by the attacks the rest of us were experiencing. If anything developed, Tony and Stoneman were to prevent them."

"Stoneman?" Ortega asked.

"Alan Stoneman," Guerrera said. "He's watching Kingman now. We take shifts."

Jimmy joined the others by sitting next to Guerrera.

"As long as Kingman skated through all of this unscathed, it would lend credibility to our contention that the attacks on the rest of us were springing from him," Guerrera said.

"So you're saying he really *isn't* making a move into Cuba?"

Estévez shook his head. "On the contrary, he *is* trying to move into Cuba. He has been to Havana on several occasions. His most recent trip was two days ago." Estévez tasted the scotch and soda, wrinkled his nose, and tasted it again. "The man is planning on moving into Cuba as soon as he can. But he isn't interested in drugs."

"He'd have to fight the Colombians on that," Guerrera said. "Just like we've had to fight them here."

"Kingman isn't interested in blow," Estévez said. "He's looking to move into entertainment."

"Entertainment?" Ortega asked.

"Women, gambling, things like that. Kingman is thinking he will profit off the euphoria that will inevitably come when the government in Cuba is solidified and things settle down," Estévez explained.

"Won't that leave everything intact here then?" Ortega asked.

Estévez shrugged. "Sure. If you're happy with that. I'm not." He took another sip of his drink.

"But the others are," Ortega said. "So that's why they've been so reluctant to get involved."

Jimmy had been drinking silently during the conversation. As he set his empty glass on the coffee table, the ice clinked.

"No, they're not," Estévez said. "I'll admit they were, but that has all changed.

Now that they understand what Kingman is up to, they understand what can be lost."

"If not in the short run," Guerrera said, "certainly in the long."

"The others needed a wake-up call. They needed something to jar them from their slumber," Estévez said, pausing to finish his drink. "They became content. Satisfied. They didn't see that the lion was upon them until it was nearly too late."

"And even then," Guerrera said, "we had to show them how vicious he was."

"It's the American way," Estévez said, with a grin. "No one wants to fight until it's nearly too late."

"What does all of this have to do with Mikey?" Ortega asked.

"Torres met with Kingman a couple of times yesterday," Guerrera said. "It's the first time I've seen him come around."

"So we used Mikey to set Torres up with the law when, in fact, he may have been working with Kingman all along?"

Estévez pursed his lips and nodded. "Looks that way."

Ortega sighed. All of his effort to sweep Mikey off the street had been for nothing.

"Don't sweat it, Ron," Estévez said. "We all acted on the best information we had."

"The guys that jumped us," Jimmy asked, breaking his silence, "do they belong to Torres?"

"We don't know for sure," Estévez said. "It's probably reasonable to assume they do, but it's probably also reasonable to assume that some of them were hired in."

"I still think Deets and Highsmith are good for it."

Estévez ignored Caltabiano's remark.

"So where do we go from here?" Ortega asked.

"We arrange a meeting with the others," Estévez said. "We tell them what we know." He turned to Jimmy. "Set it up for late morning tomorrow."

"Okay."

"Won't that trigger the war we're trying so hard to avoid?" Ortega asked.

Estévez shrugged. "It'll trigger Torres's death, but it won't be much of a war. The idea behind your plan was to let the law take him down so the others would assume it was part of the current crackdown." He paused to extract a cigar from the humidor. "And that may still happen. After all, they have Dowd and

Hurst, the coke, and the information Jimmy planted on them." He reached for the dolphin lighter and held the flame to the end of the cigar, puffing until it was fully lit. "But the landscape has changed for us." He set the lighter down. "Someone tried to kill you guys. You specifically, Ron. No one knew Jimmy and Frankie were going to be there."

Estévez was right. No one knew that Jimmy or Frankie would be on site. But O'Connor knew that Ortega would be there. And that meant the agent's lifeline was nothing of the kind.

CHAPTER *Fifty-Four*

The meeting in Estévez's office didn't last long, but it ended better than it could have, given Ortega's failure. He chided himself for having missed the obvious. He knew his mistake had been born out of his eagerness to please Estévez, as well as his sudden and pressing need to get Mikey off the street. But he also knew his inexperience had been at the root of it all, and that was what cut him most deeply.

When he left Estévez's office and crossed the dance floor, he saw Chipper sitting at one of the tables with her green vest in her hand and her purse over her shoulder.

"Can you give me a lift?" she asked. "My car won't start."

"Sure. But maybe it's the battery. I can check it if—"

She wrinkled her nose. "Bernie already tried that. It just won't start."

Ortega nodded. "Okay. I'm parked in the lot."

He led the way across the lot to his new Lexus.

"This yours?" she asked.

"Yeah. Just got it."

"Nice. Really…nice."

He opened the passenger-side door for her. Once she was settled, he got in and she gave him directions to her apartment.

"What do you do?" she asked as he backed out of the lot.

"I tend bar," he said, with a look of confusion. "In fact, I work for you. Or have you forgotten already?"

Despite the hour and the fact that most of the clubs were either closed or in the process of closing, traffic along the famous Miami strip remained heavy. He waited at the exit for an opening.

"No, Ron. You tend bar, but you work for Mr. Estévez."

He turned to look at her. Concern was etched on her face. "We all do," he said. "Directly or indirectly."

"That's not what I mean, and you know it."

He pulled from the lot and tried to focus on the moving flow and ignore her penetrating stare. But the woman knew more about Estévez's operation than he had hoped, and he knew he had been naïve to believe otherwise.

He sighed. "You've been at the club long enough to know things aren't what they appear."

"Yes."

"And that means you know what goes on."

"I've known for a long time," she said. "Guys like Jimmy, Frankie, Guerrera, and others aren't hanging around in Mr. Estévez's office until all hours for no reason."

"And what about you?" he said, steering the conversation away from himself. "What do you do?"

She rested her elbow on the door frame and her chin on her hand. She was silent for a few moments, content to watch as the world passed by. "Remember when you said things aren't what they appear?"

He passed the car ahead of him. "Yes."

"And do you remember when I was tending bar at the party?"

"Yes."

"That's what I do, Ron. I go to parties."

He turned to her.

"I'm a party girl. Or at least I was. Now I belong to Estévez when he wants me, and to anyone else when he doesn't."

Ortega felt sick. He hadn't seen this coming…at all.

"Do you understand?" she asked.

"Yeah, I guess." He turned back to watch the road and tried to not look back at her. He didn't want her to see his disappointment. "And the boat? Was that…?"

"No. That was strictly work. But I don't have to do it. I can leave if I want—if *you* want."

He did want. He had liked the girl from the beginning. Found her attractive, fun, and more than a little alluring. To deny those feelings would be dishonest. And he was tired of living a lie.

"I do want you to."

She leaned across the center console and kissed the agent's cheek.

"How long have you been…" he paused. The balance of the phrase would be too cold, harsh.

"Since I began working for Mr. Estévez," she said.

Mister. She called a man she had slept with *Mister.* What was it about Estévez that he engendered such respect? How did he inspire such loyalty?

"It began as a way to entertain his guests. *Special* guests. But as time went on, the visits became much less frequent and eventually Mr. Estévez began to—"

"I don't really want to hear this," he said, pulling into the complex.

"I'm sorry, Ron. I like you. I like you a lot. Ever since I saw you for the first time."

"Why do you do this?" he asked. "You could do anything you want." He worked the car around the U-shaped entryway and back to the rear of the complex.

"I want to be a nurse someday. Probably sounds silly. Just a dream, I guess. I've been saving to go to school."

"There are loans," Ortega said, aware of the anger in his voice. "Grants, scholarships."

"I didn't qualify for a scholarship and I was turned down for grants. Loans seemed the only way I could go, but that would leave me with more debt than I could handle."

He glanced at her. Saw her wipe a tear from her cheek with the back of her hand.

"So when I began tending bar it was to put money away so I could go to school. In a place like The Oasis, the tips are always good."

"Did Estévez make you manager of the bar because of your…other activities?"

She nodded. "Yes. I was making too much money, so to avoid rousing suspicion in the others he gave me the position."

"But the position didn't exist until he gave it to you," Acuna said.

"Yes."

"But the money from tips and tending wasn't enough."

"No, it wasn't. But the extra money came in handy." She turned to face Ortega as he parked in front of her building. She put a hand on his arm. "I haven't been foolish with it. I've been putting it away. I've almost got enough to pay for my education."

He killed the engine. The car was silent. Her hand remained on his right arm. He put his left hand on top of hers. "I want you to get out of there. I want you to leave with me."

She squeezed his arm and gave him a thin smile. "I'll tell Mr. Estévez tomorrow. I'll—"

"No. Don't tell him at all. Just go. Go tonight. Pack your things and take whatever money you've got and go."

She withdrew her hand and shrank back against the passenger door. "I can't do that. He's been good to me. If I—"

Ortega snorted. "Good to you? He's using you."

"He didn't make me do anything. I did it because I needed the money."

"And now you know too much."

She shook her head. "No, I—"

"Yes, Chipper. You know too much, whatever it is." He turned in his seat and clasped her face with both hands. "You've been around him too long. You can't just walk away." He wanted her to be afe. "I'm leaving too. We can have a great life together," he lied. "Just go. Call me and I'll join you."

She smiled. "I'll go back to Louisville. I'll call you as soon as I get there."

He kissed her, glad to have her safe.

CHAPTER *Fifty-Five*

Ortega arrived at his apartment at four a.m. He was awakened by a phone call at four-forty-five. It was the SAC.

"O'Connor is dead."

Ortega swung his legs out of the bed. "When?"

"We don't know for sure, but we suspect early this morning. Some beach strollers found him."

"Murder?"

"What do you think?"

"How?"

"Get dressed and meet me at Sunny Isles beach. Know it?"

Ortega rubbed his limited sleep from his eyes. "Yeah. Bayview to 194th."

"See you there."

Ortega met the SAC at the surfline. A couple of klieg lights had been set up by the crime-scene investigators and the boss was in the lighted area, talking to a uniformed officer taking notes. O'Connor's body was lying facedown in the surf.

"Took a shot to the head," the uniformed police officer was saying as Ortega approached. Rojas vouched for Ortega and the officer handed the SAC a plastic evidence bag. O'Connor's credentials were in it. "This guy was set up," he said.

"Somebody out for this guy?" the cop asked. "Because this looks like a hit."

He pointed with his pen. "His car is parked up there and he walked down here. Looks like he was meeting someone. My guess is that whoever it was set him up."

Ortega knelt by the body. O'Connor's skin was pale in the harsh light. A large-bore hole was in the back of his matted hair. His head was partially turned and Ortega could see that part of his face was missing.

"It could've been anyone," the SAC said. "He might have been meeting an informant. I'll pull his case files and let you know what we find."

"Not me," the cop said. "Give it to the detectives. I just find them. I don't solve them."

"He was expecting trouble," Ortega said. "He's wearing his holster, ammo pouch, and another holster. An ankle holster."

"We've got his weapons," the officer said. "Neither has been discharged."

SAC thanked the officer and told him he'd be in touch with the detectives.

Walking back to the pier, Ortega asked, "Why didn't you tell him what we know?"

"That O'Connor is dirty?"

"Well, yeah, for starters. Whoever did this is probably the same guy—or guys—who tried to kill me."

The SAC shook his head. "We don't know that for sure, Ron. But when we do, I'll tell them. Until then, let them work it as a homicide."

Ortega couldn't think. He was tired. His eyes felt as gritty as the sandy pier beneath his feet. "Were you able to get anything out of Santiago?"

"We've grilled him all day. Once he realized we're the only real friends he has, he loosened up."

Ortega was surprised. Men like Santiago survive by playing their cards close to their vest. The fact he was willing to talk meant he fully understood his situation. It also meant the man could change. He could alter a lifetime code of conduct, what the Mafia used to refer to as *omertá*—the code of silence—and work with the people who could save his life. That alone said a lot about Mikey.

"Has he said anything? Anything I can use?"

"He's telling us he really has no idea what's going on. If there are any hits on anyone, he doesn't know about them."

"What about Kingman? What's he know about him?"

"Only that the man is seriously ill and is working hard to hold his organization together for his son." The SAC sighed. "Someone's out for you, Ron. O'Connor's dead and that means whoever took him out may be gunning for you too."

Ortega shook his head. "O'Connor was the one gunning for me. He was the one who set up the hit on Dowd and Hurst—and me."

"I don't think we can say that for sure," the SAC said. "Remember, both of you guys are on the same team. That makes you enemies of the same guys."

Ortega nodded toward the beach. "That guy and I are not on the same team. He rolled over. He was playing for the other side."

"I think we can assume your cover is blown. Someone knows who you are."

"I'm not coming in yet."

"It isn't up to you, son."

"I'm asking you to hold off," the agent said, "for a little while longer."

The SAC leaned against his car and folded his arms. He studied his agent.

"Just a little bit longer," Ortega said. "I've given you the recordings and you have my reports. Let me finish the job."

The SAC began to speak. Ortega cut him off.

"Wouldn't it be nice to catch all of these guys in their own net? We would have murder charges, conspiracy charges, drug peddling, you name it. If we can get Estévez and his crew and the others too, wouldn't that make it worth it? Besides, we don't know who O'Connor was working for. We don't know who had their claws in him or how far they go."

The SAC sighed. "Okay." He pointed his finger into Ortega's face ."But this needs to end soon. And I mean *soon.*"

"It will. There's a meeting tomorrow morning. Things are beginning to move."

This new revelation cooled the SAC down. "Who's going to be there?"

"The others. Most of them, anyway. Torres won't be there since he'll undoubtedly be the topic of conversation, but I expect everyone else to be present."

"What time is the meeting?"

Ortega shrugged. "Late morning. Jimmy is supposed to call me."

The SAC refolded his arms and pursed his lips. "Okay. I want you in my office first thing."

"First thing?"

The DEA chief glanced at his watch in the light from the pier. "That'll be eight o'clock. Ninety minutes from now." He turned to open his car. "You better get some sleep. You look worse than O'Connor."

CHAPTER *Fifty-Six*

Agent Ortega was in the SAC's office by eight o'clock. His eyes were red and his hand trembled as he drank a cup of the secretary's coffee. The overbrewed sludge did little to compensate for lack of sleep.

The SAC was seated behind his desk. The USA was present, seated in the same chair he had been in during the previous meeting. Ortega was next to the attorney.

The stoic officers of the Broward County Sheriff's Department, however, had not been invited. Ortega knew the decision to keep them out of the loop would further serve to alienate him from the good deputies. But then, he didn't know who had their clutches on O'Connor or who else was on the payroll. The fewer who knew about the meeting, the better.

"What happened to O'Connor?" the USA asked.

"He's dead," the SAC said, matter-of-factly.

The attorney rolled his eyes. "I know that, Juan. *Why* is he dead?"

"Someone killed him."

Before the attorney could respond the SAC held up a hand.

"Look," he said, "the man worked for me. I knew him better than you. I introduced him to his ex-wife. But all I know for the moment is that he's dead and it looks like a hit."

"That means someone may be onto Eliot Ness, here," the attorney said, gesturing toward Ortega without looking at him.

The Cuban agent was tired. More than tired. He rose from his seat prepared to take the attorney off at the knees, when the SAC interceded for him.

"And it could have been an unrelated incident. O'Connor didn't spend all his time watching over Ron. The man had his own cases to work."

"And you're looking into them?"

The SAC sighed. "Yes, Dillon. I'm looking into them. At least I will be as soon as this meeting is over."

The government attorney glanced at Ortega, who was easing himself back into his chair. "I think we need to assume the worst. We need to assume this man's cover is blown."

"Or not," the SAC said.

"He's meeting with them this morning, isn't he?"

The SAC gave the prosecutor a weary "yes."

"Then this could be a sanctioned hit."

Ortega finally spoke. "The meeting is at ten. I heard from Jimmy just before I left my apartment. If this was a hit they'd just come to the apartment and do it. They've already had a thousand opportunities."

Since the first meeting at the beginning of the investigation, Ortega hadn't liked the United States attorney much and was sure the attorney felt the same way. The man made it clear he viewed Ortega with the same disdain a jogger held for people who walk their dogs in public parks.

"You'll be wearing a wire," the attorney said.

"A wire may get me killed," Ortega said.

The attorney snorted. "A wire or the case ends right now."

"You need to wear a wire, Ron," the SAC said. "It's not up for negotiation."

"I'm in pretty tight with this group, now," the agent countered. "If something happens where I could be exposed with the wire, I'm dead."

"We're trying to build a case, and without a wire we have much less to go on," the SAC added.

"And you know that, Agent Ortega," the attorney said. "Unless, of course, you have something to hide."

"Dillon," Rojas said, holding up a hand toward his agent, "we don't need any friction here. What we need is cooperation."

The attorney held up a hand of apology. "Someone in our own ranks knows something, Juan. O'Connor didn't exist in a vacuum."

"Did Caltabiano tell you who's going to be there?" the SAC asked Ortega, trying to steer the conversation away from personal animosities and back to the business at hand.

Ortega glared at the USA a moment longer before listing the names for his boss. Jimmy had told him who to expect, so Ortega was more specific than he'd been with the SAC at the pier.

"And where is this meeting to be held?" the USA asked.

"In Estévez's office," Ortega said without looking at the attorney.

"And where is that?" the attorney asked, condescendingly.

"In the back office of The Oasis," Ortega said.

"Is there a private access?" the SAC asked.

"Of a sort," the Cuban said. "There are two private doors leading into the club. One is located on the side of the building and is the one most often used by the employees. The second door is at the rear of the building. That door leads to a central hallway that leads to another hallway where Estévez's office is located."

"So there is no door that leads directly from his office to the outside?" the USA asked.

"No."

"That could make it hard to bust them if things start going sour," the USA said to the SAC.

"Bust them?" Ortega asked.

"That's what this is all about," the USA said. "We're all on the same side here, right?"

"Are we, counselor?" Ortega asked.

"We're all on the same side," the SAC said firmly. "And we're going to work together for the good of the public."

The United States attorney snorted and re-crossed his legs, turning his head slightly away from the Cuban agent.

"So what's this thing about a bust?" Ortega asked again.

The SAC folded his hands on top of his desk. "You're going to be wearing a live wire."

"What?" Ortega was incredulous. He rose out of his chair. "A live wire?"

"It's the only way," the SAC said.

"We only use a live wire in case of imminent danger. I'll be in no danger—at least not then."

"Ron, it's not open to discussion," the SAC said.

"You haven't had a problem with the recordings I've given you so far. Why do we—"

"Whoa, whoa," the USA said, suddenly sliding to the edge of his seat and staring at Ortega. "What's this about recordings?"

Ortega opened his mouth but was cut short by the SAC.

"I have them, Dillon."

"The larger question, Juan, is why don't I?" the attorney asked.

"I've been holding them until I thought we had enough to bring you into it," the DEA chief said.

"In case you haven't noticed, I'm already in it."

"I know," the SAC said.

"I'm the government's prosecutor here. This case doesn't go anywhere unless I say it does."

"I'm sorry, Dillon," the boss said. "I'll get everything to you. I didn't mean any disrespect."

The attorney glared at Ortega. "And you will wear the wire we tell you to wear. Got it?"

Ortega was about to unleash on the man when he noticed the SAC giving him a nod and a grin.

"Sure. Whatever you say."

CHAPTER *Fifty-Seven*

The meeting was to begin at ten. By the time Ortega arrived at nine-forty-five, all were present except for Jimmy.

Estévez was seated on the end of one of the sofas. Jiménez was on the opposite end, across from Lopez who sat on the facing sofa. Next to him was Delahoy, and next to him was the open seat Ortega took.

Estévez glanced at his watch. "Jimmy wants to be here. If it is okay with you gentlemen, can we wait for a few more minutes?"

The men indicated they could wait. Estévez caught Ortega's eye. The Cuban left his seat and went over to the club owner.

"See if Chipper can serve some coffee or something."

Ortega left the office and walked toward the bar. He had entered the club without noticing whether the woman was present or not. She wasn't. He felt relieved. Grateful she had taken his warning to heart. He returned to the office.

"She's not here," Ortega said quietly to Estévez. "Do you want me to make some?"

Estévez frowned. "That's not like her. She's never late." He kept frowning for a moment longer, then said, "Yes, go ahead, Ron. The good stuff is under the bar."

Ortega left the office. The wire he was supposed to wear had been replaced by the recording variety. After the meeting with the SAC and the USA, the DEA chief had had his agent fitted with a recorder rather than a live wire. It was the SAC's way of letting his man know he was behind him. But it was just as much a slap at the USA.

Ortega knelt behind the bar, found the custom-blended coffee, and measured it out. As it brewed, he found a large cocktail tray and loaded it with cups, creamer, various kinds of sweetener, and stir sticks. As the last of the coffee drained into the pot, he saw Jimmy enter the club through the side door. The man was dripping sweat and massaging his chest.

"Hey," Ortega said, startling the enforcer. "You're late."

The big Italian lumbered toward the bar and dropped himself onto a stool.

"You okay?" the agent asked.

Jimmy nodded slowly. "Yeah, I'm fine. Just a little short of breath, that's all."

Ortega was about to argue the point, when Estévez came out of his office. "Is the coffee ready?"

"It's ready," Ortega answered.

"Let's get started." The man didn't glance at his enforcer.

The meeting started as soon as the coffee was poured. Estévez spoke first.

"Gentlemen, Torres has joined forces with Kingman. This I know to be true."

"How, Ricardo?" Jimenez asked. "How do you know this?"

"As I have said in the past, my friend. I have my sources. But let it be plain to all of you." He turned to Jimmy.

Although the Italian continued to mop his brow, his color had returned. He told the men, "Ron Acuna, Frankie Gatto, and I were attacked by Torres's men. I can vouch for this, as can Ron. Frankie was killed."

The others in the room looked at each other with expressions of astonishment. It was Lopez who spoke next.

"Where did this attack occur?"

Ortega answered. "We discovered that police officers Dowd and Hurst were working on their own. They had been commissioned by Torres to flood the market with product. His product. And they were to offer it without charge." The others began to grumble.

"Gentlemen," Estévez said, holding up a hand, "I don't need to tell you how costly this type of blatant attack could be. It is hard enough to make a profit during this current crackdown without the market being pumped full of free product."

Lopez said, "What were your men doing?"

Estévez nodded to Jimmy.

"We were going to stop the delivery of free product by turning Dowd and Hurst over to the authorities. We contacted the two officers, told them where to find the stuff, and then took two kilos of our own and left it for them as bait," Jimmy said, lying with ease. "When the officers arrived on the scene, Dowd and Hurst began to battle them. Ultimately they were killed."

"You haven't answered my question," Lopez said. "Who shot at you?"

"Mr. Acuna, Frankie, and myself were up the hill from the arrest, when we suddenly came under fire from behind. As I said earlier, Frankie was killed, but we managed to escape with his body. We believe Deets and Highsmith were the shooters."

"And the cops just let you slide out of there?" Delahoy asked. "With all that gunfire going on behind you, they didn't ask questions?"

"They had their hands full too," Ortega said.

"So what do you want us to do, Ricardo?" Lopez asked.

"I want your permission to sanction a hit on Torres."

Delahoy sighed. Jiménez ran a hand across his face.

"Won't that cause more problems?" Lopez asked.

"Yes. But it will cause considerably fewer problems than an all-out war," Estévez said.

The faces of the men in the room showed they were divided on the strategy. Their alliance was still new, still untested. Estévez leaned forward and smiled reassuringly.

"Gentlemen, it is the only way. I am committed to our new partnership. I could act unilaterally against our enemy, but I am asking for your blessing. And," he stressed, "your blessing *only.* My men will carry out the hit. You will have no part in it. You will be free of any reprisals."

Delahoy, Jiménez, and Lopez's resistance seemed to relax. Their concern that they would somehow face the wrath of Kingman for the hit on Torres was allayed by Estévez's offer to take responsibility.

"You have our blessing, Ricardo," Lopez said. "But your source, the one that has kept you informed of these goings-on, should be watched."

Estévez said, "My source has not steered us wrong yet, my friend."

"Perhaps. But I have found that a mouth can always be bought. What is one man's violinist can be another man's trumpeter."

CHAPTER *Fifty-Eight*

The hit on Torres was quickly scheduled for later that evening and was to occur in Torres's home. Ortega was told to meet Jimmy and Tony at the club no later than eight o'clock. After calling in the information to his SAC, the agent got some much-needed sleep. He awakened at seven, tucked the Beretta into his waistband, and drove to The Oasis. Jimmy and Tony were waiting in Estévez's office. The club was in full swing.

During his conversation with the SAC, Rojas told Ortega that he and his men would be at the house prior to the hit. As soon as Ortega and the others arrived, the DEA and Miami PD would arrest Jimmy and Tony and the case would be shut down. Although this wasn't the way Ortega had envisioned the conclusion of the investigation, he understood his superior's concern. The hit could not go down as planned.

"Where's Mr. Estévez?" Ortega asked.

"He had some personal business to tend to," Jimmy said, looking better than he had earlier in the day.

Tony was loading 9mm cartridges into a magazine. When he was finished, he slammed the load into the butt of the gun.

"We ready?" Jimmy asked.

Both men indicated they were.

"Okay, then," the enforcer said. "Let's take care of business."

The three men left by way of the back door and slid into the unmarked panel van. Ortega drove. The wire he had worn earlier was still on him.

The Cuban pulled out and followed Jimmy's directions to South Dixie Highway.

"I've been watching and protecting this guy for weeks," Tony said. "Every night at this time he goes to Barrels."

"Barrels?" Ortega asked.

"A nightclub in Coconut Grove," Jimmy said. "But it has a restaurant too. Nice place. Good food. Great stone crab."

"He'll leave the club with his driver about nine o'clock," Tony said. "We can take them out and be home by ten-thirty."

Ortega felt his palms go moist. "I thought we were going to hit him at home."

"Yeah, that's what I know," Jimmy said. "But hard case here," he thumped Tony on the back of the head, "said he knows the mark's schedule better than anybody."

"Hey," Tony said, "I've been following this clown around for a long time. If Mr. Estévez wants this dude iced tonight, it's going to have to be in Coconut Grove. I'm telling you, that's where he's going to be."

For the next few minutes, the men were quiet. Ortega continued to work his way southwest along the highway. Ortega felt sick. Torres was going to be hit and there was nothing he could do to stop it. If he tried to intervene he would be killed. If he didn't intervene, Torres would be hit. And all of this would happen while the SAC and a team of officers were waiting patiently at Torres house. When they reached Coconut Grove Jimmy said, "Turn onto Grand Avenue. When you see the place, find a spot to park."

Ortega did as he was told. After making several go-rounds, he found a place to park less than a half block from the restaurant. He kept an eye on the street, hoping to see a squad car.

"Go ahead and scope it out, Tony," Jimmy said. "When they come out, we get it done and go home."

Tony left his gun in the van with Jimmy. He bolted across the street and went into the restaurant.

"How we going to do this?" Ortega asked.

"We?" Jimmy slid forward. "You ain't doing nothing. You missed your shot at Dowd. That's why we're in this mess now."

Ortega felt his back muscles tense. It was the first time he had experienced any problems with Jimmy.

Before Ortega could respond, Tony returned to the van.

"He's in there," he said, sliding into the front seat next to Ortega. "He's with his driver and they're just about finished."

"You got that right," Caltabiano said with a grin. "Now we just wait."

For the next twenty minutes the talk in the van was light—food, wine, women, vacation spots. There were no more remarks from Jimmy about Ortega's inadequacies.

"Here he comes," Tony said, breaking off the small talk. "And they're heading for the car." He screwed a silencer into his pistol's barrel.

"Start the engine," Jimmy said. "Spin this thing around in the middle of traffic. Cut them off before they cross the middle of the road."

Ortega started the van, looking for a squad car, as he floored the accelerator as it pulled away from the curb, and spun the wheel sharply to his left. The vehicle lurched in an ungraceful one-eighty in the middle of the street. Other drivers in traffic jammed on their brakes.

"Stop!" Jimmy yelled.

Ortega slammed his foot down on the brake pedal, stopping the van in the middle of Grand Avenue. Torres and his bodyguard were to the right. Tony fired two shots into Torres's driver and leaped out. He put the barrel of the gun to Torres's ear.

"Go! Get in!"

Jimmy slid the van's side door open and pulled the drug king into the vehicle. Tony climbed in after him.

"Go!" Jimmy yelled.

Ortega floored the accelerator, heaving the van forward through a red light, leaving traffic and shocked pedestrians behind. In his rearview mirror, Ortega could see the body of Torres's driver in the middle of the street. Still no squad car.

"What do you guys want?" Torres said, wide-eyed and breathing hard.

"We want to know what you know about Kingman," Jimmy said.

Tony kept his gun trained on the much older man, who was sitting askew on the rear seat.

"Hey," Torres said, catching sight of Caltabiano. "I know you. You were on the boat. You're with Estévez."

Jimmy slapped the man hard across the face. Torres reacted with wide-eyed surprise, holding his hand to his cheek. "I'm not working with Kingman. I don't—"

Jimmy punched the man in the face. "You had a chance to come in with us. Mr. Estévez extended every possible courtesy to you."

"What can I say?" Torres asked. "I'm not working with anyone. I'm just trying to make a living. I don't care what you guys do. I—"

Jimmy grabbed the gun from Tony and fired three shots into Torres.

"Here," Caltabiano said, passing the gun back to Guerrera.

"Why'd you do that?" Tony asked. "Now we'll never know."

"I was getting tired of his noise."

Despite the silencer, the gun's report left a ringing in Ortega's ears. "Where we going?" he asked Jimmy.

"Get us to the plant. We got to get rid of this guy."

CHAPTER *Fifty-Nine*

The ride to Crown Meats was quiet. Jimmy made a phone call and told someone to "meet us at the plant" before closing his eyes and leaning his head back. He remained relaxed, even nodding off as the van rocked him to sleep. Tony slid up to the front seat next to Ortega and drummed his fingers on the armrest as he watched the world pass by.

By the time they reached the packing plant, Jimmy was snoring. Ortega pulled up to the familiar dock. "We're here," he said, reaching behind his seat and shaking the big enforcer's knee as Tony jumped out of the van.

Caltabiano rose slowly from his seat. Ortega noticed that for the first time all day, the man was not sweating.

"Let's get this taken care of," the ex-cop said, working his ample frame out of the van.

Ortega jumped from behind the wheel. A man he had never seen before was approaching the van with a skid. Tony opened the rear door of the van.

"Take care of it, will you?" Jimmy asked.

The man said he would and asked Tony and Ortega to help. Tony pulled the dead crime king out of the van by his shirt collar and Ortega grabbed the corpse's ankles. For the second time since going undercover, the Cuban agent was assisting with the dismemberment of a body.

The three men hauled the body and skid onto the same elevator that had been used for Frankie. As Ortega was about to enter the elevator with Tony and the other man, Jimmy tapped him on the shoulder.

"You come with me," he said.

Ortega again felt the muscles of his back tighten. He followed the big man along the catwalk and down the steps to the floor of the plant. The place was vacant now, and the meat-cutting saw and the rotating carousel were silent.

Ortega kept an eye on Jimmy's hands as they entered the office. Any concealment of them could mean the big man was using his bulk to conceal the drawing of a weapon. But there were no suspicious moves. Jimmy dropped himself into the desk chair and motioned for the agent to have a seat in front of the desk.

"Sit," he said.

Ortega sat.

The office was small and simply furnished. The desk Jimmy sat at was gunmetal gray, with two file cabinets behind it and a computer and rolodex on top. A small table with an empty coffeepot and a stack of car magazines stood off to one side. A water cooler and coin-operated candy machine were near the door, which had a large window for the supervisor to keep an eye on the activities on the floor.

"What was all of that about back there, Jimmy?" Ortega asked.

"You'll know in a few minutes," Caltabiano said.

Something was up. Maybe the USA had been right after all. Maybe he should have worn a live wire.

Ortega sighed and tried to remain as nonchalant as possible. He reached for a magazine, but kept an eye on Jimmy's hands.

For the next few minutes neither man said a word while Jimmy ate a bag of peanuts he had gotten from the machine. A half hour had passed when Tony came into the office. He glanced at Ortega and nodded to Jimmy.

"Okay," Caltabiano said. "But I haven't heard anything yet."

Tony gave Ortega a second glance before dropping a few coins into the machine. As soon as a Three Musketeers bar dropped into the tray, he grabbed it and sat in the chair next to Ortega.

Jimmy glanced at his watch. It was nearly eleven o'clock. The enforcer had said everyone would be home by ten-thirty, which meant that whatever he was waiting on had not happened yet.

Ortega dropped the magazine onto the table and rose from his chair.

"Sit," Jimmy said.

"I'm going to get a candy bar," the agent said.

"Get him a bar," Jimmy said to Tony.

Guerrera went to the machine and dropped some change into the slot. "What do you want?"

"Same thing you had."

The man selected a second Three Musketeers and tossed it to him.

As the agent began to unwrap the bar, the man who had met them on the dock came into the office and looked at Jimmy. The enforcer shook his head.

Another ten minutes passed, along with one candy bar and two cups of water, before Jimmy's cell phone rang.

"Yeah?" he said. "Uh-huh. Okay. So that was it?" There was a pause. "We're here now, so we can take care of it. No reason to wait." Another pause.

Ortega saw Tony ease back in his chair, exposing his gun. The agent began to calculate his move. He would throw the cup of water in his hand at Tony. The sudden movement should give him time to draw his own weapon and fire. He would hit Tony first, the man at the door next, and then two shots into Jimmy before repeating the pattern. DEA agents were trained in tactical shooting—especially when their life depended on it. Hitting the other two men first would put them down, even if not out, until he could finish the third man with two shots. Then each of the first two men would get another round apiece. The plan wasn't foolproof—no plan is—but it was the best he had on short notice. He wasn't sure why he was suddenly suspect, but it was clear that whatever had gone wrong had gone wrong in a big way.

"Okay," Jimmy said. "We'll take care of it." He ended the call and slid the phone into his pocket. He looked at Tony and said, "It's okay. Acuna's clean."

"I could've told you that," the agent said, suppressing the fear in his voice.

"Yeah, sorry about that," Jimmy said. "But we know someone set us up. Deets and Highsmith didn't do it, so that left Mikey or you. Mikey's dead, so that leaves you."

"Mikey's dead because of me."

Jimmy nodded. "Yeah, I know. But that don't mean you didn't talk."

"You have some evidence I did?"

Jimmy grinned an *aw-shucks* grin. "No, not really. Circumstantial."

"You were planning on cutting me up too?" Ortega asked. He was angry. Very angry—and he didn't try to hide it.

"It's over. I'm sorry to have suspected you. Mr. Estévez is sorry."

"Is that why I got the car? To throw me off track? Make me think that—"

Jimmy held up a hand. "Like I said, it's over. Besides, we found the leak."

Ortega was confused. He ran the list of possible suspects through his mind and came up with the same list of names as Jimmy.

"That call was from Mr. Estévez. He took care of this one personally and then had to go back to the club to take care of some business there. He apologized for calling so late." Jimmy rose from the desk. "Can you get the skid?" he asked the unidentified man.

The man left the office.

"And can you guys take care of the body? It's in the freezer."

Tony climbed out of his chair and motioned for Ortega to follow him. Jimmy lumbered along behind, pausing long enough to get another bag of peanuts.

Tony reached the freezer first and opened the locker door.

Jimmy stood behind Ortega.

"When Lopez told us our source could be used against us as well as for us, that got Mr. Estévez to thinking," Jimmy said. "If our source turned on us there could be a lot of damage. Too much to repair. So Mr. Estévez checked it out. He's convinced we were betrayed." Jimmy shook some peanuts into his hand before slapping them into his mouth. "So we're going to have to hit the others and Kingman. Take our chances, you know?" He shook his head. "All because she turned on us."

"She?"

Jimmy nodded toward the freezer. "Chipper. She didn't show up today and Mr. Estévez caught her trying to leave town. That cinched it for him. Chipper was our source—and our traitor." He shook his head. "Ain't that just like a woman?" he said, as a peanut fell from his mouth and onto his shirt.

Ortega saw Tony drag the woman's frozen body through the door with a meat hook.

"Get her downstairs, will you guys?" Jimmy said. "I want to get out of here. This place is cold."

CHAPTER *Sixty*

Ortega knelt next to the van and vomited for the third time. His hands shook as he steadied himself by hanging onto the passenger-door mirror.

"I know you liked her," Jimmy said. "We all did. But she was hanging us out to dry."

Ortega struggled to breathe. Struggled to control himself. Struggled to keep from pulling his gun and killing the fat slob where he stood.

"Mr. Estévez used to loan her out. She'd sleep with guys we needed information from and bring back anything she'd hear. It's how we first caught on that Kingman is planning on making a run at Havana. She was our source." He patted Ortega on the back. "What'd you think? That we were making stuff up?"

Ortega struggled to keep from hurling again. He lost.

"She betrayed all of us," Jimmy added. "And then she was planning on leaving town. Mr. Estévez told me she didn't show this morning, and that was something she'd never done before. She must've known we were on to her." He laughed. "She was cleaning out her bank accounts. That girl had been socking it away for years. Solid evidence she knew the day would come when we'd find out what she'd been up to and she'd have to leave town in a hurry. And she had to know we were looking at you too. The girl wasn't dumb." He shook his head. "Nope. Not dumb at all. She was looking out for number one, kid. She had to know we were looking at you, while all along she was the problem. She was going to let us go after the wrong man while the right woman walked."

Ortega took a deep breath. Although the nausea had passed, tears began to sting his eyes. He fought to subdue them.

"She was calculating, cold. We even found out that she had bought herself a plane ticket to Louisville this morning. When Mr. Estévez went to talk with her he saw it lying right out in the open. He could see she wasn't sick so that left one explanation. He got the rest of it out of her the hard way."

"Wasn't there another way of handling it?" Ortega asked, in a choked voice.

"How would that be, kid? Huh? If we just ignore it, we're dead. If we slap her on the wrist, she gets mad and switches allegiances to where we can't get at her. I've seen it happen before." He shook his head again. "You can't glad-handle traitors. You've got to deal with them and you've got to deal with them in a way that sends a message. Just like you did with Mikey. He was a traitor." He paused to shrug. "Of course, we didn't know at the time that he wasn't, but for all intents and purposes, he was. So you iced him. And it doesn't take long before the word gets out." He gestured toward the plant. "Those two guys in there. You think they aren't wondering about her? They know she was hung in the freezer. Now, before they ever think of doing the same thing, they'll remember her. And that means they'll think twice."

"Estévez let her freeze to death?"

Jimmy put a hand on the agent's shoulder. "Look, he had to do what he had to do. He liked her too. And he liked her in a way you didn't. But business is business. She knew that. And she chose the wrong side. It could've been worse. He could have told you to do her."

Ortega rose to his feet and gave Jimmy a hard stare.

"I know you're mad," Caltabiano said. "And if I was new like you, I'd be mad too. I was mad when Pablo got killed and I wanted revenge. And I wanted it bad. But Mr. Estévez taught me to take the long view. It was a hard pill to swallow and it didn't go down easy. But I learned to get past it, and I learned that Mr. Estévez was right." He paused to pop a stick of gum into his mouth. "And you'll learn to get past it too."

CHAPTER *Sixty-One*

Ortega was in no shape to drive, so Guerrera drove, taking Jimmy and the agent back to The Oasis. By the time Ortega reached his apartment, he was approaching meltdown. Chipper had died as a direct result of his advice to leave now. And she had died in a meat locker, symbolic of the value Estévez had placed on her.

The Cuban vented his rage. He punched holes in the walls. He smashed the TV and kicked it across the room, where it landed in a mound of faux cabinetry and glass.

He pulled the mattress from his bed. And then he sobbed. And he sobbed uncontrollably. And still the pain wouldn't subside.

Like a film loop in which the scenes repeat in a never-ending fashion, his mind replayed the drama. Chipper's smile. Their last conversation. Her concern over his drinking. Her desire to become a nurse…Her frozen body dragged out of the locker at the end of a hook.

The agent trembled with remorse. His hands shook as he sat alone in the smashed-up apartment. The place was quiet. But inside himself, he was at war.

Do the right thing? Or do the desired thing?

He had chosen the desired thing. And it was that knowledge, as much as Chipper's death, that drove him to tears again.

For yet another time in his life, he had chosen style over substance. Like the drinking he had once chosen over Libby, he had again chosen the vanishing things over the eternal.

The promotion, the title, the increased pay, the desk in his own office...all of these were nice on the surface, but they could never replace the love of Libby, his wife. Or the peace of God.

He had lost sight of the *real* goal, and people were dead because of it.

Estévez was a dealer in false dreams. He sold drugs to people who were searching for something—anything—to fill the void in their lives. He sold pain to people who needed healing. He sold despair to people who sought hope. And he sold misery to people who were searching for happiness.

Ortega jerked the Rolex off his arm to fling it across the room, when he noticed the inscription *RON ACUNA* on the back casing.

Ron Acuna? It was a lie. His name was *Ron Ortega.* But somewhere in his zeal to belong, to secure the better life, he had sacrificed the truth for the lie and had begun to see himself in terms that fit his new world. He could easily have *become* Ron Acuna. In his quiet moments he had even begun to see himself as the mythical character he sold to Estévez and his men. And with Chipper—yes, they could have had something. Ron Acuna could have stepped across that line and found what passed for success in Ricardo Estévez's world. He had somehow gotten to the point of living with one foot in each of the two worlds. How easily it could have been to move that one foot over to the life Estévez had promised him.

Before he accepted this assignment, he had thought he was secure from temptation. Able to see Satan and his tactics coming a mile away. But his nemesis had not approached with fangs bared. He had come with offerings extended. An angel of light, offering the desires of his victim's heart. He had come as beauty in an ugly world.

Ortega threw the watch against the wall.

He knew that his wavering commitment had left him open and unprotected. Without the means to resist, he had succumbed as so many before him had. He had chosen the desired thing over the right thing. And in tasting the sweetness of sin, he had allowed Satan to gain a foothold. That was all it had taken. The pleasure had lasted for a season. But now Chipper was dead, and the consequences of his choices would last a lifetime.

He buried his face in his hands.

He hadn't seen it coming. He'd expected that if he fell, he would *fall.* But it hadn't been a fall at all. Instead, it had been a steady decline. A decline he had willingly participated in and initiated by choosing the desired thing over the right thing. Like Estévez's patrons, who took the first hit of his free coke without concern, so too had he taken the first hit of success in a world he could never be happy in.

Other loops of film played now in his memory. The time when Jimmy was scalding Mario, and later, during the beating of Hoppity-T, when Ortega had fought to restrain himself from stopping the violence and blowing the case. And then tonight, he had been the wheel man for an event that resulted in the deaths of two men. And yet his concern had been over Jimmy's attitude toward him.

He wept again.

He had left his wife alone to deal with their problems...*their* problems... any way she could, and then had reamed her out for the way she did it. And while she was struggling to keep things together at home, he had been slowly falling for another woman. A woman who was not his to have.

He lowered himself to his knees. The gun still tucked into his waistband pulled at him, made him aware of its presence. It would be so easy to escape this guilt now. But that would mean choosing the desired thing over the right thing. No, there was a better way. For Ron Ortega sensed another presence. One that offered the only true way to the peace he sought. The agent could sense the whisper of God's Spirit as He brought to the agent's mind another story of betrayal. A man who had denied his Master, not once, but three times. A man who, after that betrayal, found a restoration that took him to a far better future than he no doubt had imagined for himself.

And Ron Ortega began to pray. He prayed that God would forgive him and restore him to the man he was meant to be. It was the only thing he knew to say. And praying for God's strength was all he knew to do.

CHAPTER *Sixty-Two*

The phone rang at precisely seven a.m. Ron Ortega raised his head from his facedown position on the floor.

The apartment was a mess—things shattered, scattered, and broken.

He rubbed his eyes and crawled to the couch, where he saw the phone cord peeking from underneath. He grasped it and began to pull, finally dragging the base and the receiver into view.

"Yeah?" he croaked into the phone.

It was Jimmy. "Get your tail to Mr. Estévez's house. We got hit last night."

Less than an hour later Ortega drove up the winding driveway to the mansion. He was met by Jimmy as soon as the car was parked. The Italian's face was pained and characteristically beaded with sweat.

"He's out back, Ron," Jimmy said. "He's not happy."

"What happened?"

"Someone torched two of our warehouses last night." He wiped his brow. "And Guerrera is dead."

Ortega paused. Even though he had become grafted into a world where life could be snuffed out as easily as a candle in the wind, he never ceased to be startled by it.

"Dead?"

"I went to the club this morning to clean out some of Chipper's things and I found the van in the lot. Someone had shot him through the windshield. His body was still behind the wheel and the engine was running." He shook his head. "It had to be after we left, and that was late."

"He was with us at the club last night," Ortega said, more to himself than to the enforcer.

"Yeah," Jimmy nodded, mopping his brow again, "Sometime after we left, somebody did him and left him there. I found him this morning and came here to tell Mr. Estévez. We found out about the warehouse fires on the news."

The two resumed their walk around the house, coming on the expanded view of the Atlantic. The horizon that had at one time seemed blurred, with ocean blending into sky, was now sharply defined. Ortega could clearly see the boundary that lay between heaven and earth.

Jimmy spoke in whispered terms. "There's going to be trouble over this. Big trouble."

"He says he doesn't want a war," Ortega said. "If he loses control and attacks someone now, there *will* be one for sure."

"We're past all of that now. He's angry and he isn't listening to me. Maybe you can talk some reason into him."

The two crossed onto the veranda. Estévez was wearing a floral-print Hawaiian shirt, white shorts, sandals, and shades. He was sitting on the seawall, staring blankly at the ocean. Caltabiano and Ortega paused.

"Chipper did more damage than we knew," Estévez said, without looking at either man. "She told someone about our efforts to paint Kingman into a corner. Someone hit us last night and hit us hard."

"I told Ron everything," Jimmy said. "You want something to drink?"

Estévez held up a bottle of Corona that had been hidden from view.

"Ron?" Jimmy asked.

Ortega shook his head.

"We have to act quickly," Estévez said, tipping the bottle to his lips. "We have to act broadly."

"You have an idea who's behind this?" Ortega asked.

"It's not Kingman."

"How do we know that?" Ortega asked.

"Because I had Stoneman on him. There hasn't been any activity at all. Nothing."

"He could arrange a hit with a phone call," Jimmy said.

Estévez cursed and threw the half-empty bottle at his enforcer.

Caltabiano ducked and the bottle passed overhead, landing on the flagstones, where it shattered. The Italian seemed unperturbed.

"I had his phone bugged, you idiot," Estévez said. "I didn't have Stoneman and Guerrera eavesdropping on him, I had them there to protect him. I had his phone tapped and used Chipper for pillow talk." He shook his head. "It was a good system till she got it into her head she could cut and run. Nobody does that with me. Nobody." He glared at Jimmy and Ortega.

Jimmy mopped his brow but said nothing.

"You think it's one of the others?" Ortega asked.

Estévez gave the agent a look of blunt disbelief. "Don't you?"

The club owner looked toward the ocean and sighed. It was the first time Ortega could recall seeing the man under duress. Or had it been there all along?

"I'm sorry, Jimmy," Estévez said.

Caltabiano acknowledged the apology. "Where do we go from here?"

Estévez turned to face Ortega and Jimmy. "We don't know which fish knows what, but we know which sea they swim in. We've been working on shutting Kingman down, pulling the alliance together, and eventually bringing The Corporation under one umbrella." He flashed a wry grin. "And of course, take Havana." He remained sitting on the wall with his feet dangling over the edge. His folded hands rested on his legs. "But that isn't going to happen now. The best we can hope for is to protect what we have, regroup, and return to fight another day."

Ortega was astonished he hadn't seen the shallowness of the man. The desire of Estévez's life, even at the risk of harm to himself and his family, was money, and the power that comes with it.

"Jimmy, we've got to take them out."

"Who?"

"All of them. Delahoy, Jiménez, and Lopez. It has to be one of them, and since we don't know who, we hit them all."

Jimmy shot a sideways glance at Ortega. "When?"

"As soon as you can set it up."

"Where do you want to meet?"

Estévez paused to think. "Let's get it done at the plant. Afterward we can dispose of the bodies and torch the place." He paused to think, before nodding to himself. "Yeah. That's the best way to do it. We've got to get rid of the bodies, torch the plant, and cut our losses."

"If you're going to torch the plant, why get rid of the bodies?" Ortega asked.

"Bodies will always be found, even in a fire. Since it's not only possible, but likely these men will tell someone where they're going, we need to be sure no evidence is found."

Jimmy said, "I can arrange to have Donnie there. He can cut them up, then—"

Estévez shook his head. "No. *Ground up.* Then I want the place to burn, Jimmy. I want it burnt to the ground."

CHAPTER *Sixty-Three*

Jimmy and Ortega walked back to the agent's Lexus without saying a word. When they reached the car, Jimmy put a hand on Ortega's shoulder.

"Go home and stay there. I'll arrange the hit and let you know when and where. You'll need to be there. It's for your own safety." He slid his hands into his pockets and shook his head. "The man is brilliant. I owe him everything. But I've never seen him like this. This whole Kingman thing is taking a toll."

"It's going to take a bigger toll on three men," Ortega said.

Jimmy grinned. "Most likely. But all of these guys know the score, Ron. We all do."

Ortega entered his apartment and frowned at the mess. Jimmy had told him to stay put and that meant he would have to do just that.

He picked up the phone and set it on the table next to the couch. Estévez had bugged Kingman's phone. The possibility he would tap Ortega's line had been considered by the DEA. The administration had placed safeguards on the line, which would notify them the minute it had been breached. They could then tell Ortega, who would exercise caution when speaking. Scramblers were not an option, since a coded signal would be as revealing about Ortega's true identity as a tapped phone conversation. The DEA had long ago tapped Estévez's line, but since the man also used safeguards, no evidence of wrongdoing ever came across the line, and the courts ordered the tap removed.

Ortega dropped onto the couch and called the SAC.

"A lot happened last night," Ortega told him. "Things are beginning to spin down."

"How so?"

Ortega told his boss about Chipper. He told him about the hit on two of Estévez's warehouses and the murder of Tony Guerrera. He reported the impending strike against Lopez, Delahoy, and Jiménez.

"Any idea when all of this is going down?"

"No. Maybe tonight. I was told to stay put until they call."

"Do it. Do what they say."

"I have to be there," Ortega said. "We all need to be there."

"Call me as soon as you know when and where the hit is to occur. I'll have a team of agents ready and we'll be nearby ahead of time."

"The hit is going down at Crown Meats."

"You sure?"

"Yes. I think he's going after Kingman next."

"Why?"

"I don't know. Gut feeling, maybe. He's taking out all of his enemies with one drop of the ax.

The SAC was silent for a moment. "That's all I need to know?"

"Isn't that enough?"

The boss ignored his question. "That means you'll need to wear a live wire. We'll be listening, and when things begin to heat up you'll need to give the word."

Ortega thought for a moment. "I'll say 'Chipper.' She ought to have some role in this bust."

"'Chipper' it is. I'll have the wire delivered to your mailbox. Anyone observing will see nothing more than a delivery service."

After ending the call, Ortega hung up and called his wife on his cell.

"Hi," he said.

She didn't respond the way he expected. She seemed to have forgotten their recent fight.

"I'm sorry," he said. "I'm sorry for what I said and why I said it."

"It's okay."

"No, it's not. But it will be. This thing is about to wrap up and then I'll be home." He wanted to tell her everything. About how he had lost his bearings. About his temptations. He wanted to tell her he had slipped away and God had brought him back. He wanted to, but he didn't. There would be time later. When he could see her face and hold her again.

"Be careful," she said.

"I will." *And in more ways than one,* he thought.

CHAPTER *Sixty-Four*

The call from Jimmy came at three o'clock. Ortega was wearing the wire sent by Rojas and was dressed casually in a pair of khaki Dockers, a blue oxford shirt, brown loafers, and a navy-blue sport coat. Underneath the coat, he was carrying his government-issue Glock, two extra magazines, and a pair of handcuffs, laced through his belt. He left the apartment feeling like a cop—a *good* cop—for the first time since beginning the operation.

When Ortega reached the plant he saw Estévez's Caddy, retouched since the gunfire at Hoppity T's, parked next to Lopez's Mercedes. Jimmy's Lexus was next in line, followed by another Mercedes and a late-model Corvette. When Ortega entered the plant, the others were already gathered on the cutting floor. It had been cleaned of its normal debris and shined like a gymnasium floor. A long table sat in the middle of the room, adorned with food of all kinds and decorated with fresh-cut flowers in crystal vases on a pristine white tablecloth.

Lopez, Jiménez, and Delahoy were already seated at the table with their wives. Estévez sat at the head and was talking to Jimmy, who was standing next to the drug lord's seat. A small bandstand, with string instruments sitting ready for use, stood less than forty feet from the table.

As soon as Ortega entered, he saw Estévez smile and gesture toward an empty seat.

"So glad you could come, Ron."

Ortega wasn't surprised to see the wives of Estevez's intending targets. Although the man had always expressed a desire to never hit a man in the presence of his family, given the situation and Estevez's meltdown, it was clear the rules had changed. The slate was going to be wiped clean. And that meant no survivors.

Ortega smiled. "Thank you for the invitation." He took a seat at the table, next to Lopez. The two men made small talk for a few moments, before Estévez stood and tapped on his glass with a spoon. Jimmy took his seat.

"Gentlemen…and ladies," Estévez said, acknowledging the presence of the men's wives. "I am so glad we could gather for a time of friendship and relaxation." He gestured about the plant. "And I am pleased you could all come on such short notice. But I wanted you to hear the news from me, first. Our nemesis was arrested this morning and is now under federal indictment. The path to Havana has been cleared for us, my friends." Estévez smiled winningly. The silence from the others was deafening, but it soon gave way to applause. The Cuban held up his hand.

"And I apologize for the location, but I have begun renovations on my home and felt that this location, as crude as it is, would afford us a chance to talk freely out of the prying eyes of the government. I would also like to add that my men will deliver a dozen of our best steaks to your homes no later than tomorrow evening." He raised his glass. "That is my gift to you." Estévez raised his glass higher. "To our new venture. May it be profitable."

The others raised their glasses in acknowledgment of the toast. Three men adorned in tie and tails appeared, lining up along one side of the table opposite Ortega. Another group, consisting of two men and a woman, stepped up to the platform and began playing softly as the waiters served an appetizer of fried clams, shrimp, and mussels.

Ortega made small talk with Julio Lopez. The man's wife gave the Cuban agent the same warm smile she had given him during the party at Estévez's home. That smile now made Ortega exceedingly uncomfortable.

Estévez seemed as jovial and lighthearted as Ortega had ever seen him. If any of his guests had suspicions something was amiss, they would be hard-pressed to find any evidence of it in the drug lord's demeanor. By all appearances, he was offering just what he had declared. Good food and fellowship.

And the food *was* good. Very good. Following the appetizers, salads were brought on. And after the salad came a dinner of prime rib that Ortega suspected came from Estévez's own stock.

As dessert was served, Jimmy rose from his chair, excusing himself, and gave Ortega a look that made it clear he wanted the agent to follow him.

Ortega excused himself, dabbing his mouth with the cloth napkin before discreetly setting it on his chair. He met Jimmy in the office.

"Close the door," Caltabiano said, glancing at his watch.

"What, Jimmy? What's going to happen?"

The ex-cop stood near the door where he could watch events unfold. It wasn't until Ortega saw the waiters return with serving towels draped over their arms that he realized the massacre was about to occur.

"He isn't going to put them in the freezer like he did with Chipper, is he?" Ortega said, passing the code word through the wire to the listening SAC.

Jimmy gave the Cuban a confused look. "You've got to be kidding me. He wants this over and done with. You and I are going to torch this place as soon as those guys do their job."

Ortega slipped behind the big Italian, pulling his Glock and his credentials from under his coat. "I'm afraid not, Jimmy. You're under arrest."

Caltabiano turned from the door to face Ortega. His eyes focused first on the gun, then on the credentials that Ortega displayed. He snorted. "You're kidding me."

"I don't kid, Jimmy," Ortega said, sliding the credential case into his pocket and pulling the handcuffs forward. "Put these on. And keep your hands where I can see them."

Ortega didn't want to cuff the man himself. Although the Italian was big and slow, he was heftier and more powerful than the DEA agent.

Caltabiano sneered at him before turning around and putting his hands behind his back. "Mr. Estévez was right. You hit wide of the mark with Dowd and Hurst and we should've known."

The Cuban agent dropped the cuffs into one of the man's hands. "Put 'em on, Jimmy."

As the ex-cop cuffed himself, Ortega glanced around the man's body, hoping to see the SAC and a swarm of agents. There was no one.

"Chipper," he repeated, directly into the wire under his shirt. "Chipper, Chipper."

Caltabiano turned with his hands cuffed and gave Ortega another confused look. "You really have a thing for that broad, don't you?"

Ortega ignored the man's remark and looked past him to the cutting-room floor. His eyes widened as he saw the waiters drop their towels and bring their Uzis to bear on their guests.

CHAPTER *Sixty-Five*

Ortega bolted around Jimmy on his way to the door. The Italian responded fast, slamming into the agent, driving him to the wall, and causing him to drop his weapon as he spilled onto the floor. From where he lay, Ortega could hear the screams of those on the cutting-room floor as the reality of their impending doom enveloped them like a shroud.

Caltabiano, too big and slow to reach for Ortega's gun, struggled to get his hands into position where he could reach his own.

Ortega climbed to his feet in time to hear a burst of gunfire erupt from the cutting-room floor. Through the window in the office door, he could see the SAC running along the catwalk overhead, firing an Uzi on the waiters below. Estévez looked startled. His guests looked confused.

Caltabiano had his weapon in hand and maneuvered to bring it down on Ortega. The agent grabbed the barrel and easily wrested it from the cuffed hands of the enforcer. The weapon in hand, the agent knelt to get his own.

Jimmy kicked him hard enough to send him reeling into one of the chairs. The wind had been knocked out of him, and as the big enforcer moved in, the agent struggled to ward off more blows.

As Ortega struggled with Caltabiano, the sound of multiple Uzis being fired told the agent that an all-out battle was erupting between Estévez's men and Ortega's fellow agents. Things were spiraling out of control.

He struggled to his feet.

Caltabiano kicked him, knocking him to the floor again.

"Mr. Estévez trusted you," Jimmy said, red-faced and sweating. "You betrayed us all." He kicked at the Cuban again.

Ortega timed his response to Jimmy's next blow and latched onto the man's leg, pulling him down. He landed on the floor like a side of beef.

The undercover agent crawled over the enforcer's torso to try to reach the weapons. But as he reached, Caltabiano kneed him in the groin throwing him backward.

Ortega groaned and rolled off as the bigger man cursed and kicked at the agent again.

Ortega fought to regain his breath as he struggled to defend himself against another attack.

"You betrayed us," Caltabiano repeated as he continued kicking, landing another blow on Ortega's side, spinning the smaller man across the floor.

The sound of gunfire from the cutting room was laced with the screams of the dying. The acrid stench of gunpowder began to find its way into the office.

Ortega rose to his knees, fighting to subdue the pain. Jimmy rolled to his side and reached for the revolver.

The agent threw himself onto the Italian, barely missing yet another kick.

Jimmy cursed again. The man's face was purple. His words were barely audible as he fought for breath.

Ortega wrested the gun from the man's hand, punched him twice, then a third time.

Caltabiano coughed and gasped for air.

Ortega stuffed the enforcer's gun into the back of his waistband, under his coat.

Creeping slowly to the door, he pulled himself above the window line. He could see that Estévez's men were not going down without a fight. Two of them were lying on the floor, presumably dead, along with the three band members, and two of the wives, who had probably been hit by cross fire. The third waiter was kneeling in the open, blasting away at Ortega's boss as he returned fire. Estévez and his guests had dived under the table, taking the only cover available.

"Stay put," Ortega said to Jimmy's back. As the undercover agent opened the door the brutal sound of gunfire filled the room. The reverberation was deafening.

Ortega, gun in hand, crawled to a position of relative safety behind the corner of the wall just outside the office.

His eyes locked briefly on Estévez's, and the Cuban agent saw a brief glimmer of hope that somehow his protégé would rescue him. Ortega motioned for the drug lord to stay down. The agent no longer felt the perverted sense of loyalty to Estévez he once had. But he also did not want the man to die. Not here. Not like this. He wanted him to stand trial, where justice under the law could be served and where Estévez would, perhaps, be willing to deal and hand over others in an effort to save himself.

Ortega lay on his stomach, shielding himself behind the corner of the wall, and steadied the pistol with both hands as he aimed at the lone waiter. As soon as there was a break in the exchange of fire, the agent ordered the man to drop his weapon.

The man spun in Ortega's direction, forcing him to fire. The impact knocked the waiter off his knees. He landed on the floor, his weapon spinning several feet away.

Estévez was stunned.

Ortega emerged from his position and walked steadily to the area where the man was lying. He knelt and put two fingers to the man's neck. There was no pulse.

"All of you," Ortega said to Estévez and the others who had sought refuge under the table, "come out from under there. With your hands in the air." He held his credentials at chest level with his gun trained on them. The unbelieving look on Estévez's face was priceless.

"It was *you,*" the drug lord said. "It was you all along."

The SAC came running down from the catwalk. He ejected the empty magazine from the gun. It clattered on the metal steps as he slipped another magazine into the butt of the gun.

"It wasn't Chipper," Ortega said. "You killed her for no reason. No reason at all."

Estévez's eyes narrowed. His face contorted from anger. "This isn't over until it's over."

"It's *over,* Ricardo," Ortega said as the SAC approached. "It's over for all of you."

The SAC was dressed for a day at the office. A white shirt, dark slacks, and subdued tie were set off by his badge and cell phone, clipped to his belt. He had an Uzi in his hand. "Is this all of them, Ron?"

Ortega gestured toward the office. "Estevez's enforcer is in there."

Lopez and his wife said nothing. Delahoy and Jiménez were sobbing. The wives of both men lay sprawled on the cutting room floor.

"Where are the others?" Ortega asked.

"What others?" Rojas asked, before spraying Estévez and his guests with gunfire.

CHAPTER *Sixty-Six*

Ortega reacted on instinct. Instinct that had been honed by his training. He fired a shot at the SAC, striking the man in the chest just above the bulk of the protective vest he wore. The man went down. Down, but not out. The DEA chief returned fire from his position on the floor. He missed Ortega as he ran toward the catwalk from which the SAC had descended. As the agent ran, a second burst of machine-gun fire nipped at his feet, pocking the floor and sending bits of concrete shrapnel shooting upward.

Ortega returned fire blindly as he hurled himself up the stairs, taking two steps at a time. Below, he could hear the clatter of a magazine hitting the floor as the SAC slammed yet another into place.

He had hit the boss. He had hit him in a vital area. If he could just make it to a phone, he could—

Another burst of gunfire from the SAC.

Bullets pinged and sparked as they made impact on the metal of the catwalk. Ortega continued to run for the safety of the locker, returning fire as he went.

By the time he reached the freezer, the SAC was no longer visible on the floor.

Ortega opened the meat-locker door and moved twenty feet away to hide behind his second corner of the day. He ejected the empty magazine from his Glock and rammed another into the pistol. He was breathing hard—his palms were growing moist.

The SAC's labored footsteps echoed off the metal steps. By the time he reached the catwalk, Ortega could hear the man's breathing.

He peered around the corner just as the SAC came into view. His face was ashen. There was a large red stain on the front of his white shirt. His tie was saturated with blood.

Ortega passed the Glock from one hand to the other as he wiped his palms against his pants leg before gripping the weapon again and training it on the man he had entrusted his safety to.

The SAC held the Uzi in both hands at waist level as he slowly peered into the locker.

Ortega waited.

The SAC eased one foot around the doorway before taking the bait and stepping into the freezer.

Ortega lowered his weapon and bolted across the slick floor to close the door on the SAC. As he reached the freezer, his boss appeared from behind the door and fired a short burst that hit Ortega in the leg, knocking his feet from under him.

The agent lost his grip on the Glock and saw it clatter away as he slid over the lip of the stairs, rolling down them one at a time until he landed on the concrete floor below. From above, the SAC began to descend the steps.

Ortega struggled to rise to his feet. His legs were numb, his pants blood-drenched. He placed one hand on the floor to hoist himself to his feet. But another burst from the SAC's Uzi convinced the young agent it was futile.

"Ron," the ashen-faced SAC said. 'You know I can't let you walk out of here. Not now."

Ortega was breathing hard. Losing blood fast. His heart raced as his vision dimmed.

"You were the one," Ortega said.

Rojas opened his mouth to respond but was cut short by Estévez.

"You deserve each other," he said, his voice trembling.

Ortega and the SAC turned in the direction of the dying man. He lay on his side, his head resting on the blood-stained floor.

"You two are worse than us. We have rules. But you..." he coughed on the blood that had filled his mouth. "You people don't care about anything."

Ortega's vision began to dim. "I don't play by this man's rules, Ricardo. Or yours. It isn't he and I that are the same. It is you."

Estévez licked his parched lips. A grin slid slowly across his face. "We shall see what our maker has to say." His grin broadened. "I'll see you both in hell. Soon."

Ortega shook his head. "No, Ricardo. You won't."

Rojas fired a burst from his Uzi. The drug lord was silenced.

Ortega groaned and turned to face his approaching enemy. "You were the one," he repeated. "You were the one who set us up."

The SAC shook his head. "Not really. For the most part it was O'Connor."

Ortega recalled the first meeting in the SAC's office. "So that's why you recommended him. When you told the USA you had 'just the man,' this thing was planned all along."

"When you dropped Estévez into our laps, it was a godsend. O'Connor was supposed to keep an eye on you. Use you to get the information we needed from Estévez."

"We?"

"Kingman." The boss stopped. He was standing directly over Ortega.

"So Estévez was right. Kingman is engineering a takeover."

The SAC shook his head. "Not really. Not here, anyway. He knows that Cuba is where the action is going to be and he's made deals with the Colombians to provide the peripheral ventures to their trade."

"They do the coke," Ortega said, "while he provides the inducements for foreign travel to Cuba."

"That's an oversimplification, but...yeah. He wants to ease out of the drug business. Go legit in a few years and pass the thing on to his son. The arrangement with the Colombians can help him do that."

"So Garcia and Torres weren't working with him?" Ortega asked, eyeing the puddle of blood that had begun to form at Rojas' feet.

"Torres was. Garcia was just bitter toward your Cuban friend over there," the SAC said, gesturing with the machine gun to Estévez's lifeless body.

Ortega blinked his eyes. His vision was dimming fast. "So when O'Connor hit Dowd and Hurst, did he use Kingman's crew?"

"Yep."

"And you were the one who was shooting at us from the bushes?"

The SAC smiled a weak smile. The red stain had now taken over his shirt. "That'd be me."

"Why?"

"Because we had all we needed from you. You told us what Estévez was planning. Kingman wants to reach out to the others." He looked around the room. "They're gone." He shrugged. "Kingman wants to build alliances with them."

"*Use* them."

He shrugged again. "Isn't that what Estévez was doing?"

Ortega felt his strength ebb.

"What happened to Mikey?"

The SAC rolled his eyes. "Come on, you know."

Ortega knew the diminutive Mexican had, in all probability, been tortured for the information he had before being weighted and dumped into the Atlantic.

"Why?"

"Why? The war is over. It's been over for some time now. We've lost. It's time to throw in the towel. There's money to be had here." He tilted his head to study the agent like a specimen. "You're not just playing dumb, are you? You really don't get it."

"If 'it' is what you have, I don't want it. You've betrayed every good cop and every good agent in the—"

"Oh, please," the SAC said. "Save that for St. Peter."

"Is the USA involved?"

The man laughed. "Are you kidding? He's a bigger boy scout than you are."

"He has the tapes," Ortega said. "The transcripts."

The SAC slowly shook his head. "No, he doesn't."

Ortega recalled the last meeting in the boss's office. He recalled how the attorney had expressed concern he didn't have the evidence the SAC was supposed to pass on to him.

"Did you kill O'Connor?"

"Had to. He knew too much. Had too much leverage over me." He raised the barrel of the Uzi. "Sorry, Ron."

Ortega grabbed the man's ankle with both hands and pulled with all that he had left. The boss slid in his own blood and fired the Uzi as he went down. The shots went wide and the gun clattered to the floor.

Ortega hoisted himself onto the man. Despite the blood loss, the SAC was able to put up a struggle. Ortega punched the man once, twice, and a third time, but his own loss of blood and his awkward position kept him from getting power behind his blows.

Rojas kneed the younger man, forcing him to roll off to one side.

Ortega gasped and fought to stay conscious. His boss slowly rolled to his knees and crawled toward the Uzi.

Ortega struggled to rise, but his weakness made him slip on the blood-slick floor.

The SAC continued toward the Uzi. It was less than five feet away.

Ortega rolled to his right and tried to pull Jimmy's revolver from his waistband.

The SAC's fingers touched the machine gun—spun the gun's grip into his hand.

Ortega tugged on the revolver. The gun's hammer was snagged. He struggled to roll farther to his left. Pain seared through him, as hot and penetrating as molten steel. His vision began to tunnel down.

"I'm sorry, Ron," the SAC said, raising the barrel of the Uzi.

Ortega jerked the pistol free.

"I really am."

The two men fired simultaneously.

CHAPTER *Sixty-Seven*

Jimmy died as a result of his struggle in the plant office. The medical examiner called the event "inevitable."

Juan Rojas died, along with Estévez, his gunmen, and the band in the carnage at the meat plant. Ron Ortega survived.

Two weeks after the incident, and two days after his release from the hospital, a press conference was held in the DEA's Miami office. By all accounts, Ortega's penetration into the Estévez organization had made the young agent an icon within the city's law-enforcement community. His name had been honored by his superiors, and he was scheduled to receive an award for heroism.

But none of that mattered. Not anymore.

"I'm afraid that your face has been plastered all over America," the USA said, settling himself behind the SAC's desk. "The press conference has made it impossible for you to work undercover again."

That didn't matter either.

"But you can have this," the attorney said, gesturing around the office. "It's yours if you want it."

He didn't.

"I've had enough," Ortega said, glancing at his wife and new son.

"I understand, Ron," the man said, in tones more civil than Ortega had ever heard him use. "But you're a good agent. You did the job you said you would do." He lowered his voice. "I'm just sorry there were others here who didn't."

“There are bad apples everywhere, Dillon,” Ortega said, opting to use the man’s given name. “Even in the garden of Eden.” He grinned.

“Yes, well, at any rate, I apologize and I hope you’ll reconsider. It isn’t often that the DEA will leap someone so far ahead as to make him the SAC of an office like Miami. Especially with only three years’ experience. But—”

“Three years? Is that all?” he asked, smiling as he squeezed Libby’s hand. “It sure seems like a lot more than that. Besides, I committed crimes. I’m not in a position to supervise anyone.”

“The government won’t pursue charges against you. As for supervising anyone else, the DEA has told me you’re exactly what they want. A man who’ll stay the course. Someone who can inspire others to do the same.”

Ortega shook his head. “Things have changed for me now. I see life differently.” He rose from his chair. “And that means I won’t be needing these anymore.” He dropped his badge, credentials, and gun onto the desk.

“Ron, I really wish you’d reconsider. Everything you want is right here,” the attorney said. “It’s your whole life. It’s your dream. Don’t walk away because of a few guys that went bad.”

Ortega smiled. “Those are the things I used to want. But now I see more clearly. Everything I want is sitting right next to me.” He extended a hand to the USA. The attorney rose to take it.

“Nothing I can say?”

Ortega shook his head. “Estévez already said it.”

The attorney gave the agent a confused look.

“We all chase after the thing we think will fill the void,” Ortega said. “For Estévez it was power. For his clients it was the drugs he traded. For me,” he nodded toward the desk, “I thought it was this. But I was wrong. What I want neither money nor the government can give me.”

He turned to smile at his wife and baby. “I’m not leaving because of a few bad apples. I’m leaving because one apple that went bad has been given a second chance. I can do the right thing or I can do the desired thing. And for the first time in my life, the two are one and the same.”

© Susan Gerth 2005

MEET BRANDT DODSON

Brandt Dodson was born and raised in Indianapolis, where he graduated from Ben Davis High School and, later, Indiana Central University (now known as the University of Indianapolis). It was during a creative writing course in college that a professor said; "You're a good writer. With a little effort and work, you could be a very good writer." That comment, and the support offered by a good teacher, set Brandt on a course that would eventually lead to the Colton Parker, P.I., series:

Original Sin

Seventy Times Seven

The Root of All Evil

The Lost Sheep

Brandt comes from a long line of police officers spanning several generations and was employed by the FBI before leaving to pursue his education.

A former United States Naval Reserve officer, Brandt is a board-certified podiatrist and past president of the Indiana Podiatric Medical Association. He is a recipient of the association's highest honor, the Theodore H. Clark Award.

He currently resides in southwestern Indiana with his wife and two sons and is at work on his next novel.